PETER I
TUNE TO A ⌣⌣ʌ∣ ⌣ʟ

ERIC ELRINGTON ADDIS, aka 'Peter Drax', was born in Edinburgh in 1899, the youngest child of a retired Indian civil servant and the daughter of an officer in the British Indian Army.

Drax attended Edinburgh University, and served in the Royal Navy, retiring in 1929. In the 1930s he began practising as a barrister, but, recalled to the Navy upon the outbreak of the Second World War, he served on HMS *Warspite* and was mentioned in dispatches. When Drax was killed in 1941 he left a wife and two children.

Between 1936 and 1939, Drax published six crime novels: *Murder by Chance* (1936), *He Shot to Kill* (1936), *Murder by Proxy* (1937), *Death by Two Hands* (1937), *Tune to a Corpse* (1938) and *High Seas Murder* (1939). A further novel, *Sing a Song of Murder*, unfinished by Drax on his death, was completed by his wife, Hazel Iris (Wilson) Addis, and published in 1944.

By Peter Drax

PETER DRAX

TUNE TO A CORPSE

With an introduction
by Curtis Evans

DEAN STREET PRESS

Published by Dean Street Press 2017

Introduction copyright © 2017 Curtis Evans

All Rights Reserved

First published in 1938 by Hutchinson & Co. Ltd.

Cover by DSP

ISBN 978 1 911579 61 8

www.deanstreetpress.co.uk

INTRODUCTION

ERIC ELRINGTON ADDIS, aka "Peter Drax," one of the major between-the-wars exponents and practitioners of realism in the British crime novel, was born near the end of the Victorian era in Edinburgh, Scotland on 19 May 1899, the youngest child of David Foulis Addis, a retired Indian civil servant, and Emily Malcolm, daughter of an officer in the British Indian Army. Drax died during the Second World War on 31 August 1941, having been mortally wounded in a German air raid on the British Royal Navy base at Alexandria, Egypt, officially known as HMS *Nile*. During his brief life of 42 years, Drax between the short span from 1936 to 1939 published six crime novels: *Murder by Chance* (1936), *He Shot to Kill* (1936), *Murder by Proxy* (1937), *Death by Two Hands* (1937), *Tune to a Corpse* (1938) and *High Seas Murder* (1939). An additional crime novel, *Sing a Song of Murder*, having been left unfinished by Drax at his death in 1941 and completed by his novelist wife, was published in 1944. Together the Peter Drax novels constitute one of the most important bodies of realistic crime fiction published in the 1930s, part of the period commonly dubbed the "Golden Age of detective fiction." Rather than the artificial and outsize master sleuths and super crooks found in so many classic mysteries from this era, Drax's novels concern, as publicity material for the books put it, "police who are not endowed with supernatural powers and crooks who are also human." In doing so they offered crime fiction fans from those years some of the period's most compelling reading. The reissuing of these gripping tales of criminal mayhem and murder, unaccountably out-of-print for more than seven decades, by Dean Street Press marks a signal event in recent mystery publishing history.

Peter Drax's career background gave the future crime writer constant exposure to the often grim rigors of life, experience which he most effectively incorporated into his fiction. A graduate of Edinburgh Academy, the teenaged Drax served during the First World War as a Midshipman on HMS *Dreadnought* and *Marlborough*. (Two of his three brothers died in the war, the elder, David Malcolm Addis, at Ypres, where his body was never found.) After the signing of the armistice and his graduation from the Royal Naval College, Drax remained in the Navy for nearly a decade, retiring in 1929 with the rank of Lieutenant-Commander, in which capacity he supervised training with the New Zealand Navy, residing with his English wife, Hazel Iris (Wilson) Addis, daughter of an electrical engineer, in Auckland. In the 1930s he returned with Hazel to England and began practicing as a barrister, specializing, predictably enough, in the division of Admiralty, as well as that of Divorce. Recalled to the Navy upon the outbreak of the Second World War, Drax served as Commander (second-in-command) on HMS *Warspite* and was mentioned in dispatches at the Second Battle of Narvik, a naval affray which took place during the 1940 Norwegian campaign. At his death in Egypt in 1941 Drax left behind Hazel --herself an accomplished writer, under the pen name Hazel Adair, of so-called middlebrow "women's fiction"--and two children, including Jeremy Cecil Addis, the late editor and founder of *Books Ireland.*

Commuting to his London office daily in the 1930s on the 9.16, Drax's hobby became, according to his own account, the "reading and dissecting of thrillers," ubiquitous in station book stalls. Concluding that the vast majority of them were lamentably unlikely affairs, Drax set out over six months to spin his own tale, "inspired by the desire to tell a story that was credible." (More prosaically the neophyte author also wanted to show his wife, who had recently published her first novel, *Wanted a Son*, that he too could publish a novel.) The result was *Murder by Chance*, the first of the author's seven crime novels. In the United States during the late 1920s and early 1930s, recalled Raymond Chandler in his essay "The Simple Art of Murder" (originally published in 1944), the celebrated American crime writer Dashiell Hammett had given "murder back to the kind of people who commit it for reasons, not just to provide a corpse; and with the means at hand, not with hand-wrought dueling pistols, curare and tropical fish." Drax's debut crime novel, which followed on the heels of Hammett's books, made something of a similar impression in the United Kingdom, with mystery writer and founding Detection Club member Milward Kennedy in the *Sunday Times* pronouncing the novel a "thriller of great merit" that was "extremely convincing" and the influential *Observer* crime fiction critic Torquemada avowing, "I have not for a good many months enjoyed a thriller as much as I have enjoyed *Murder by Chance*."

What so impressed these and other critics about *Murder by Chance* and Drax's successive novels was their simultaneous plausibility and readability, a combination seen as a tough feat to pull off in an era of colorful though not always entirely credible crime writers like S. S. Van Dine, Edgar Wallace and John Dickson Carr. Certainly in the 1930s the crime novelists Dorothy L. Sayers, Margery Allingham and Anthony Berkeley, among others (including Milward Kennedy himself), had elevated the presence of psychological realism in the crime novel; yet the criminal milieus that these authors presented to readers were mostly resolutely occupied by the respectable middle and upper classes. Drax offered British readers what was then an especially bracing change of atmosphere (one wherein mean streets replaced country mansions and quips were exchanged for coshes, if you will)—as indicated in this resoundingly positive Milward Kennedy review of Drax's fifth crime novel, *Tune to a Corpse* (1938):

> I have the highest opinion of Peter Drax's murder stories....
> Mainly his picture is of low life in London, where crime and
> poverty meet and merge. He draws characters who shift
> uneasily from shabby to disreputable associations....and he
> can win our sudden liking, almost our respect, for creatures
> in whom little virtue is to be found. To show how a drab
> crime was committed and then to show the slow detection
> of the truth, and to keep the reader absorbed all the time—
> this is a real achievement. The secret of Peter Drax's success
> is his ability to make the circumstances as plausible as the
> characters are real....

Two of Peter Drax's crime novels, the superb *Death by Two Hands* and *Tune to a Corpse*, were published in the United States, under the titles, respectively, *Crime within Crime* and *Crime to Music*, to very strong notices. The *Saturday Review of Literature*, for example, pronounced of *Crime within Crime* that "as a straightforward eventful yarn of little people in [the] grip of tragic destiny it's brilliantly done" and of *Crime to Music* that "London underworld life is described with color and realism. The steps in the weakling killer's descent to Avernus [see Virgil] are thrillingly traced." That the country which gave the world Dashiell Hammett could be so impressed with the crime fiction of Peter Drax surely is strong recommendation indeed. Today seedily realistic urban British crime fiction of the 1930s is perhaps most strongly associated with two authors who dabbled in crime fiction: Graham Greene (*Brighton Rock*, 1938, and others) and Gerald Kersh (*Night and the City*, 1938). If not belonging on quite that exalted level, the novels of Peter Drax nevertheless grace this gritty roster, one that forever changed the face of British crime fiction.

Curtis Evans

CHAPTER ONE

IN A BED-SITTING-ROOM on the first floor of No. 5 Bury Square, in the Borough of Southwark, Captain Eric Macrae lay on his back on a divan bed. The room had started life, in the days of the hop merchant who had built the house in 1820, as a drawing-room; a very grand drawing-room with a deep pile crimson carpet, gilt chairs with brocade seats and backs, a dozen occasional tables, and a cosy corner of white-painted wood.

This morning, by the light of a July sun filtering through a holland blind, it appeared singularly unattractive, for there was oil-cloth on the floor, a rag mat in front of the marble fireplace, and a white pine dressing-table in the bow-window. There was a wicker chair with its cover torn, and grey padding showing.

Macrae woke slowly; slowly stretched his arms above his head and yawned. Then he turned on his side and looked at the watch on his wrist. It was five minutes past eleven, and he was lunching with Mrs. Keene at her flat at one o'clock. There was plenty of time. He put out a hand to the trousers on the back of a chair, groped deeply in a pocket, and brought out six coppers and a box of matches.

He laughed. Sixpence! Well, he'd been broke before and had found a way out. Mrs. Keene would give him lunch, and she owed him a couple of quid. He wouldn't worry if it wasn't for that damn' bill at the club. Forty pounds! . . . And he hadn't a notion how to raise it.

He kicked back the bedclothes and swung his feet to the floor, walked unsteadily to a corner of the room, and took a dressing-gown off a peg. Then he went to the fireplace and turned on a tap. There was a hiss of escaping gas. That was a bit of luck, for he hadn't got a shilling for the meter. He filled a kettle and put it on the ring.

While the water was heating he opened a drawer in the dressing-table and took out a clean shirt. It was the last one. The right cuff was frayed, and as he shaved off the threads he thought, "I must get Mrs. Finch to do something about this." The front was all right, and the collar he had worn yesterday would have to do.

When the water in the kettle was hot he propped a six-inch square of looking-glass on the mantelpiece and shaved; when he had finished and had wiped off the outlying fringes of soap he rubbed cold cream into his skin. As he did so he drew down his lower jaw until the skin was stretched tightly and the wrinkles round his mouth disappeared. They returned as the muscles relaxed.

Then he wiped his hands on a towel, put the lid back on the pot of cold cream, and dipped a rag into a saucer half-filled with an oily black liquid. He squeezed the rag half-dry and dabbed it on the grey hairs at the sides just above the ears and on the temples.

Some damn' fool had said that a man at forty was in his prime. He felt old at thirty-nine.

He had barely completed one side when he put down the rag and turned his head, listening to the sound of footsteps on the bare wooden treads of the staircase. There was a shuffling on the landing outside. The door opened and a very small but very penetrating voice said:

"'Morning, Captain. Sorry I'm late."

It was Mrs. Finch. Macrae pushed the saucer of hair-dye out of sight behind a photograph frame.

"That's all right," he said, and thrust his hands into the pockets of his dressing-gown.

Mrs. Finch, who stood five foot nothing in her broken-down boots, looked up at Macrae. The top of her head was on a level with his shoulder.

"I've brought your trousis and I've sponged them and pressed them. They don't look so bad, do they?"

Macrae took the pair of dove-grey trousers from her arm and turned them over. There was a white ring in the place where they had been stained.

"That's fine." He held them up, folded them, and laid them across the arm of the wicker chair.

Mrs. Finch put her bag on the bed. It was rumpled and the top blankets and sheet were hanging to the floor. An ash-tray on the floor was full of cigarette-ends and grey ash. She walked to the kitchenette, built out from the back window. There was a plate on the window-sill containing two sardines lying in a pool of green oil.

"What did you have for breakfast?" she asked in a voice which could have been heard in the street if the window had been open.

"I wasn't hungry," Macrae replied evasively.

"You ought to have something hot like I told you. Herrings is cheap enough, and so is bloaters."

"I never care for much breakfast."

Mrs. Finch looked at him and opened her mouth as though to speak. But she changed her mind after a moment's thought. "When things get this way, it's better to keep your trap shut," she thought, and carried a dirty cup to the basin in a corner of the room.

When she had washed and dried it she hung it on a hook and then set to work to make the bed.

Macrae picked up a cuff-link and put it into the clean shirt. It was a gold link, one side torpedo-shaped, the other flat. On the flat side there was a date engraved: 15.11.17. He had been eighteen when he had found these links at his place on the breakfast-table of Grove Hall, the year he went to Sandhurst. He had almost forgotten those days.

Mrs. Finch was sweeping the floor now, with little strength or purpose. A handful of dust was the result of her labour. She put down the pan by the door.

"I'll come back and finish off when you're dressed. I've got a bit of shopping to do."

Macrae turned as she opened the door. "Oh, wait a minute. There's something I want to ask you."

Mrs. Finch stopped with one hand on the door-knob. "Yes, sir?"

"I was walking through Bulmer Court last night and I saw rather a pretty girl. She wasn't wearing a hat and her hair was black and curly."

"That must have been Peggy. She works at Mr. Crick's, just opposite my place."

"She's a good-looker."

"She's not so bad, but she'd look a lot better if she was to take more pride in herself. Got her hair done proper and wore a dress that suited her."

"Her name's Peggy, is it?"

"That's what I said. Peggy Nichol."

"I'd like to meet her."

"You meet Peggy Nichol!" A cracked laugh followed the words. "She's not your sort, Captain."

"That doesn't matter."

Mrs. Finch looked doubtful. "I don't know what she'd say—I don't really. She's a funny girl some ways. Independent. And besides that she's walking out with my son Bert, and when a girl's got a steady man she don't want to start going out with some one else. Bert would have a lot to say if she did, I can tell you that."

"Bert needn't worry. I only want her as a dancing partner. She's got just the right figure."

"Well, I'll see what I can do about it." Mrs. Finch took her hand from the knob and put it under her chin. "She finishes with Mr. Crick along about six o'clock most nights, and if you was to come to my place afore that, say half-past five, I could ask her to look in on her way home."

Macrae took a packet from the mantelpiece and lit a cigarette. "Then that's settled," he said through a cloud of smoke.

"Of course, I can't promise nothing, and if she won't come, she won't come, and that's all there is to it."

"Yes, I understand that. And now I'll have to be getting dressed."

Mrs. Finch still stood in the doorway.

"Mr. Crick, him that she works for, is a decent old stick. Clever, too."

Macrae hummed a tune and picked up a day-old paper.

"He had a murder case once and got the bloke off, what was more than any one round here thought he'd do. But for all the good it did he might have saved himself the trouble. The bloke killed himself the week after."

Macrae nodded, untied the cord of his dressing-gown, and took the newly pressed pair of trousers off the chair. The hint was broad enough even for Mrs. Finch.

Macrae dressed slowly and with care, for his clothes were his stock-in-trade, his sole capital. He would sooner have gone hungry than appear badly dressed. He was hungry now. He consoled himself with the thought of a free lunch to be provided by Mrs. Keene and counted out the coppers which would take him to it. Sixpence! He smiled, and his thin mean lips spread in a hard line beneath his black moustache. Life was a game—the life he led. Sometimes rich, but more often poor. It had been fun for a time, but now that he was nearing the forty mark it wasn't quite so amusing.

He looked into the glass and took up the rag again and started on the left side. Damn these grey hairs! When he had finished he put on a double-breasted coat which still fitted without a wrinkle, though it was more than four years old. The slim gold cigarette-case which he slipped into the breast pocket did not show. Book matches in a waistcoat pocket; a silk handkerchief in his cuff; the six pennies in a trouser pocket, and he was ready for the road.

It cost two-pence to ride in a tram to Charing Cross Underground, and there he got down and bought a midday paper. Racing that day was at Haydock Park, and he turned to the program. The Mayfly filly was running in the second race and ought to have a pretty good chance. Perks was riding her. The betting forecast gave the price as 100 to 8, and with a fiver each way he could pick up enough to pay the club debt and leave a bit over. He would try to touch the old woman for a tenner.

At a quarter to one Macrae entered the hall of Mortlake Mansions, a block of very new flats near Sloane Square. The porter saluted him, said that it was a lovely day, and asked if the Captain knew anything for Haydock. Macrae replied that he thought the Mayfly filly had a pretty good chance, and pressed the lift button.

Outside the door of a flat on the third floor he fingered his tie, smoothed his hair, and then rang the bell. The maid who opened the door smiled at him. He got on well with women of every class.

"Madam is changing, sir. She won't be long."

Macrae put his hat on a table in the hall and sauntered into a long, low room which could not have been mistaken for any other than the room of a single woman. Bright chintzes of flamboyant design covered the chairs and a massive chesterfield. There were no ash-trays. The walls, the colour of overripe corn, were bare of pictures. A walnut stand held the morning papers neatly folded. A cold, white marble figure of a naked woman held up a primrose-shaded lamp.

There was no sign of the careless, untidy presence of a man.

From behind a door came the fruity voice of Mrs. Keene saying that it was wonderful of Eric to have come, that she wouldn't be a minute, and would he get himself a drink?

Macrae, with his hand already on a bottle of gin, said he would. Mixing a drink for himself at some one else's expense was one of the things that gave him the greatest pleasure. He filled a glass half-full of gin, added a quarter of French vermouth and a few drops of orange bitters.

He sipped his drink. It tasted very good to him. One more and he would be ready for lunch.

Mrs. Keene came flowing in as he was repeating the dose; a large, middle-aged woman in a startling dress of black, gold, and crimson. "Eric, my dear. So good of you to come." She kissed Macrae and subsided into a chair, which took her weight without one protesting creak from its expensive, coppered springs. "My dear, I've had such a rush. I never thought I'd get away in time for the train."

Apparently her toilet was still incomplete, for she opened an elaborate compact and got busy with a lipstick. She spoke in jerks. "I saw Lady Danesbury in Debenham's. She asked me to tea next week. . . . We must go to the Savoy one night. . . . When I come back of course. . . . I'll let you know."

"Yes, rather. Great fun." Macrae forced enthusiasm into his tone and half finished his drink.

"And I want to see the new show at the Gaiety. I met some one the other day who said it was wonderful, and Milly said that I must see . . ."

As she talked, Macrae was looking round the room. There wasn't anything worth lifting that he could see. The clock might be worth something, but it was too bulky.

Mrs. Keene looked at her watch. "Heavens! It's after one. Come along, we must lunch or I shall miss the train."

As she was fussing with her bag, Macrae walked to the door. There were times when she got on his nerves, and this was one of them.

They lunched quickly but expensively in the restaurant on the ground floor and returned to the flat. The maid, wearing her hat and coat, was waiting in the hall beside a pile of luggage.

"Have you packed everything?" Mrs. Keene asked.

"Yes, ma'am. I'm all ready." There was a suggestion of reproof in her voice.

"All right, then. Order a taxi." Mrs. Keene swept round the flat. "I think we have everything." She collected a pile of letters from a marquetry desk, stuffed them in her bag, fastened the catch, and then kissed Macrae. He had trained himself not to flinch, and took it well. "I'll be back next week. Friday probably. Now, do you think I've really got everything?"

Macrae said he was sure she had and then asked with affected carelessness if she could let him have his money.

"Yes, of course. Stupid of me to have forgotten." She unlocked her desk and took a cheque-book out of her bag. Macrae supplied a pen, which he shook gently over a pink virgin blotting-pad until ink fell in a shower of tiny drops.

Mrs. Keene wrinkled her brow. "Now, let me see. Dinner and dance on Tuesday. Tea Dance on Thursday. How much is that?"

Macrae told her, and when she had signed her name he took the cheque and blotted it. Then he said: "I wonder if you'd mind backing a cheque for me for a tenner? I'm rather short of cash."

As he spoke the words Macrae realized that he had made a mistake. Mrs. Keene looked away from him as she got up, and there was a hard edge to her voice as she replied:

"No. I'm afraid I can't."

He shrugged his shoulders and followed her out to the hall. The bags were gone, but the maid was still waiting.

"We'll have to hurry," she said, and opened the front door.

As Macrae watched the taxi drive away there was a thoughtful expression in his eyes. Two pounds twelve and sixpence. That was the hell of a lot of good to him. He stood on the edge of the pavement until the porter of the flats had disappeared into his office. Then he walked back into the hall and ran up the stairs to the third floor. There was no one about; no one to see him open the door of Mrs. Keene's flat with a key which he had had cut at a stall in a street market.

The lock fell with a click as he shut the door behind him. A handkerchief, a scrap of white lace, lay on the polished oak floor. He picked it up and put it on the hall table. Then he lit a cigarette and opened the door of the living-room. He wasted no time there, but went straight through to Mrs. Keene's bedroom.

The dressing-table was bare, but there was a pile of small change on the mantelpiece. He put the coins in his pocket. A pair of silk pyjamas lay on the bed. On a side table was an onyx box containing cigarettes and an ash-tray to match. They were no good to him.

He went back to the dressing-table and opened the top drawer; in it were a jumble of red morocco jewel-cases. He opened the first one. It was empty; so was the next; and the next.

"Gosh! Here's a bit of luck." Macrae spoke the words half aloud as he looked at a rope of pearls nestling in a bed of white satin. He snapped the case shut and slipped it into his pocket.

Then he went to the front door and opened it a couple of inches. He could hear the whine of the lift and a moment later saw it going up. The way was clear. He ran down the stairs and waited a moment on the bottom step. There was no sign of the porter. He walked quickly into the street and got a bus at the corner which took him to Piccadilly.

From a viewpoint ten thousand miles distant Piccadilly is always attractive; the centre of the hopes and expectations of those who resolutely keep the Old School Tie waving in the uttermost outposts.

Macrae, who had never suffered from seasickness, prickly heat, or frost-bite, looked on the pavements of Piccadilly only as a well-stocked covert where game may be flushed, run down, and subsequently plucked at leisure. But to-day his mind was not on the chase. He had a cheque to cash, but, unfortunately, he was not on the best of terms with his bank manager. There was, of course, his club, a curious place situated in a dirty little street not far from Cambridge Circus.

At the moment he wasn't too keen on going there either, for until he could pay the forty-pound debt his welcome would be wanting in warmth. And, moreover, the proprietor had made a rule that cheques were not to be cashed under any circumstances. Twelve stumers neatly framed and hung in the bar were twelve excellent reasons for this harsh measure. The rule had also been neatly framed, and, together with the cheques, served the dual purpose of a decoration to the room and a warning to those who might think of trying it. The majority of the members were adepts at that game.

"Sammy's," was that sort of club.

Macrae stopped outside the Criterion and counted the money that he had taken from the mantelpiece in Mrs. Keene's bedroom. It amounted to the sum of three shillings and ninepence, and he felt very annoyed with Mrs. Keene that it wasn't more, until the bulge in his side pocket reminded him of her other involuntary gift. That made him feel better. It would serve her right if he sold them outright.

If any one had read his thoughts and had asked, with pardonable curiosity, why Mrs. Keene should be thus punished for her carelessness, Macrae might have replied that she should have backed his cheque, which would have been no answer at all. She had paid what she owed. But with a man like Macrae logic counted for nothing where his own desires were concerned.

He thought over what he should do with the pearls. As he did so he crossed over to Shaftesbury Avenue and walked up the south side. There was a man ahead of him; a man with a thick red neck.

Tim Daly, though he usually dressed in a blue serge suit, shiny and tight round his chest, looked very much like a pig if you looked at his face. If, however, that doubtful pleasure was denied you, and you were forced to deduce his calling from an eyeful of chest and a glimpse of his left ear, the verdict would be "prize-fighter," without a doubt. A native of Chicago would have classed him as a tough guy.

A police constable had placed him in this class without a second thought at the end of a three-minute round with Tim. On that occasion, if help in the shape of a sergeant had not arrived on the scene, it is probable that Tim would have stood his trial for murder. As it was he was awarded a three-year stretch which had ended just two days ago.

Macrae lengthened his step and came up level with Tim Daly. He said: "What cheer, Tim?"

"Huh?"

"I want a word with you. Private."

"Come along to the club. I'm going that way."

"I haven't time for that."

Tim grunted and turned into a side street. There weren't many people about. "What's your trouble?"

"I've got some stuff to get rid of."

"Let's have a look."

"I haven't got it on me," Macrae lied.

"What is it?"

"Stones."

They walked on a hundred yards and then Tim said:

"You might try Abie Russ. The dicks aren't on to him yet."

"Where does he hang out?"

"Fenwick Street. Opposite Bulmer Court."

"Is he safe?"

"As good as any of 'em, but you won't get much of a price unless you let me handle the job."

Macrae refused. "I'll go and see him myself."

"O.K."

Tim Daly was smiling as he watched Macrae walk quickly away. Abie Russ! Well, he knew who'd come out top of that deal.

CHAPTER TWO

BULMER COURT is a wide alley paved with flagstones, on either side of which is a row of trim, prim little houses, each one boasting a brightly painted front door and polished knocker, a window with a fern, or a palm set on a bamboo table, and, behind the table, looped lace curtains.

The Court connects the quietly decaying gentility of Bury Square with that noisy canyon of stone and brick which is Fenwick Street. Stout iron posts ensure that nothing on wheels except a bicycle can invade this stamping-ground of gossips. Even the milkman has to leave his handcart on the other side of the iron posts and carry his bottles clinking in a wire basket.

Half-way down the Court in the direction of Fenwick Street the bow front of Danny Levine's shop makes a pleasant break in the flat front of the houses on the northern side. It is shaded by the leaves of a plane tree springing from the flagstones. How it thrives and every year produces shiny green leaves, how rain ever percolates to its roots, is one of London's mysteries which few bother their heads over. Peggy Nichol certainly did not, as she sat in its shade with her back against its sooty trunk and her slim, sheer-silk-clad legs stretched out before her. She was eating a Bath bun.

A flying squad of pigeons from St. Paul's, led by a bellicose gentleman pigeon with a crop of iridescent purple and green, had also decided that Bulmer Court was as good a place to feed in as any other on a hot day. There was a pool where they could drink after lunching off the crumbs of office-workers' sandwiches—and Bath buns. There was also a dusty flower-bed wherein they could squat and droop their wings and ruffle out their feathers.

The chief of the squad watched Peggy with his boot-button eyes as she bit into her dry bun; his head jerked backwards and forwards, and his pink legs marked time with nervous indecision.

Peggy picked up a pebble and threw it into the pool. The pigeon looked first startled and then offended. Peggy laughed and broke off a piece of her bun. He cocked his head on one side as though asking: "Now, what?" The crumbs fell within a few inches of his feet. He waited for three seconds, then made a sudden dash and carried off the loot. Several of his friends, waiting in the background, very kindly helped him to eat it.

Beyond the shade of the plane tree, at the Fenwick Street entrance to the Court, an old man leaned against the wall of a house. A wide leather strap around his bowed shoulders supported a large piano accordion. He was droning out "September in the Rain." A flat tweed cap sat like a plate on a head of thick white hair. Beneath a nose the shape and colour of a ripe strawberry his lips moved as he muttered the words of the song.

Old Lampy. Peggy thought of him with the tepid interest which the young accord to those who are old and poor. Sometimes she gave him a copper when she passed him on her way home, and felt guilty if she forgot. She was wondering idly how he lived, when the bell on the door of Danny Levine's shop clanged and Danny himself came out and stood with his thumbs in the armholes of his waistcoat.

He was a spare little man with a mouth that never stayed the same shape for long; his hair was thin and sandy and his eyebrows and eyelashes were of so pale a colour that you had to look twice to make sure that he had any at all; if you didn't particularly notice his eyes you were apt to receive the impression that they were pink, like a white rabbit's.

A smile split Danny's monkey face and he jerked his head in the direction of old Lampy. "Enjoying the music?"

Peggy nodded.

A man came up the alley; he was walking quickly, and as he passed Danny he handed him something, but didn't speak.

Peggy finished her bun, got up, and dusted the crumbs from her skirt. Six pigeons toed the line, waiting for her to leave the way clear for a quick peck all around. But Peggy stood looking down the Court towards Fenwick Street.

Danny took a match out of his mouth and said: "I wouldn't be surprised if Bert was late to-day. He's always terrible busy in the shop on Mondays."

"Yes, I know, but I did want to see him. There's a picture on at the Palace with that girl Rosabelle Lee in it, and I—"

"I shouldn't count on him, if I was you," Danny advised. "He's going to be busy to-night."

"What d'you mean?"

"I don't know."

"Yes, you do! Tell me!"

"Ask Bert." Danny, with a half-smile on his face, went back into his shop.

Peggy stood for a minute or two staring at the closed door. Then she turned and walked up the Court.

A group of women were standing outside an open door gossiping. On one of the door-posts was a brass plate which read: "Benjamin Crick. Solicitor. Commissioner for Oaths." The words, once etched deep into the metal, were worn shallow with five-and-thirty years of rubbing.

Two of the women made way for her, but a third caught her by the arm. "I've been waiting since ten o'clock, deary."

Peggy smiled as only Peggy could smile. "I know, Mrs. Flynn, but he's been frightfully rushed. It won't be long now." She drew up her skirt above her knees in order to attack the stairs, which were as steep as a ladder. It ran up in a dark tunnel to a landing ten feet by three. At the far end there was a half-glazed door of cheap deal. The last two letters of the word "Push" had been worn away by impatient hands.

Peggy kicked it open and let it bang to behind her. She was now in the main office of Benjamin Crick, solicitor. It was a long, narrow room, and on the right was a window which looked out into Bulmer Court.

On busy days Peggy would lean out of the window and summon Mr. Crick's clients like a barber, except that she only said "next" and omitted the "please."

There were two desks, three chairs—one broken—a cupboard with a door that would never stay shut, and a bookcase filled with out-of-date law books, which were never used.

A trap hatch snapped up and Mr. Crick's voice came through the opening. "Come on. What are you waiting for?"

Peggy picked up a sheet of paper and went through the banging door into Mr. Crick's office. It was a small room. Mr. Crick was a big man, and his desk very nearly filled the remainder of the available space. Sitting in a swivel-chair with his back to the window, Mr. Crick looked fat. When he stood up he was merely big. His black coat was unbuttoned and on the spread of his waistcoat was a drift of white ash lately fallen from the twopenny cheroot he was smoking. Surprisingly blue eyes looked out from under two craggy eyebrows.

"You're late," he barked.

"No, I'm not. I'm three minutes early."

Mr. Crick glared at a black marble clock. It said twenty minutes to seven, and had been telling that lie for the last five years. Peggy had long ago given up suggesting that it should be repaired or sold. Sold! That clock had been presented to his father in the year 1895 to mark his golden jubilee as a shopwalker.

"Anyway, I wish you wouldn't bang that door."

"It wouldn't bang if you'd let me take that spring off it."

"Then it would be always left open and there'd be a draught." Mr. Crick pulled at his cheroot and, when he had blown out a great cloud of blue-grey smoke, said: "Well, let's get on. Who's first?"

"Mrs. Flynn."

"What's her trouble?"

"Same as last time. Her old man's been picked up."

"Flynn? That'll be Toby Flynn. I suppose he's been mooching."

"I don't think so."

"What do you mean?"

"Flynn doesn't beg."

"Nonsense. He's the same as all the others. Bone lazy. He could get work if he tried."

"He's sixty-five."

Mr. Crick, who was on the down grade from fifty, said that that wasn't old.

"He kept his last job for forty-three years," Peggy said quietly. "You know what happened. The firm he was with went bust."

"Yes, but this isn't the first time he's been in trouble with the police."

"He was framed that time, the same as he was yesterday."

"Framed?"

"That's American for fixing it so that he could be pinched."

"I suppose it's a begging charge?"

"Yes, and I don't think he'll get the option this time."

Mr. Crick took his cheroot from his mouth and blew out a thin stream of smoke through pursed lips. "When is he coming up?"

"To-morrow, at Howard Street."

"I'll go along and see what I can do."

"That's the story." Peggy laid a sheet of paper on the blotter and went out.

Ten seconds later her voice rang out through Bulmer Court. "Mrs. Flynn. You're next."

Mr. Crick had read Toby Flynn's history by the time Mrs. Flynn came sidling into the room. She was wearing her best "black," a brooch she'd borrowed from her sister, and a bonnet with a hearse-horse plume. In her hand she carried a bead bag. A visit to a solicitor demanded only the very best.

"Sit down," said Mr. Crick. He tried to knock his ash into a saucer, but failed. It fell in a shower on the blotter. He blew it away and then looked up at Mrs. Flynn and said, "Well?" so fiercely that she quite forgot the story she had been rehearsing all the morning. Her lips moved, but something seemed to have gone wrong with her voice.

Mr. Crick tapped on the desk with his pen and looked at the marble clock, which still said twenty minutes to seven.

"It's me husband."

Mr. Crick glared at her. "This is the third time since—since— well, whenever it was. What has he got to say?"

Mrs. Flynn began to cry without any apparent effort.

Mr. Crick waited until the flow had been partly stemmed by a rag of a handkerchief, and then he said: "Tell me what happened."

Mrs. Flynn gulped twice and sniffed. "He was at his stand outside the A.B.C. at the corner of Albert Street when a lady came along and gave him sixpence. She was gone before he had time to make her take something. Then a man did the same thing, and after him another lady, and then a slop came up and pinched him for begging. He couldn't help hisself."

"Did he get a sixpence each time?"

"No. It was two sixpences and a bob."

"What does he usually take in a day?"

"About five bob."

"In coppers, I suppose?"

"Yes—mostly."

"I see." Mr. Crick leaned back in his chair and looked at the ceiling.

Mrs. Flynn blew her nose vigorously on her overworked handkerchief. "And it's not as if he hadn't been careful; because, you see, Mr. Russ got him the pitch and told him he'd got to be very particular that he always offered people a box of matches or a stud or a bootlace or something."

"But this time he hadn't a chance to do that?"

"That's right, sir." Mrs. Flynn, having told her troubles, began to feel better. "You will say a word for him, won't you?" She opened the catch of her bead bag and scrabbled about in it. Five pennies and a shilling came to light. She laid them on the desk.

Mr. Crick pushed them away. "What did you have for breakfast?" he asked.

"Breakfast?"

"Yes. What did you eat?"

"I had some bread-and-dripping. I can manage all right." There was dignity and reproof in Mrs. Flynn's tone.

"What about the rent?"

"I'm a bit behind, but I'll be able to make it up if Toby can get a job."

Mr. Crick fumbled in his trouser pocket. "Take that." He put a two-shilling piece on the desk. "Get yourself something to eat. Steak-and-kidney pie. Sausages. Anything. But feed. Do you understand?"

Mrs. Flynn made grateful noises, got up, and backed towards the door. When she had gone, Mr. Crick rang for Peggy.

"There's something in that woman's story. Something I don't quite understand. Flynn's not a bad fellow."

"What are you going to do about it?"

"I don't know yet. I'll have to think up something." As he spoke, Mr. Crick searched back in his memory of countless police-court cases. Most of them had been dull, many sordid, but none devoid of that human interest which had compensated for long hours spent in the frowzy atmosphere of stale air and disinfectant.

"What did you give her?" Peggy asked.

Mr. Crick looked guilty. "Two shillings," he mumbled.

He was thinking how he could excuse his weakness, when Peggy said: "She can do with that. She's not far off starvation."

"Well, I'll do what I can for her husband." Mr. Crick stubbed out his cheroot and felt in the box for another. It was empty. "Damn!"

Peggy smiled. "I took them. You've been smoking too much."

"No, I haven't." Mr. Crick picked up his pen and dipped it into the ink. It came out with a hair on the nib. "I wish you'd have this pot cleaned out. It's full of muck."

"It wouldn't be if you kept the lid on." Peggy swung out of the room and let the door shut with a bang.

St. Peter's clock was chiming six when Peggy watched Mr. Crick's back disappearing down the passage. She tidied up the papers on her desk, put the cover on her typewriter, and ran down the stairs to the Court. The stones underfoot threw back the heat they had absorbed during the day, but it was better here than in the stuffy office. She sat on the brick surround of the pool, opened her bag, and took out a comb and a mirror. Bert would be along any minute now.

Bert was no rival of Owen Nares, but as some one had once said, he wasn't no Hunchback of Notre Dame neither, and if it hadn't been for the cast in his left eye Peggy's first glance at him wouldn't have led to a second; but it had.

They had gone for a walk and that had cost nothing. Then Bert had suggested the pictures. Peggy had repaid that entertainment with supper at her home, which had been an ordeal for Bert. Luckily for Peggy he bore up well under Mrs. Nichol's withering and critical scrutiny, and three days later had spent one-quarter of his week's pay on two ports-and-lemon, fish and chips, and seats at the Southwark Palace.

After that little burst the pace had slackened and had soon subsided into that state known as "walking out," which they did economically on five days of the week and expensively on Saturdays.

And then one night, when he was saying good night, Bert had said, quite casually, that he wouldn't be able to do more than Saturdays in future. Peggy had asked why, and Bert had replied that he'd got a job that would keep him busy in the evenings, but as it would mean more money it was all for the best. They'd be able to get married sooner.

Peggy stood it for a fortnight and then rebelled. The cause of the rebellion was a girl called Rosabelle Lee, who lived several thousands of miles away in Hollywood, but who was appearing in celluloid at the local picture-house for three nights only. And not one of these three nights included Saturday, when Bert would be free.

Peggy finished combing her hair, put away the comb and mirror, and snapped her bag shut. Every word of the ultimatum was clear in her brain. St. Peter's clock chimed the first quarter. She wouldn't be cross and start a row. She'd just tell him quite quietly, but firmly of course, that if he didn't take her to the flicks she'd . . . well, she'd find some one who would.

Peggy was quite warm both inside and out when she saw Bert come walking up the Court from the direction of Abie Russ's shop. He was warm on the outside only. He gave her one of his shy, furtive glances and said: "Sorry not to have got here sooner, but you know the way it is Mondays."

"Yes, I know, and you needn't have hurried." Peggy mentally kicked herself for being so pleasant. This was no way to lead up to an ultimatum. But he was so apologetic, and she didn't want to be nasty, and, after all, what did Rosabelle Lee matter, anyway?

But determination to make her point returned when she remembered the arid Bert-less days of the past two weeks. As they walked down the Court she said: "I want to go to the pictures to-night."

"Sorry, but it can't be done." Bert took her arm in his and squeezed it. "You'll have to wait till Saturday."

Have to! Peggy retrieved her arm. "Oh, no, I won't!"

"But what does it matter what day we go?"

"The picture I want to see is only on till Wednesday."

"Then I'll give you the money and you can go by yourself."

"That's no good. Pictures aren't any fun if you're on your own."

"Well, then, take your mother with you."

"Why can't you come?"

Bert refused to answer this question.

"What's this job that takes you out night-times?"

"I can't tell you that, except that I get good pay."

Peggy became very pink about the nose and she held her head high. "You could tell me all right, if you wanted to."

At the point where the High Street crosses Fenwick Street the traffic had been released and barred their way. "Well, if that's all you've got to say, I can go home by myself."

Bert said, "All right, then," and disappeared.

Before he was out of sight Peggy realized that she had probably made a fool of herself, but she still held her head high and did not see Mrs. Finch until she laid a hand on her arm.

Mrs. Finch had been shopping. A bulging string bag hung from one skinny wrist and under her arm was an elderly cabbage.

"What's the matter with Bert?" she asked sharply.

"Nothing." Peggy tried to get away.

Mrs. Finch nodded her head. "You've been having a bust-up with him. That's what it is, and I'm not surprised."

"What do you mean?"

"Bert's been acting funny for some time back. He's been going off after he's had his supper every blooming night and he doesn't get back till long after I'm in my bed."

"What does he do?"

Mrs. Finch gave one of her steam-whistle laughs. "That's what I'd like to know. I asked him once, but he only told me to mind my own business and not to interfere with him. Interfere with him, indeed! I'd like to know where he'd be if I didn't darn his socks and sew on his buttons. He wants a lot of interfering with."

The traffic lights turned to green.

"Well, I must really be getting along," Peggy said.

"Wait a minute, deary. I've got an idea. You come and have a bite with me." She held up her bag. "I've got plenty for the two of us."

Peggy hesitated for a moment and then accepted the invitation.

"That's fine," said Mrs. Finch, smiling. "And I'll be able to in-troduce you to some one who's been very anxious to make your ac-quaintance."

"Who's that?"

"A gentleman. A real gentleman. The bloke I does for."

Peggy looked doubtful. "But I don't think I ought to meet him before I have a word with Mother."

"He's all right. Don't you worry. It was only this morning that he asked me if I could fix it so that he could take you out. I said I would because I couldn't very well say anything else, but I didn't mean to do it, seeing as how you and Bert were walking out."

"What's made you change your mind?"

"You having a row with Bert, of course. Now, what you've got to do is to go out with the Captain. That'll make Bert jealous, see?" Mrs. Finch put her arm through Peggy's and started to lead her back in the direction of Bulmer Court.

"I'm not sure that I want to. I'd like to give Bert another chance."

"Well, there's no harm in having a look at the Captain, is there? It'll be time enough to make up your mind after you've seen him."

Still doubtful, Peggy walked by Mrs. Finch's side along Fenwick Street. Old Lampy was on his pitch. He bobbed a greeting to Mrs. Finch over the top of his accordion.

When they were a few paces past him, Peggy said: "I can't think how he makes a living playing here. No one hardly ever gives him anything."

"That's just what I was saying to Mr. Levine only yesterday. He kind of shut me up same as Bert might have done. But I was still cu-rious, and to-day I asked the old geezer in to have a cup of you-and-me. I said to him straight: 'Look here, Lampy,' I says, 'why don't you try some other pitch? There must be lots of places up West or around about the stations where you could pick up more in half an hour than you get here in a week.'"

"What did he have to say to that?" Peggy asked.

"He didn't say nothing," Mrs. Finch replied peevishly. "He only smiled and waggled that old head of his." She became confidential. "If you ask me, I'd say he was crazy." She stopped outside her front door and felt in her bag for the key. Then she led the way into her front room and decanted the contents of the string bag on to a table.

A ragged end of smoked ham lightly clothed in newspaper rolled out. "Sevenpence I paid for that," Mrs. Finch announced with pride. She prodded its tenderer portions with a grimy forefinger. "And the bone'll do for soup." She handed the cabbage to Peggy. "Give that a wash, will you, dear? And chop it up. Not too small."

She put the ham in a saucepan, added water, and put it on a gas-ring. Then she looked at a battered tin clock on the mantelpiece. Like Mr. Crick's clock, it was permanently stopped. "What time is it?" she asked Peggy.

"A quarter to seven."

Mrs. Finch went to the window and leaned across the sill. "He said he'd be here at half-six. Are you sure your time's right?"

Peggy said that her watch might be a bit fast, but not more than a minute or two.

Like Sister Ann, Mrs. Finch kept her watch, but it wasn't until the water in the saucepan was boiling that she let out a squawk that brought Peggy to the window. "It's him," she said in a whistling whisper. And then, aloud: "Evening, Captain. I was beginning to think that you wouldn't be coming."

Peggy looked out across Mrs. Finch's flat back. She drew in her breath quickly. Gosh! He was a good-looker and no mistake; something like Ronald Colman with that thin black moustache. Peggy forgot all about Bert and their silly quarrel. Something had happened inside her. It made her feel that nothing else mattered as long as she could be with him, could talk to him. She made a desperate effort to tidy her hair, and looked round for a mirror. But it was too late to do anything; Mrs. Finch, clutching at her dress in an agony of nervousness, was at the front door welcoming her guest. Peggy heard her say: "She's here."

Then he came in with Mrs. Finch fluttering behind. "Peggy. Meet Captain Macrae."

Captain Eric Macrae smiled as he held out his hand. Peggy took it shyly, limply, and murmured: "Pleased to meet you." She stared at the carpet, at a point a foot to the right of Macrae.

He threw his hat on to a chair and turned to Mrs. Finch. "You've got a nice little place here." He picked up a photograph framed in red plush.

"That's my old man. I told you what happened to him, didn't I?"

Macrae hurriedly said that she had, and offered Peggy a cigarette. She blushed as she fumbled in his case. His hand touched
hers. She withdrew it quickly and looked up at Macrae. Apparently
he had not noticed anything. "Are you doing anything to-night?"
he asked.

"No."

"Would you care to come out with me?"

"I'd love to," Peggy answered shyly.

"Righto! Then let's be moving." He opened the door and then
turned to Mrs. Finch, and slipped two pound notes into her hand.

"But you don't owe me all this," she protested. "It's only—now,
let me think. Three bob for the washing, and—"

Macrae put a hand on her shoulder. "That's all right. You keep
the change. I've had a bit of luck to-day."

"Well, I'm sure it's real kind of you, sir, and welcome, too."

Macrae picked up his hat, said "Good night," and joined Peggy,
who was waiting in the passage.

Old Lampy was playing "Lily of Laguna" when they reached the
end of the Court. Macrae dropped half a crown into the tin hanging
on his coat. Lampy mumbled his thanks.

Peggy laughed. "I'll bet that that's more than he's taken all day.
I expect he'll get tight on it."

"Where shall we go?" Macrae asked.

"Well, I do rather want to see the picture that's on at the Palace." Peggy's shyness was beginning to wear off.

"All right. Let's go there. Is it far?"

"We could walk it in ten minutes," Peggy replied.

Macrae wanted to take a taxi, but Peggy said that a bus would do
just as well. They went by bus.

Macrae paid for two of the best seats at the cinema with a
pound note, and as they mounted the stairs to the circle Peggy was
thoughtful. It was wonderful, of course, and she knew she ought
to be thrilled, but she wasn't. When she'd been with Bert they'd
always gone to the ninepennies. She knew where she was with him
because they were both on the same financial level; but a man who
gave beggars half-crowns and handled pound notes as if they were
shillings frightened her.

A dancing spot of light led them to seats in the front row. The news was on. A band was blaring on the occasion of the presentation of a city's charter to a fat old hen of a man, wearing a cloak, a three-cornered hat, and a chain round his neck.

Peggy sighed her relief; they hadn't missed Rosabelle Lee's picture. She drew down her skirt over her knees and sat back luxuriously.

Two minutes later the lights went up and Macrae slipped from his seat. He returned with a box of chocolates and put them in Peggy's lap.

"Oh! How lovely! Thanks ever so much." She thought of the supper she was not having with Mrs. Finch and felt a little bit of a cad for having gone off without a word of apology. Then the lights began to fade; the curtain on the stage parted, and the familiar certificate flashed on the screen: "Passed by the Board of Film Censors . . ."

Peggy bit into a coffee cream as she snuggled down in her seat. This was real bliss.

It was the old, old story of the beautiful girl who slaves all day in a spotless and most becoming overall until the nice young man comes along, gawky and shy, but devastatingly good-looking. A crabbed old aunt with a Heart of Gold. Comic relief by the village idiot. A domineering mother. . . .

Then enter the villain from the Big City with a smile which wins the heart of the mother. He owns a two-seater as long as a Green Line bus, smokes cigars after breakfast, and lives in a flat with rooms the size of a village hall.

To Macrae, who had not served his apprenticeship as a picture fan, it was all utter tripe. A play—make-believe. He, who never read one word of fiction from one Christmas to the next, simply could not understand why people paid money to see such stuff.

He crossed and uncrossed his legs and turned in his seat to look at Peggy. He could just see her face. She was certainly a good-looker—no mistake about that; but why, exactly, she attracted him he could not have said, any more than he could have explained the fascination which the turn of a card at poker had for him, or the pleasure he drew from a really good cigar.

It was amazing to find a girl like Peggy working in a scrubby little office in Bulmer Court. Of course, she would have to be educated a bit, and taught how to wear decent clothes, but all that could be done in time. He had the money. Money! The feel of the wad of notes in his breast pocket was most comforting.

The girl in the picture had left her home and, at the expense of the crabbed old aunt with the Heart of Gold, was dressed in a black velvet frock which revealed every line of her figure.

Peggy saw herself in that dress; saw herself sitting in a deep arm-chair with a man in evening dress bending over her. . . .

Enter the gawky young hero. What is his fiancée doing here he asks. What, indeed! Sardonic smile by crabbed aunt.

Macrae turned in his seat and said: "What the blazes is it all about?"

Peggy said, "Hush," and put out a hand. Macrae, ever an opportunist, took it and pressed it.

Peggy, with her eyes on Rosabelle Lee, at first did not realize what was happening. When she did so she drew her hand away and felt uncomfortable. She had let Bert hold her hand, but that was different. Macrae did not protest. He was a good tactician and knew when to hold back.

"Have a chocolate?"

Macrae refused. He had lost his taste for sweets when he had acquired a liking for whisky.

Peggy snuggled back in her seat and soon forgot the incident. The picture was getting exciting, and it was not until Rosabelle was firmly clasped in the arms of her true lover, and the villain as firmly held by two policemen, that she realized that she was sitting in the two-and-sixpennies with a half-empty box of chocolates on her knee.

Macrae pulled himself out of his seat and said: "Well, what about a spot of eats? Is there anywhere near here we can go?"

Peggy thought of the supper-room where Bert took her on Saturday nights; of the trays of sizzling food in the window and the constant smell of cooking; of the proprietor, fat and dirty. It was not the sort of place that the captain would care for. She was sure of that. And there wasn't anywhere else near that was much better.

"Well?" Macrae said impatiently, for he was hungry, and was longing for a drink.

Peggy said that there was a café near Bulmer Court.

"I know that one. It's no good." Macrae hailed a taxi.

The entrance to Sammy's Club was an open doorway between two shops. Macrae pressed a bell-push and then went inside and struck a match. Peggy saw a steep flight of stairs leading upwards, very like those in Mr. Crick's office, except that here there was a hand-rail and a carpet.

Before they were half-way up the stairs a door at the top opened and a man wearing a short white coat came out. He said, "Hullo, Mac," looked with undisguised interest at Peggy, and then winked at Macrae.

When they had entered the club he shut the door and locked it.

"We want supper, Tony."

"That'll be O.K.," the barman replied, and then drew Macrae to one side and whispered in his ear.

Macrae smiled and nodded, and brought out the wad of notes from his pocket.

"You'd better see the old man first."

"I will, in a minute." He signed to Peggy and opened a door. "Come in here."

Peggy saw a small room, softly lit. Deep, comfortable arm-chairs. There was a low coffee-table of figured walnut standing in the glow of an electric fire.

The proprietor of Sammy's called this the conference-room and charged five pounds a night for its exclusive use, which was not a great deal when the credit side of the account was examined. A card-party in the "con" room usually netted anything up to a century for three of the players. The record was twelve hundred and fifty, the result of a particularly dishonest game of poker.

On the morning after that party there had been a blackguard rush to a bank in St. James's to cash the cheques of the fourth member before he recovered consciousness and stopped them. Macrae had shared in that cut-up and had seen New York as a result.

To-night he didn't reckon on any monetary return for his outlay.

"Would you like a glass of sherry?" he asked Peggy.

"Yes, thanks."

She wasn't educated up to cocktails yet.

"Well, if you'll excuse me a minute, I'll go and order supper." Macrae went out, along the passage and into a room crowded with men. There was a bar across one corner. Tony was behind it pouring out drinks. Macrae walked up to the bar. "A double White Horse. And how I need it!"

Tony grinned and his teeth showed whiter than his coat. "What have you been doing, Captain?"

"The flicks." There was pain in Macrae's voice. "Do you ever go to them, Tony?"

"Only Mickey Mouse."

Macrae splashed soda in his glass and raised it to his lips. "The first to-day, if you'll believe me."

Tony didn't, but didn't bother to say so. He only laughed.

"And send a couple of sherries into the con room."

A man with his nose in a long glass withdrew it to say: "Sherry? You won't get nowhere on sherry."

Macrae finished his drink and told Tony to order supper. Then he elbowed his way out of the room. At the end of the passage was a door with a heavy curtain draped across it. Macrae pulled it aside and knocked twice, waited a moment, and then knocked again. A muffled, booming voice called out, "Come in."

The room was in darkness except for a desk light with a blue globe. Behind it, half in shadow, Macrae saw the face of Big Bill Connor. A heavy jowl made two black lines from cheek to chin. Between them was a small, mean mouth pursed as though their owner had smelled something bad.

"'Evening, guv'nor." Macrae's greeting was self-conscious and his movements nervous as he groped for a chair. "I've come to pay that bill of mine. Sorry I'm late with it."

Big Bill Connor didn't speak. That wasn't his habit unless he had to. A pudgy white hand stretched out across the desk.

Macrae counted out forty one-pound notes. Connor took them, checked the number, and dropped them into an open drawer. "O.K."

Macrae began to get up.

"Just a minute." The fat lips pouted the words.

Macrae sank back slowly into his chair. "Yes?" he said.

Bill Connor picked up a pen and stared at it for ten seconds without speaking. Then he put it down, hunched his shoulders, and twisted back into his chair. "Who's the woman?"

"A girl I picked up."

"What's the idea?"

"Nothing."

"I don't want women round here."

"Yes, I know that, but I had to give her supper and I wanted to settle what I owed, so I thought it wouldn't matter for once in a way."

"All right, but don't do it again." Connor dismissed the subject of Peggy Nichol. He was silent for half a minute. Macrae could hear the ticking of the silver clock on the desk; could hear Connor breathing heavily, wheezily, like a man who has eaten too much.

"How are you fixed?"

"I'm all right."

"I've got a job going."

Macrae knew better than to make objections. He said that he was free.

"The pay's good and there's no risk." None of Bill Connor's jobs had any risk—to Bill Connor. "I will tell you about it later. That is all."

Macrae felt better when he had got out of the room and a great deal better when he saw Peggy. There were two full glasses of sherry on the table by the fire. "Come on. Drink up. You shouldn't have waited." He rang the bell. Tony came in with a tray of *hors d'oeuvres* and a bottle of Chablis.

"I have ordered a sole *à la maison*," Tony said. "What would you like to follow?"

Macrae looked at Peggy. "What about a Pêche Melba?"

Peggy hadn't the slightest idea what he meant, but replied blindly: "Yes, that would be awfully nice." As she tasted her very first mouthful of smoked salmon Peggy forgot Bulmer Court, Mr. Crick, Mrs. Finch, and Danny Levine.

It was nearly midnight when Tony brought in coffee and asked if they wanted anything else. Peggy looked at her watch and got up in a panic. "Heavens! I never thought it was so late. I must go."

"All right. Have a cigarette and I'll tell Tony to get a taxi."

"I'd rather go by Tube, and I mustn't really wait a minute. I don't know what Mother'll say."

As he helped her on with her coat Macrae said: "It's been a wonderful evening. We must do it again some time."

"Yes. I have enjoyed myself and I'm terribly grateful."

Macrae saw her into the Tube station at Leicester Square and then went back to the club.

CHAPTER THREE

OLD LAMPY finished the tune he was playing. Then he took the half-crown which Macrae had given him and bit it. It was all right. He shuffled up the Court to Danny Levine's shop and opened the door.

At the sound of the bell Danny poked his head out of the back room.

"I'm going along to have a wet," Lampy mumbled.

Danny grinned. "Thirsty weather. See you later."

Old Lampy stepped backwards into the Court and with his accordion slung across his bowed back made his way to the "Goat."

At nine o'clock he was back on his pitch, and stayed there playing until the church clock struck eleven. Then he fumbled in a pocket and took out a packet of cigarettes, lit one, and sucked in the smoke.

He crossed the road, passed the pawnshop, and turned into a doorway. On one side of it was a board with faded lettering, "Practice Rooms," and underneath the words "Daniel Levine, prop."

Lampy reached up and pulled a wire. A latch clicked and the door swung open as he leaned against it. He shuffled down a passage slowly, with his toes splayed, and up a short flight of steps. The door at the top was open. Ahead of him was a long, low room. A naked bulb hung from the ceiling on a short flex. There were several small tables, benches against the wall, and half a dozen wooden chairs. The floor was bare boards.

At the far end of the room, almost beyond the range of the light, there was a raised platform, and on it was an upright piano with the lid open.

Danny Levine, stripped to a singlet and trousers, was sitting at the keyboard thumping out "Red Sails in the Sunset."

Lampy slung the accordion off his shoulders and put it on the floor as he sat on a bench with his back against the wall.

Danny stopped playing and twirled round on his stool. "Now try it," he snapped. His face was screwed up like a monkey's.

An old man, older than Lampy and more bent, got up from a chair and nestled a violin under his chin. Gnarled, knotted fingers gripped a bow and began scraping the strings.

Danny sat for a minute quite still, then he waved his arms and shouted at the old man. "Nothing like it. Listen!" He sprang back to the piano. His fingers flashed over the keys. When he came to the part where the old man had failed he played more slowly. "Like this." And when he had finished: "Now try again."

He picked out the tune with one finger as the violin wailed and sobbed out the melody.

"That's better. Now try again. Quicker this time."

Old Lampy was very tired of "Red Sails in the Sunset" before Danny Levine was satisfied and demanded sixpence from his pupil. He threw the coin into a cigar-box, lifted down a can of beer, and drank deeply.

"You want to practise that," he said. Then he slipped off his stool and came down off the platform, lit a cigarette, and saw old Lampy. "You're early."

Lampy said: "It's gone eleven."

Danny nodded and looked round the room. "How she go?"

"Not so bad."

Danny ran his fingers through his hair and turned back to the piano. "I got something new. Listen."

Old Lampy's head nodded to the rhythm: "Where Your Love Is, There I'll Be."

"How d'you like it?"

"Not so bad."

Lampy picked up his accordion and began to finger out the tune. "What cheer, Lampy!"

He came back to the present with a jerk. It was Chalks O'Callaghan. A man with sleek black hair, long nose, and a sad mouth. The fingers which held the glass were long, tapering, and seldom still. The voice was soft, low, and vibrating.

Lampy turned to look into eyes the colour of ripe sloes. They made him feel uneasy.

"Do you think we'll get our money?"

"Money? Why not?"

"I don't know. There's been trouble."

Lampy clutched at the skirts of his ragged coat, and for a moment cold fear made him shiver. The fear of hunger; nights in doorways with rags and old papers for bedclothes. And in the end—the institution. Chopping wood. Big, cold, comfortless rooms; greasy stew out of a tin. Getting up when a bell rang. . . .

Lampy said crossly: "What the hell's got you?"

"There's trouble. And you know how it is once it starts. There's no knowing how it'll finish up."

Lampy was anxious. "Abie didn't say anything last night. I saw him."

"It was all right yesterday." Chalks stared at the floor as he drew at his cigarette. Then he blew out the smoke and said: "There's a bloke got a pitch in King's Road. Outside a pub. He paid his squeeze and Abie told me to fix him up with the gear. I sat up most of one night doing them. Good stuff they was, too. One of Lloyd George. And another of Winston Churchill in a funny hat. And the usual lettering: 'All my own work. No dole.'"

Lampy chuckled. "That's a ruddy lie."

Chalks went on: "Well, this bloke got the daubs set up and he laid out his cap and was sitting with his back up agin the wall of the pub when a guy came along. He'd a can of oil under his coat and that was the finish of the daubs."

"Who was it?"

"That's what I'd like to know."

"That kind of thing happens now and again and nothing comes of it."

"You know Toby Flynn?"

Lampy nodded.

"The rozzers have took him. Said he was on the mooch. I saw his missus. She said it'd been fixed."

"She would say that."

Chalks, still staring at the floor and thinking of his spoilt pictures, said: "Anyway, Abie's got the wind up. Else why'd he have Crick up at this time of night?"

The door burst open and Bert came in. He walked unsteadily down the centre of the room. He was holding a handkerchief to his face and there was blood on his hands.

"D'you see that?" Lampy put out a hand and touched Chalks on the knee. He looked up slowly and stared at Bert. "That's the third of our bunch as has copped it. Now what d'you say?"

Lampy got up and followed Bert. He caught him by the sleeve. "What happened, mate?"

Bert swore and shook him off. Danny Levine stopped playing. He filled a glass with beer. Bert took it and drained it in one long, gurgling swallow.

"Where's Abie?" he asked.

"He'll be along any minute." Danny crooked a foot round the rail of a chair and drew it towards him. "Sit down."

Bert took the handkerchief from his face and looked at it stupidly. Then he felt his cheek. A gash ran from his cheek-bone almost to his mouth. There was dry blood round it and the flesh was swollen and coloured red and purple.

Lampy went back to his seat. Chalks gave him a twisted smile and spat on the floor. "What did I tell you?"

"Razor," Lampy muttered. "That's what that was done with." He drew his ragged coat closer about him and shivered, though the night was warm.

Mr. Crick worked late in his office after Peggy had gone.

It was nine o'clock when he finished with Toby Flynn's case. He sighed as he tied up the bundle of papers with a piece of red tape and put it on one side. Then he wiped his pen and put it in its rack, tipped down the lid of the inkwell, and got up, dusting the ash of his cheroot from the wide spread of his black waistcoat.

The black marble clock still said twenty minutes to seven.

The droning wail of Lampy's accordion came in through the open window. Footsteps approached and faded. A house-door slammed.

He locked up the office and walked down the precipitous stairway slowly, with his toes turned out. Down the Court; Lampy nodded to him as he passed; across the street to the pawnbroker's shop.

There was a light in the first-floor window and before the bell had stopped pealing he saw Abie Russ looking down at him.

The door-latch clicked, released by a wire, and he walked into a wide, tiled hall, cool even on this hot summer night.

A single gas-jet burned in a gilt chandelier which had once held twenty wax candles.

He mounted the broad, shallow steps of the uncarpeted staircase, his hand sliding easily over the polished mahogany rail. That wrought-iron balustrade, with its broad rail, had cost eighty pounds. The chandelier twenty.

Abie Russ was waiting in an open doorway; a slim young Jew of twenty-eight, eyes of such a dark shade of brown that they looked black, a blue suit with padded shoulders, light-blue shirt and collar, a blue tie sprinkled with yellow half-moons, in his cuff a mauve silk handkerchief, hair that started well back and rippled in steep, short waves, black and glinting in the light.

He smiled and said: "Good evening." Somehow he managed to put an "s" or two into the words.

Before Abie had shut the door, Crick was well bedded down in the best arm-chair.

He didn't like the room, with its self-coloured russet carpet, dull gold walls, shaded lights, massive wireless set standing four feet high, and a cocktail cabinet like a cabinet-maker's nightmare in walnut.

"Cigarette?"

Mr. Crick stared at the inside of the slim gold case Abie held out to him as though it smelt bad. "No, thanks. I'll have one of my own." He dragged a leather case from an inside pocket. It was full of cheroots. He'd filled it when Peggy had been looking the other way.

Abie lit a Turkish cigarette and leaned against the mantelpiece. "Hot to-night."

"You know Flynn, don't you?" Mr. Crick wasn't in the mood for small talk.

"Yes, I fixed him up with a pitch in Albert Street."

"That's the man." Mr. Crick rolled his cheroot in his fingers. It wasn't drawing well.

"I suppose he's in trouble again."

"Then you know what it's about?"

"No." Abie smiled, though he wasn't amused. It was a habit with him to smile without reason. He had no sense of humour. "But you never come to see me unless there's something wrong."

"You won't be disappointed this time."

Abie tapped the ash off his cigarette. Then he looked at Crick. "What is it?" Smooth tones gave way to a note of urgency.

Crick met his gaze, held it for seconds, and then said: "Some one's trying to break the racket."

"I'll fix that. It's happened before."

"This is different."

"What do you mean?"

"I'll tell you." Mr. Crick crossed his legs, took a pull at his cheroot, and then told the story of Toby Flynn.

When he had finished, Abie left his stand at the mantelpiece. He walked up and down the room three times. Then he stopped and said: "You've got to clear Flynn."

"I'll try, but it won't be easy."

"You've got to do it."

Crick looked up. "Got to? That's easy to say."

"But don't you see?" Abie dropped a hand on Crick's shoulder. "If Flynn goes down it's going to make trouble. The boys'll begin to lose confidence, and I can't afford to have that happen."

Crick twisted his shoulders, and Abie took his hand away. "I know what you mean," Crick said. "That's why I came up. I'll do the best I can about Flynn, but it's up to you to see that this sort of thing doesn't happen again."

"I don't want trouble." Abie walked to the cocktail cabinet, opened it, and picked up a decanter. "Scotch?"

"Thanks."

"I don't want trouble," Abie repeated. "Maybe it's nothing to worry about." He took a drink from his glass and put it on the mantelpiece.

Before his hand was off the glass he froze. There was a noise of scratching in one corner of the room, two knocks, and then two more.

He relaxed and took three strides across the room.

Crick, looking over his shoulder, saw him reach up and press on a section of the beading. There was a faint creak and a square of the panelled wall swung inwards.

A man stumbled into the room.

"Bert!" Abie shut the panel and then swung round. "I told you not to come in this way!"

"I know, but I thought it would be better, seeing as how—"

Abie saw the livid slash across Bert's cheek. "What happened?"

Crick half turned in his chair and said: "You seem to have been mixing in bad company, Bert. Better give him a drink, Abie."

"I'm all right." Bert tried to smile and stopped. Smiling hurt.

Abie poured out a whisky and gave it to him.

"That's what I've been wanting. Danny ought to be shot for that beer he sells. I'll bet it's never seen a hop."

"To hell with Danny. What's been going on?"

"It was in Rupert Street. I'd finished collecting and I'd started back home. Two blokes came up from behind. One on each side. 'Out with the gelt,' one of them said. I tried to make a break, but I hadn't a chance. They closed in and took the sack. Then I felt this." Bert put his fingers on the raw wound. "The bloke that did it laughed and said, 'We'll know you again.' Then they piled into a car that was cruising, and that's all there was to it."

Abie stood staring at Bert for a full half-minute. Then he looked at Crick.

"There's trouble about, all right."

Crick finished his drink and put the empty glass on a table by his side. "Not so good," he muttered, and threw the stub of his cheroot into the fireplace.

"And that's not all. Chalks says they've slopped the daubs he sent out this morning. Oil."

"Where is he?"

"At Danny's. He's in there now."

"Have you any idea who cut you?"

"No."

"What kind of car was it?"

"I don't know."

"A car," said Mr. Crick slowly. "They got away in a car?"

Bert nodded. "It could move, too."

"All right." Abie felt in his pocket, took out three one-pound notes, and gave them to Bert. "You'd better go back by the yard."

Bert nodded, and was on his way to the door, when he changed his mind. He drew back a curtain and looked down to the street.

Abie asked sharply: "What's the matter?"

"Come here." Bert took a pace backwards, still holding the curtain open. "There's a bloke in that doorway across the street. You can see his shadow."

Abie didn't say anything for nearly half a minute. Then he walked slowly to the fireplace and picked a cigarette from an open box. As he was lighting it he said to Crick: "Now what are we to do?"

Crick was still lying back in his chair puffing at his cheroot. He turned his head towards Abie. "You'll have to hit back."

"I don't want trouble. Once we start the strong-arm business you don't know how it'll end." He sat on the edge of a table and stared at the fireplace. It was filled with a pink paper fan, and on the fan was a dusting of soot. "I don't want trouble," he repeated, half to himself.

Bert coughed, and when Abie looked up he said: "Can I go the way I came? It'll be best."

Abie nodded and watched him go.

"What are you going to do about Flynn if I get him off?" Mr. Crick asked.

"Find him another pitch." Abie got to his feet and opened a cupboard on the right of the fireplace. He took from it a map, unfolded it, and spread it on the top of the wireless set.

Crick grunted and levered himself forward with his elbows. "Why not try him in the Strand or Fleet Street? The police won't be wise to him there."

"I'll fix it." Abie made a cross on the map. "This sort of thing would happen just when I'm a bit short of cash."

Crick looked first at the radio set and then at the cocktail cabinet. Abie read his thoughts.

"They haven't been paid for," he said.

"I see." Crick finished his drink and got up with difficulty.

"I'll let you out through the yard."

Abie opened the door and led the way downstairs to the hall, turned right past the door which led to the shop, and unlocked and unbolted the back door.

Mr. Crick walked slowly and not too steadily over the uneven cobblestones of the back yard. Past a row of open sheds where barrows and barrel-organs were ranged; through a gate into a narrow alleyway which came out on Fenwick Street near the door of the Practice Rooms.

He could hear the sound of many men talking and the tinkle of Danny Levine's piano.

It was a dirty racket, he thought, and wondered if it wouldn't be better if he broke with Abie Russ.

He had thought of doing so a dozen times before, but the few pounds he got out of it paid the rent of his office.

The shillings and half-crowns of his respectable clients only supplied the necessities of life, which of course included cheroots.

CHAPTER FOUR

ABIE SHUT the door when he had seen Crick out of sight and looked at his watch by the dim light of the single gas-jet in the chandelier.

It was later than he thought—after eleven. The boys would be waiting for their pay.

He unlocked the door of the shop, went in, and struck a match. The gas on a mantle popped with a blue flame and spread into a ball of hard white light, revealing a long room which ran the whole length of the house.

There were shelves rising to the ceiling, piled high with bundles of clothes, cameras, fenders, pictures, tea-pots, umbrellas, hats.

Opposite this array was a broad counter, divided off into cubicles.

Abie unlocked a safe under the counter and, squatting on his heels, took out a wad of one-pound notes, a bag of silver, and one of coppers. He put the bags on the counter and then felt along a shelf in the safe until his fingers touched a parcel bound with tape. He carried it to a high desk under the gas-light, untied the knot, unfolded the blue tissue-paper, and held up a string of pearls.

They looked all right and they felt all right as he rubbed them against the flat of a front tooth—just that faint roughness that a genuine pearl should have.

He screwed an optician's glass into his right eye and examined each individual pearl. They were the real thing. Six hundred pounds, seven hundred. He wouldn't like to say what they were worth.

The acquisitive greed of a man who has made every penny he has spent in the last ten years showed in his eyes, in the restless, nervous fingers, and the glance over the shoulder into the deep shadows of the shop.

Slowly, lovingly, regretfully, Abie gathered the string into a heap of milky shiny beads, wrapped it in the blue tissue-paper, and tied it up with a length of tape on which was threaded a tag. On the tag was scribbled a short description of the necklace.

He put the pearls back on a shelf of the safe. Then he sat quite still while his thoughts ranged back two hours, to the time when Macrae had come hesitantly into the shop, had refused Bert's services, and had asked to see the boss.

Seven years in the trade had taught Abie Russ to spot at a glance the man who was making his first pledge. The shy advance, then the too-aggressive demand, and later the reluctance to give his name and address. Edward Morrison., he'd called himself, and the address, 93 Clarges Street.

Abie reached across the desk and turned over the leaves of a street directory, Clarges Street did not have ninety-three houses.

And the name, Morrison, Edward James, wasn't in the telephone directory.

Six hundred pounds! He knew where he could sell the string and get paid in treasury notes. Six hundred pounds.

Abie got up suddenly, filled his pockets with the money he had taken from the safe, locked it, and after a look around he turned off the gas. The mantle, fading to a faint red glow, gave sufficient light to show the way to the door. He walked down the hall to the back door, the steel tips on the heels of his shoes making a brisk click-clack on the tiled floor.

He took the same way which Mr. Crick had followed, across the yard and up the alley to the street. There he stopped and looked across to where Bert had pointed out the watcher. The man was still there. He could see the red pin-point of a lighted cigarette.

Though the breadth of the street separated him from the man, though there were passers-by, and a policeman at the crossing a few hundred yards away, Abie felt a rising, sickening fear; his hands went cold, and a sweat broke out on his scalp.

He ran up the steps leading to the entrance of the Practice Rooms and stumbled up the stairs. The sound of many voices and Danny Levine singing was comforting. There were men there; men who would help him if he called. Then he remembered Bert and saw again the livid scar. A razor! Abie shuddered even as he pushed open the door of the Practice Rooms.

No one noticed his entrance for a moment. Then as he walked towards the platform the talk and laughter died. Old Lampy called out, "'Evening, guv'nor." Some one else followed suit. Danny stopped playing. A little wisp of a man took a cornet from his mouth and drew back from the piano.

Abie forgot his fear. He was boss here. They were waiting for him. Awaiting his pleasure. He took the bag of silver from his pocket and dumped it on a table. "Sorry if I'm late."

Sycophantic voices said it didn't matter. Greedy eyes fastened on the bags of money which spelled beds, food, beer, and smokes. Abie tipped a shower of silver on to the table, followed it with the coppers, and set the wad of notes beside the two heaps. Chair legs scraped on the bare wooden floor. Shuffling steps advanced to the platform. There were whisperings, chuckles, and an occasional burst of laughter. It always took them that way.

"Where's Bert?" Abie looked round the room, and like mechanical dolls worked by one string, twenty-five heads followed his movements.

Bert came out of a corner like a shy child at a grown-up party. His right hand concealed his right cheek. With his other hand he fumbled awkwardly in his breast pocket and produced a black note-book.

Abie took it and Bert retreated. The eyes of the crowd switched back to the money on the table.

"You read 'em out," Abie said to Danny Levine.

One by one they were paid. Some took their pay sullenly, silently; others mumbled a word of thanks; but each and all, as soon as they had been paid, hurried from the light so that none should see where they hid their money.

The last man to be paid was Chalks O'Callaghan. Abie said to him, "I want a word with you," walked to a table behind the piano, and pointed to a chair.

Chalks sat down and stared at the floor. Abie lit a cigarette. Danny brought a glass of beer. "And one for him," Abie said.

Chalks looked up, gave a shy smile, and said, "Thanks."

Abie smoked, but said nothing until the second glass was put on the table. "Bert told me. I'm sorry about it."

Chalks took a long drink and then said, "It's a bad business. You don't know where it's going to finish up. I took a lot of trouble over those daubs."

"Yes, I know. They're good."

"They were." Chalks traced a line of spilt beer on the table with a slender forefinger.

"Can you do anything about them?"

"No. The wood's spoilt. That oil'll eat into anything."

"I'll get you some more frames."

Chalks's finger stopped its tracing. When he spoke he did not raise his eyes.

"I'm not sure I can do any more."

Abie's hand with his cigarette stopped an inch from his mouth. "Why?" he asked sharply.

Chalks moved in his chair. "Well, you see . . ." he said, and was silent.

Abie dropped his cigarette on the floor and trod it out with his foot. Then he turned until he was facing O'Callaghan. "Do you mean you're ratting?"

Still Chalks did not look up. He said, "No, of course not," hurriedly, and took up his glass.

"You are," Abie accused.

Chalks's stained fingers rapped a tattoo on the rim of his glass. "I don't want to get beaten up. You've seen Bert?"

"That won't happen again." Abie leaned forward with eager tension in his slim body. "That was different. He had cash on him; that's what they were after."

"They said they'd get me if—" Chalks's voice was very low, a vibrant whisper—"if I don't pack up working for you."

Fear sapped at Abie's determined optimism, and Chalks looked up curiously when Abie said quickly, nervously, "I've never let you down. I've always paid what I promised and if there's any rough stuff I can meet it." He put out a hand and laid it on Chalk's shabby sleeve. "I rely on you. The others . . ." He hunched his shoulders and his teeth showed in a smile.

Chalks looked at Abie for a full half-minute after he had finished speaking. Then his gaze wandered round the room. It was nearly empty now.

Danny Levine was collecting the glasses. His eyes came back to Abie. "When I was on my way here to-night a man came up to me in the street and said I'd got to lay off working for you."

"Where did you see him?"

"At the corner of Bulmer Court."

"What's his name?"

"He didn't say, and I've never seen him before. He's hot."

Abie got up. "I'll get some more woods and you can start on another set to-morrow." There was a question and a challenge in the words. He waited, looking down at O'Callaghan for a few seconds, and then said, "Well?" sharply.

"I'll have a go; but you've got to stop the rot."

Abie was smiling. "That's fine. Fine." He nodded a good night to Danny. "I'll take the daubs along to my room." He went through the door which led straight to his flat. It didn't matter going that way when the crowd wasn't around.

When he was gone, and the muffled sound of his footsteps had faded, Danny Levine turned to O'Callaghan. "He's windy."

Chalks said, "So would you be after what's happened to Bert."

"I saw him."

"All right, then." O'Callaghan pushed back his chair and walked to a window overlooking the street. "Seems as if it's all clear now. I'll be beating it."

When Macrae got back to the club after parting with Peggy he went straight to the bar-room. Six men were sitting at a card-table. In the centre of the green cloth there was a heap of coloured chips. Macrae was watching the play when a man who had been sitting back in the shadows in a corner of the room got up and touched him on the arm.

"Come over here a minute." It was Tim Daly.

He spoke in a husky whisper: "How did you get on with Abie?"

"I didn't go," Macrae lied easily.

"Yes, you did." Tim felt in his pocket. From it he brought a dirty envelope. "You went into Abie's shop at a quarter past six and came out at five to seven."

There was a finality about the plain statement which silenced the next lie which was forming on Macrae's lips.

"It's no use trying to put anything over on me." Tim leaned back in his chair and pressed a bell-push in the wall. When the barman came he ordered a double White Horse.

"What's yours?"

"The same," Macrae said.

"What did you raise?"

"A fiver."

Tim Daly grunted and breathed heavily through his mouth. "A fiver? You got more than that."

The barman brought the drinks, and when he had gone Tim Daly said, "I know you paid the old man forty tonight. What was it you soaked?"

"Stones. I told you that before."

"Where'd you get 'em and what were they like?"

"I won't tell you."

"Oh, so that's the line you're taking!" Tim Daly leaned forward in his chair and heaved himself to his feet. "All right. But remember!" He finished his drink, wiped his mouth with the back of his hand, and lurched out of the room.

One of the men at the card-table called to Macrae. "Want to come in?"

"No, thanks. I'm going home."

He had come back to the club to gamble, but now he didn't feel like it. He was frightened.

Tim Daly went down the passage and opened the door at the end without knocking. Big Bill Connor was still sitting at his desk.

He raised a pudgy white hand and massaged his pendulous cheeks. "Well, how did it go?"

Tim brought a handful of crumpled notes out of a trouser pocket and laid them on the desk. "That's all he had on him."

"Not so bad. Not so bad." Connor's fingers worked quickly and efficiently, smoothing the notes and packing them in a pile. He snapped a rubber band round them. "Did he fight?"

"He couldn't. Everything worked fine."

"Let's have it." Connor stretched out a hand.

Tim gave him a closed razor.

"You don't want to be picked up carrying this." Connor opened a drawer and dropped the razor into it.

"What about to-morrow?" Tim asked.

"We'll give him time to let it sink in. He's got plenty to think about." Connor chuckled fatly. He was thinking of Toby Flynn and of the set of daubs ruined by a can of oil. "How did you find out where Bert Finch would be?"

"From Danny Levine. He's ready to change over when I give him the word. And it won't need a lot to keep him sweet. Abie's been cutting down on the squeeze. I chucked a scare into Chalks O'Callaghan as well." Tim grinned.

"That's fine." Connor's fat lips pouted and then spread as he said, "But you can lay off any more of the strong-arm stuff till I give you the word."

"I get you." Tim leaned back and lit a cigarette. "You saw Macrae?"

"Yes. I told him I'd got a job for him."

"He's yellow."

"I know that. But we've got to have some one from outside and he'll do it all right. He's gabby enough."

"I couldn't get him to talk to-night."

"What about?"

"I met him earlier on, and he asked me where he could fence some stuff he'd lifted. I sent him to Abie."

"What was it?"

"Stones. That's all he'd say."

"What was the idea in putting him on to Abie?"

"Well, the way I figured it out was this: if Abie takes the stuff we could tip the slops off to him."

Connor stared at Tim for a minute without speaking. Then he said, "Yes, I see what you mean." He began to laugh. "That's funny. Damn' funny." He choked and coughed. When he had got his breath again he said, "But we've got to find out what it was Macrae fenced."

"You leave him to me."

"What did he raise from Abie?"

"He said it was a fiver, but he was lying. He paid you forty to-night, didn't he?"

Connor nodded. "I'd like to know what he's got on to."

"I'll see Danny Levine in the morning. He might know."

"All right." Connor picked up his pen and began to write.

Tim Daly got up and left the room.

CHAPTER FIVE

"WELL, HOW DID you get on last night?" The shrill tones of Mrs. Finch in full morning song woke Captain Eric Macrae. "Did you make a night of it?"

It took Macrae a little time to realize what Mrs. Finch was talking about. Meanwhile she let in an unwelcome beam of sunlight.

"What's the time?"

"Gone ten." She lit the gas-ring and put on the kettle. The money Macrae had given her had imbued her with a desire to act as a valet as well as a char. "I saw Peggy. She told me you took her to the pictures."

"Oh, yes."

"I must really give the place a proper turn-out. It could do with it."

"She's a nice kid." Macrae took a cigarette-case from the coat on the chair and lit a cigarette.

"Yes, but you've got to take her easy, if you know what I mean," Mrs. Finch replied, with her head cocked on one side and a hand on her hip. The other hand was carrying out an exploratory expedition with a match among her back teeth. "You see, she's not your sort really."

"I didn't do anything."

"She was late getting home. Close on one o'clock."

Macrae laughed. "Yes, I see what you mean. I'll be more careful next time."

"Her ma's a tiger."

"They always are."

"Who are what?"

"Nice girls' mothers. There's never a rose without a thorn."

Mrs. Finch thought over that statement for a moment and then said, "Maybe you're right. Anyway, there's the water warming up, and if you like you can come to my place for your breakfast. I've got a kipper."

Macrae politely refused the invitation.

He breakfasted largely and satisfactorily at a tea-shop in the High Street, with a morning paper propped up on the cruet. It was open at the racing news, and his coffee grew cold as he searched the list of runners at Sandown. He had over fifty pounds left, but he'd have to make it a hundred before he could redeem the pearls from Abie Russ.

Something at about thirteen to eight or even shorter odds would do for a start. There was a two-year-old five-furlong sprint at three o'clock. There might be a horse in that to suit him. The racing correspondent gave Jack o' Lantern. Forecast of the betting seven to four. He was a good horse, nicely weighted, and he didn't mind hard going. Then there was the four-thirty with only three probable starters. The favourite six to four on; the next horse at six to four against; the third, twenty to one. Twenty to one. That might be worth a gamble. Say ten pounds. A couple of hundred would put him in Easy Street for a long time to come and would give him a chance to play Mrs. Keene until she was ready for a touch.

He had a scheme all worked out. He would start by giving her a sound tip on the Stock Exchange and let her clear a nice bit of profit. He would do that three times and then make a big strike and clear out. He knew an outside broker who would work in with him.

But that sort of thing required capital. He might do it with a couple of hundred, but three would be safer, or even five.

Macrae returned to his study of the race program and finally settled on Jack o' Lantern. Forty pounds to eighty. Better keep off that four-thirty outsider.

If Jack o' Lantern came home he could have a crack at the three-thirty.

Old Lampy was on his pitch droning out "Red Sails in the Sunset," more slowly than it had ever been played before, as Macrae passed him. He missed a couple of notes as he nodded and grinned. That was the bloke who had given him the half-dollar.

Macrae gave him a shilling for luck. He always gave a beggar something before he made a big bet. He wasn't superstitious, but—well, some people said it was lucky. The same as taking off your hat to a sweep or touching a blind man.

He pushed open the door of Danny Levine's shop, and as the bell tinkled Danny came out from the back room.

"'Morning, Captain." His face crinkled in a cheery grin. "What can I do for you?"

"Jack o' Lantern. Eighty pounds to forty. Can you fix that?"

"Eighty to forty!" Danny sprawled across the paper-strewn counter. "Eighty to forty!"

"It isn't twelve o'clock yet. You've time to lay it off."

Danny pulled at the lobe of his right ear and the grin faded as he thought over the suggestion. "Cash?" he asked.

"Sure."

Danny went into the back room and returned carrying an evening paper. "That's for the three o'clock. Jack o Lantern." He pulled out a note-book and made an entry. "I'll do the best I can for you, but it may have to be starting price."

Macrae counted out forty notes and handed them over.

"I'll risk that." He went out into the Court and nearly bumped into Mr. Crick, who was hurrying along with his head bent.

Mr. Crick was on his way back from the police court, where, after a hard fight, he had managed to get Toby Flynn off with a five-shilling fine. The magistrate had had some unpleasant things to say about men who begged under the pretence of selling match-es, and hinted that the next time Toby came before him on a similar charge he would be sent to prison. He also suggested that Toby should go into an institution where he would be properly cared for.

Toby had been pathetically grateful to Mr. Crick, who only growled at him, paid his fine, and told him to be more careful in future.

Mr. Crick sighed as he settled down at his desk and counted his remaining cash. Toby Flynn was an expensive charity. He was staring at the marble clock, which still said twenty minutes to seven with implacable obstinacy, when the trap hatch snapped up and Peggy put in her head.

"I was expecting you back before this," she said sharply.

Mr. Crick didn't say anything while he lit a cheroot; as he tossed the match out of the window he smiled. "What's gone wrong?"

"Nothing. Why?"

"You're crosser than two sticks."

"I'm all right.'"

"Had a row with Bert?"

Peggy blushed and said, "No."

"Meaning yes."

"It wasn't anything."

Mr. Crick tore a corner off his blotting-pad and began to clean his pen.

"I wish you wouldn't do that." Peggy leaned across the desk and picked up a slip of nice clean blotting-paper. "I told you to use that, didn't I?"

"You did." The smile was playing about Mr. Crick's mouth. "It was very wicked of me. But tell me about Bert. What did he say? And what did you say?"

Peggy ignored the questions and asked what had happened to Toby Flynn. Mr. Crick told her, and then said, looking at the clock, "Bert's not a bad 'un."

"I've got a lot of work to do," Peggy said, and left the room.

Mr. Crick picked up the corner of the pink blotting-paper and tore it into tiny pieces. Was this another case of love's young dream going wrong, or just a passing cloud in the sky? Bert was a worker and loyal to Abie, but he'd be better out of it. Abie wouldn't last. He was smart and had made a lot of money, but . . . Mr. Crick thought of the room over the shop; the cocktail cabinet and the radio set. There was something rotten about Abie. True, he was a worker, but he only cared for what his work would bring him. Money, gaudy furniture, flashy clothes. One of these days he'd take a toss, and if Mr. Crick knew anything the toss wasn't far off.

The door of the saloon bar opened inwards and before it had finished swinging the talk had eased to a murmur. Mrs. Finch looked round and saw Detective-Constable Leith. His lugubrious face showed none of the gladness it should have borne this bright summer's day.

All the good Leith saw in the heat of the sun was the thirst it had given him. He hitched himself on to a high stool and ordered a pint of bitter.

While it was being drawn he asked Mrs. Finch what had happened to Bert's face.

She said she didn't know.

"He was up West last night, wasn't he?" Leith asked, and took up a biscuit and began nibbling it.

"Up West? What'd he want to go there for?"

"I don't know. I'm asking you."

"He hadn't no call to go anywhere near there that I knows of."

"It isn't a crime to go to the West End."

Danny Levine finished his drink and went out.

Mrs. Finch said nervously that she must be getting along. She didn't like policemen. Of course, she hadn't done nothing wrong, and she wasn't scared of Leith, but all the same there was hundreds of other blokes she'd sooner talk to.

There was slightly more rock to her walk than could be attributed to corns and tight boots as she went down the alley to the Court and into her house.

She collected a large duster, a dust-pan, and a brush.

Then she steered a moderately straight course for Bury Square and let herself into Macrae's room. It was stuffy and hot. Well, there wasn't no good rushing it. She'd sit down and get her breath, and maybe slip off her boots. Ah, that was better! A bluebottle buzzing and pinging against a window-pane was as a lullaby to Mrs. Finch.

She woke two hours later, fat-headed, drowsy, and aching in two or three new spots where the splines of the wicker chair had poked through the torn padding.

She tied up her hair with the duster she had brought and set to work with dust-pan and brush. The good turn-out that she had promised the room, however, became no more than the ordinary sweep and flick that had been its lot since she had undertaken the duties of "doing" for the Captain. There was only a handful of dust in the pan.

Mrs. Finch felt that she had done her job and felt entitled to a little recreation, and her idea of recreation was to poke her sharp little nose into things which were no concern of hers.

Every article on the top of the chest of drawers was examined. The ivory-backed brushes with their black intertwining monogram. The silver cigar-piercer. The stud-box of painted wood. The silver shoe-horn.

She pulled out the top drawer and shut it at once. There were socks in it that she had promised to darn, and she didn't feel like darning socks. She seldom did.

There was the cupboard in the wall to the right of the fireplace. She had promised herself a long time ago to have a look through it, but unfortunately it was always kept locked.

But the key must be somewhere about, surely; on the mantelpiece, in one of them jars that the Captain kept his pipe-cleaners in. She turned one upside down; two buttons and a safety-pin fell out, and—yes, that looked like a key that would fit the cupboard door.

The key fitted the keyhole all right, but it was stiff to turn. It hadn't been used for a long time most likely. She exerted all her strength. There was a creaking sound and the lock snapped back.

What she expected to find Mrs. Finch could not have said, but the locked cupboard had fascinated her. It was therefore a great disappointment to her to find that the shelves were stacked with clothes. Not a sign of a body. Not even a skeleton.

A row of dusty boots in trees filled the lowest shelf. Tall boots, black with brown tops; there were three pairs of them. Heavy brown leather shoes with nailed soles. A pair of thigh-high waders.

What they were for was a question quite beyond Mrs. Finch's ability to answer. She had never seen any one riding to hounds, walking up partridges over stubble, nor casting a fly for salmon in brown pools.

Fancy him keeping all that rubbish! And some of them hardly worn, neither.

She picked up a boot and examined the sole.

There were two shelves filled with clothes. Mrs. Finch pulled out a pair of white cord riding breeches. They were riddled with moth-holes.

"Well, if that ain't a blooming shame! Somebody might have been glad of these if they'd been looked after proper. Good stuff, too."

The top shelf looked more interesting. She could see a tin helmet, the handle of a sword, a pile of books, and a lot of maps. There was one sound chair in the room, and she pushed it close to the open cupboard and clambered on to it.

The dust lay thick on the brown leather scabbard of the sword; the hand-guard was green and slimy to the touch.

Curios. That's what they were. And they'd look all right hung over the mantelpiece in her room. At least, the sword would, and them bayonets. And the helmet, with its spike and tarnished brass badge, that would do to carry coals in. It must have been a German's, with that eagle on it. That was a real curio.

She moved the helmet to one side, and my, it was a tidy weight! She wouldn't care to have it on her head even if there was an air raid. And she wouldn't half look a scream in it, neither.

Her eager, searching fingers closed on the butt of a heavy Service revolver, and she had drawn it clear of some maps which half concealed it when the door of the room opened. It was Macrae. He was carrying an evening paper in his hand.

Mrs. Finch wobbled on the chair, caught hold of the edge of the shelf to steady herself, and dropped the revolver on the floor.

"I've just been having a clear-up," she explained. "I didn't think you'd be in so soon."

Macrae came across the room and picked up the revolver. He turned it over in his hands. "Where did you find this?"

"On the top shelf under a lot of books." Mrs. Finch got down to the floor and wiped her hands on her apron.

"I'd forgotten I had it." Macrae stood up on his toes. "Gosh, there's a lot of rubbish there!"

Hope shone in Mrs. Finch's eyes. "Well, if you like, I'll clear it out for you. I'd give you more room to put your clothes away in."

"Yes, it would. I'll see." He tossed the revolver back on to the shelf, locked the cupboard door, and put the key in his pocket.

Mrs. Finch, realizing that the chance of appropriating a curio had gone, collected her dust-pan and brush. As she was untying the duster from her head she saw the paper which Macrae had dropped on to the table.

"Do you mind if I have a look at this?"

"No, of course not." Macrae, with his back to her, was counting a number of one-pound notes.

Mrs. Finch turned to the back page and ran a finger down the stop-press column. Just her blooming luck. The horse which Mr. Godwin had chosen to carry his colours wasn't in the first three. And Star of Eve hadn't come up, neither.

"Two and thruppence down the drain," she muttered.

"Been having a gamble?" Macrae asked.

Mrs. Finch said: "Well, you can call it a gamble if you like, but it's more like blinking robbery to me. That there Godwin ought to be warned off, and I don't care who hears me say it."

"You ought to have done Jack o' Lantern." Macrae, with eighty pounds in his pocket, was annoyingly cheerful. "Have something on him the next time he runs."

"Thanks for the tip, Captain, but I've finished with horses."

Macrae held out a pound note. "You take that and back him both ways."

Mrs. Finch looked first at the note and then up at Macrae's smiling face. "Oh, I couldn't take it, sir. Not after what you gave me before—"

"Go on." He crumpled the note into a ball and threw it in to the dust-pan she was holding.

"I don't know how to thank you, sir. I'm sure I don't deserve all that money."

Macrae also was quite sure she didn't, but he enjoyed being generous when he had money to throw away.

When he had none he had no scruples in borrowing.

Mrs. Finch went off in a twitter of gratitude, and stronger than ever in her belief that Captain Macrae was a real gentleman.

He watched her through the window, hurrying along the pavement. Then he turned and looked at the cupboard and opened the door. He was a fool to keep all that rubbish when he might be able to sell it for a pound or two.

Those boots; he'd never use them again. Never? Well, if he did manage to make a big killing out of Mrs. Keene, something really big, thousands, then he could afford to live in the country. Hunt? No, he wouldn't have the nerve to start again. But fishing, that was different.

And why stay in this stinking room? Now he was on the up-grade he could afford a flat on the other side of the river. Two rooms, and a bath of his own. Central heating. Constant hot water.

He'd thought of making a move a score of times; every time he had had a bit of luck. But somehow the intention had proved to be but an intention. A stone-cold certainty had come unstuck, the shares he'd bought on margin had crashed, and he stayed on in Bury Square.

But it was going to be different this time. He would play safe. One more bet, or perhaps two, and he'd redeem the pearls, put them back in Mrs. Keene's flat, and have enough cash in hand to live on until he could land her for a packet. It would take time, but it would be worth it.

At the back of his mind he felt a slight uneasiness. He hadn't liked the way she'd looked when he'd asked her to lend him ten pounds, but the feel of the wad of notes he'd won on Jack o' Lantern restored his faith in himself. He'd land her in time; not too quick on the strike, and give her plenty of line.

CHAPTER SIX

ON THE EVENING of the same day that Captain Eric Macrae was considering the possibility of a move from Bury Square, Mrs. Keene was dressing for dinner at Longwood House, in the County of Berkshire.

To be accurate, she was sitting in a comfortable chair before her dressing-table, while her maid handed her powder-puff, lipstick, or eyebrow-pencil as required.

"I'll wear my pearls to-night, Maddox."

"Yes, madam." The maid unlocked the wardrobe and took out the jewel-case.

She put it on the bed and opened it.

Mrs. Keene bent forward to the glass and drew an orange-scarlet line along her upper lip. Then she sat back and picked up a hand-glass. It was rather a nice shade.

"Maddox, I like this stick. Remember the name of it."

There was no reply.

"Maddox, did you hear me? I said—"

"Madam! The pearls!"

"What's the matter?" Mrs. Keene, with the lipstick half-raised, turned her head and saw the girl's frightened face.

"Are you ill?"

"No, madam. But the pearls! I can't find them."

"Nonsense. Let me look."

Uneasy, but not alarmed, Mrs. Keene pushed the maid out of the way and bent over the case. "They must be somewhere. Here are the earrings that go with them." She emptied every satin-lined pocket of the case; went through them again, more slowly, more carefully.

Her voice was toneless when she said at last: "No, you're quite right, Maddox. They've gone."

The maid began to cry easily and noisily.

"Oh, stop that noise and tell me what you did with the case when we arrived!"

The story was a simple one. Maddox had carried the jewel-case up to the bedroom herself and had locked it in the wardrobe. She had then put the key of the wardrobe in her bag.

"Where is your bag?"

The maid pointed to the mantelpiece. She was still crying.

"Did you leave it lying about anywhere?"

"No."

"You must have."

"No, I didn't."

"All right, I believe you, but stop crying. You probably put the pearls away somewhere without thinking. Turn everything out."

The search continued for the best part of an hour and then the police were summoned. First there came the village constable, who, though clearly but of his depth, grappled with the problem gallantly and filled half his notebook with statements.

Then there was a sergeant, slightly blown by a five-mile cycle ride. When he was told of the value of the missing property he put through a call to his inspector, who sent a description of the pearls to Scotland Yard.

"Do you think there's any chance of getting them back?" Mrs. Keene asked the sergeant.

"Well, I wouldn't like to say, madam. It's a funny business."

"What d'you mean . . . a funny business?"

"Well, I've had a good look round, and what's troubling me is that there's no sign of any breaking-in."

He went on to question Mrs. Keene as to the character of the maid, Lucy Maddox. She had come to Mrs. Keene with excellent references, which she had taken up personally.

"I trust her absolutely."

"Has she any men friends?"

"I don't know."

"When did she first know you were coming here?"

"A day or two ago."

The sergeant searched the maid's room and found nothing, and when the inspector arrived he reported what had been done.

The inspector agreed that it was, indeed, a "funny business," and gave orders that a watch should be kept on the approaches to Longwood House, with especial reference to the movements of Lucy Maddox.

Mrs. Keene was contemptuous of the work of the police, and said some very nasty things about them.

"At least they might try and look as though they were doing something," she said.

Even as she spoke the words a hand printing-press in a basement of New Scotland Yard was turning out a special circular which, within an hour, was distributed to every pawnbroker in London.

Seven gentlemen known for their unconventional dealings in precious stones were visited by members of the Flying Squad. Pearls! A pearl necklace? No, they knew nothing about anything like that. It had been stolen? They were severally shocked, embarrassed, and offended that the police should think for one moment that they knew anything about it. If the inspector would care to have a look round?

In every case the inspector took advantage of the invitation, paying especial attention to such odd hiding-places as the insides of tea-pots, flour-bins, tea-caddies, and even cisterns.

Abie Russ was totting up his books at the end of the day when a constable brought him a copy of the circular.

"Here's a late extra special, but I shouldn't think it's much in your line."

Abie put down his pen and took the sheet. "Stolen from Longwood House . . . a pearl necklace . . ." He skipped the detailed description. "A reward of £150 will be paid to any person who gives information which will lead to the conviction of the thief or thieves and to the recovery of the necklace. Apply to . . . Assessors at . . ."

"Hundred and fifty reward." Abie looked up at the policeman. "That means it must be worth somewhere about fifteen hundred."

"Seems like it," the policeman answered. "If it's brought in here, you'll know what to do, but there won't be much chance of that."

"Why not?" Abie asked sharply.

"It'll go to a big fence. Well, I'll have to be toddling. Good night."

Abie said "Good night" and sat quite still, staring into the passage for a minute or longer. Then he smoothed out the sheet. That was the necklace all right. At least, if it wasn't, it was its twin. And pearl necklaces of that value didn't have twins.

He went out into the hall, walked to the back door and bolted it, then to the front door and shut it, and turned the key in the lock. It was past closing-time, anyway.

Excitement made him sweat. His head was buzzing and his hands trembling as he walked back to the shop. He closed the door behind him and stood for a moment looking to the right and to the left. Bert had gone. He knew that. But still he had to make sure.

He pulled up two chairs and draped two coats across them just in case any one should look in through the windows. Then he felt in his pocket for his key-ring and opened the safe.

For a moment he thought that the package had gone, and then his fingers closed on the tissue-paper and he felt the hard rounds of the pearls.

Fifteen hundred pounds. That was what they were worth, and the reward offered was only a measly hundred and fifty. He could see himself going along to the underwriters and handing them over for that sum!

He lifted down the scales from the desk and set them on a chair. Then he took a pair of scissors and cut through the silk thread. The diamond clasp alone would fetch nearly a hundred. If he could sell it!

He weighed each single bead and noted the figures on the back of an envelope, comparing them as he did so with the particulars given on the police circular.

That was the necklace all right. There was not the slightest doubt of that. The question now was, what was he going to do with it?

He had never dealt in stolen property before; at least, not in a big way. A few pounds' worth of lead stripped from the roof of an empty house; he had got rid of it quick to a dealer near-by, and there had been little risk of being found out. But this was different. It wouldn't be easy to find a buyer, and, in any event, it would take time to do so.

Fifteen hundred pounds! They would fetch that amount, Abie knew well enough, but half that figure would satisfy him. A hundred or two would be all he'd need to buy the services of the Hoxton mob to beat up the crowd who were trying to chisel in on his racket.

Abie smiled. That would fix the swine. He opened a drawer and took out a reel of fine silk thread, waxed it, and restrung the pearls. It was fine work, but his hand was steady. When the task was complete he wrapped the string in the blue tissue-paper, tied it with tape, and put the packet at the back of the top shelf of the safe. Then he locked the door and took the coats off the chairs.

He was thinking of the man who had brought him the pearls as he climbed the stairs to his flat.

Macrae sat in his room on the broken wicker chair reading the evening paper until seven o'clock. Then he got up and washed his hands. He could afford some decent towels now. He must tell Mrs. Finch to get some for him.

Seven o'clock. Peggy would be waiting for him. He smiled at the thought. They'd dine at the place he always went to in Soho. It wasn't cheap, but it was quiet. And afterwards a show. He had the tickets.

Bulmer Court was deserted as he entered it; not even a pigeon in sight. From the far end came the strains of Lampy's accordion.

He felt in his pocket for a shilling to give the old man, for he had brought him luck to-day. Eighty pounds! A window-sash went up with a slam, and Mrs. Finch's voice broke forth:

"Captain!"

He stopped and looked up, puzzled. When he saw who it was he smiled, and was about to walk on with a casual "Good evening."

"Captain. I saw Peggy and gave her your message, but she said she was sorry she couldn't come."

"Couldn't come?"

"That's right." Mrs. Finch leaned flat across the sill and lowered her voice to a piercing whisper. "It's Bert. She's going out with him."

"Damn!"

The pleasant picture of dinner and show faded.

"I did all I could, but it wasn't no good. Peggy's like that. Once she's made up her mind, it's no use talking to her."

"All right," Macrae said abruptly. "It doesn't matter." He stood for a moment irresolute and then walked on. Lampy nodded and grinned, to the destruction of half a bar of "Red Sails in the Sunset." Macrae dropped the shilling in his tin and was about to turn left into Fenwick Street, when a man came up to him. It was Tim Daly.

He said, "What cheer, Captain?" and fell into step beside him. "Going to the club?"

"No."

"The guv'nor wants a word with you."

"When?"

"As soon as you can get along."

"What about?"

"That's his business."

They walked a hundred yards before Macrae replied: "I'm not going. You can tell him I'm finished with—"

"I'd go if I was you." There was a threat in the husky tones.

"He can get some one else. Tell him I've a job on of my own."

"I'm telling him nothing, and if you want to keep your health, you'll go right along now."

It was absurd, Macrae argued to himself. He didn't owe Bill Connor anything. He wasn't one of his regular crowd, and if he, Macrae, wanted to run his own show, why the hell shouldn't he?

"Look here . . ." he began to say to Tim Daly, but Tim had gone.

Macrae walked over Southwark Bridge. At first he was weakly determined to ignore the summons. He would cut out going to the club and would stay over on the south side till Mrs. Keene came back; only go out in the daytime. He would do this; he would do that. Bill Connor could go to hell for all he cared.

But he still walked northward. At a quarter to eight he entered the club.

"Is the guv'nor in?" he asked Tony, the barman, who was passing with a tray of drinks.

"Yes, sir. He said you were to go straight in as soon as you arrived."

Macrae stiffened, pulled down his coat, and then adjusted his tie. His feelings were those of a school-boy being haled to justice. Tony was smiling as he turned away with his tray.

Macrae walked down the long passage. He wasn't feeling too good.

"Come in," said the voice of Bill Connor in answer to his knock.

Though it was still broad daylight, the heavy maroon curtains were drawn across the window. The light on the desk was burning.

Macrae took a step forward and waited. Connor raised his head slowly.

"You are late."

"I only got your message half an hour ago."

"You know Abie Russ?"

"Russ?"

"You've been seen going into his place. Tim says you soaked some stuff with him for a fiver. Is that true?"

Macrae said, "Yes."

"That is a lie. But never mind that. I said I had a job for you."

Macrae said that he was busy.

Connor ignored the plea. "You will go to Abie Russ to-night at eleven o'clock. You will not say that I sent you." Connor opened a silver box and took out a thick Turkish cigarette. As he flicked out the flame of the match with his thumbnail he said: "You will tell Abie Russ that you are willing to make a deal with him . . ." Connor spoke for five minutes.

When he had finished, Macrae left the room with the feelings of a man who has escaped from his dentist with a mere scale and polish.

Unexpectedly the job was one he really didn't mind carrying out; there was no risk. Even the sight of Tim Daly on a stool at the bar didn't depress him, and he very nearly clapped him on the back, but refrained. Clapping Tim Daly on the back was considered by those who knew him as only slightly less dangerous than monkeying with dynamite.

Instead he bought Tim a drink, and naturally did not forget himself. The guv'nor paid well, and he might reasonably expect ten pounds. More, maybe, if the deal came off.

"I'm going to see—" he said, when Tim Daly cut him short.

"I know all about that. Don't go around squawking."

Tony had his back to the two men. He was polishing glasses. There was no one else in the bar.

"What the hell does it matter?" Macrae was slightly drunk.

Tim Daly, who had been drinking off and on for the last two hours, was sober. "If the guv'nor tumbles to it that you've been blabbing, it won't be long before you're inside a wooden shirt."

Macrae stared stupidly.

"Coffin," Tim explained tersely, and ordered a double White Horse. When his glass had been filled, he took Macrae to a corner of the room. "And there's another thing. Abie's as wise as a crate of monkeys. You want to take him easy and watch your step—all the time. Make him see sense; that's your job, and cut out the booze till after you've seen him."

Tim Daly sat with Macrae until half-past ten. Then he got up and said: "You'd better get going." He followed Macrae into the hall and stood there smoking, while Macrae got his hat and let himself out of the street door.

Then he stepped back into an alcove and waited. Ten seconds passed. A door opened down the passage and footsteps came towards him.

"Just a minute." Tim came out of the shadow and stood in front of Tony.

The barman said, "Excuse me," and tried to walk round him.

"I want a drink."

"Certainly, sir," Tony said, but did not move.

"Well, what are you waiting for?"

"I'm going for some cigarettes. We're nearly out."

"It's after nine."

"I know a place where I can get them."

"Get me a double White Horse. The cigarettes can wait."

Tony went back to the bar. Tim waited till he was out of sight. Then he locked the front door, put the key in his pocket, and went to Connor's room.

CHAPTER SEVEN

ABIE RUSS OPENED the door on the chain when Macrae rang the bell.

It was dark under the porch and he could not see Macrae's face. "Who is that?" He was standing back a few feet in the hall.

"It's all right. Let me in."

"What d'you want?"

"Talk to you, that's all."

"It's too late. I'm going to bed." Abie was nervous.

"You know me. I was in yesterday."

Abie came closer to the door. "Stand back so I can see your face." Yes, it was the man. Abie's hand felt for the chain.

"Have you come to get the necklace?"

Macrae said: "Yes, that's it."

Abie shut the door, took off the chain, and opened the door again. "Come in," he said, and as soon as Macrae was inside he slammed the door and shot a bolt.

"Windy!" Macrae laughed.

"I've got to be careful," Abie muttered. "Lot of valuable stuff in the shop."

"Yes. You've got my necklace?"

Abie stopped with his foot on the first step of the stairs. In the flickering light of the single gas-jet he shot a glance charged with suspicion at Macrae. Then he said, "Yes, I've got your necklace," and went up the staircase.

He opened the door of the living-room and signed to Macrae to go in.

Macrae, with a clear picture of his own room in his mind, said: "Jove, you've got a nice place here!"

"Yes. It's not so bad." Abie switched on the wireless and tuned in to a dance-band program, opened the cocktail cabinet, and waited for further appreciation.

Macrae did not disappoint him. "That's rather nice." He thought: "I'd sooner be dead than have a thing like that in my place. Just like the filthy little beggar. And his suit! Gawd!"

"Whisky?"

"Thanks."

"It's rather good stuff. Cost me fifteen bob a bottle."

"Really? Where did you get it?"

"A friend of mine. In the trade. Cigarette?" Abie pointed to a gold cigarette-box. "And do sit down."

Macrae sat on the arm of a chair and took a sip of his drink. "Good stuff, this."

He could almost hear Abie purr.

"Now, about those pearls, Mr. Morrison."

"Oh, yes." Macrae put his glass down on a table. "Well, as a matter of fact I haven't come about them. There's something else I want to talk to you about."

"We will talk about the necklace first, if you please."

Macrae looked up, surprised. "Why?"

Abie walked to the wireless and tuned down the music. With his back turned to his guest he said: "I've heard something about it since I saw you."

"About the necklace?"

"Yes."

"Oh!"

Abie turned slowly and walked slowly to the fireplace. He leaned against the mantelpiece and looked down at Macrae. "Where did you get it, Mr. Morrison?" His tone was silky.

"That's nothing to do with you."

"I think it has," Abie smiled, and he looked at the tip of his cigarette as he spoke. "You see, if you happened not to be the owner . . . it would make things a little awkward for you. You understand that, don't you?"

Macrae drew at his cigarette, blew out the smoke in a thin, expanding, eddying stream, and said: "Yes. I suppose it would."

"Who does own that necklace?" Abie asked, and as he spoke his eyes closed to slits.

"A friend of mine. You needn't worry. She knows about it."

"A lady? Name?"

"I'm not telling you that."

"I think you will."

"Like hell!" Macrae got up. He felt better able to tackle this little blighter when he was on his feet. "If I want to, I can redeem the pearls now."

"Oh, no, you can't!" Abie was lazily, oilily insolent.

"I've got the money."

"You borrowed a hundred on them."

"Yes."

"Well, it's going to cost you a lot more than that to get 'em back. I haven't fixed the price yet."

"If I went to Court I could get an order against you to give them up on payment of the hundred pounds and interest."

"You go to Court! That's funny. Very funny. You would have to produce the lady and get her to say she'd authorized you to pawn her pearls."

"I can do that."

Abie laughed. Silently at first, and then aloud. "Excuse me one moment." He left the room and came back a few minutes later with a folded paper. He gave it to Macrae. "Read that."

Macrae spread it out on a table. "Stolen!" He muttered the word. "A pearl necklace and diamond clasp. . . . Reward . . . apply to . . . assessors."

"Now do you understand?" Abie left his stand at the fireplace and leaned on the table. "They give the weight of every single pearl. I have checked the figures. This notice refers to the necklace you brought to me last night. There is no doubt about that."

Macrae carried his glass to the cocktail cabinet and helped himself to more whisky. As he splashed in the soda he said: "The whole matter can be explained very simply. A little—er—misunderstanding, that's all."

"Which, no doubt, you and your lady friend would be prepared to explain in Court."

"Yes, of course. But we don't want any bother. I'll pay you a hundred and twenty."

"If I sold them I would get fifteen hundred pounds."

"And do you think I'd keep my mouth shut if you did?"

"That would be the best thing for you to do. It would not be wise for you to tell the police that I had the pearls, because if they came to get them they would not be here. They would ask you to explain why you should think that I had them. The explanation might lead you into trouble."

"And what d'you think I'd be doing?"

"If you were wise you would forget that you had ever seen the necklace."

"Like hell I would! One word from me to the police and you'd be sunk."

"There's no need to get excited, and I'll give you a cut. Thirty per cent."

Macrae looked at Abie steadily for seconds. Then he said: "I'll think it over."

"I'm glad you see it that way. Perhaps we could do another deal in the same line. There must be a lot more good stuff where the necklace came from."

"When we clean up on the pearls that'll be the finish."

"We'll see about that later." Abie folded the circular and put it in his pocket. "And now, if you will excuse me, I must go to bed."

"I've got something else to talk to you about. It's nothing to do with me personally, but a friend of mine asked me to deal with it."

"Who is the friend?"

"That doesn't matter."

"Well, let's hear what it is, quick," Abie yawned. "I'm tired."

"There's a man who works for you, Bert Finch. He was held up last night."

"What's that?" Abie's voice was harsh.

"And then there was that little affair of a pavement artist's pictures. Oil, I'm told, was used. And Toby Flynn. You know him, don't you? He was lucky to get off."

The colour came and went from Abie's cheeks. He was breathing quickly, as though he had been running.

Macrae was satisfied with the effect of his words. The tables were turned, and it was now his turn to take the upper hand. "You're in for a spot of trouble; unless, of course, you like to make a deal."

"A deal?"

"Yes. I've got a proposition to put up. You're working a big area, and my friend thinks more could be made of it."

"I'm satisfied the way I'm going."

"I dare say you are, but he's not."

Abie's fear was ebbing. "Then you can go to hell!"

"I wouldn't fight, if I were you." Macrae traced the pattern of the chair-cover with his forefinger. He didn't look at Abie. "You don't want your crowd beaten up."

"There's not going to be any more of that."

Macrae looked up and raised his eyebrows.

"That's not a question that you can decide."

"I can fight."

"Yes. I dare say you can, but it'll mean the end of your racket in about two weeks."

"You'd better get out."

"Not till I've finished." Macrae settled back in his chair and lit a cigarette. "You haven't heard the interesting part."

"All right, let's have it."

"That's better. Now, this is how it'd work. We'd supply the protection and the organization. You carry on with the crowd you've got and work them south of the river."

Abie laughed. "South of the river! It's the West End that pays."

"And it'll pay a lot better when we get it reorganized. There's a number of streets you've never touched yet. We could treble the takings and you wouldn't be out of it. You'd get a fair whack."

"How much?"

"I don't know yet. We can fix that later."

"We'll fix it now." Abie spat out the words. He was trembling with a sudden rage. "I told you before that you can go to hell, and I say it again. All you want is to squeeze me out. I've built up a good business; it's taken me years, and now you come along and want to grab the lot. You'd give me a share! Like hell you would! Get out!"

Macrae got up quickly. "You're a fool! You don't know what you're up against. Don't forget what Bert Finch got. You'll get the same, or worse, one of these days."

"And what do you think I'm going to do? Lie down and take it?"

"You'll have to."

"Strong-arm mob, eh?" Abie sneered. "I can meet that."

"All right." Macrae squashed the butt of his cigarette in an ash-tray and turned towards the door. "You'll have forty-eight hours to think it over. I'll come back on Thursday for the answer."

Macrae was opening the door when Abie said: "Wait a minute, Mr. Morrison. There's no need to be hasty." Abie's voice became silky again. "I've an idea. You and me can work it."

"Alone?"

"Yes."

"Go ahead."

"You hold off your crowd until I give you the word I'm ready to meet them."

"And what then?"

"After that I'll expect you to tip me off to anything they're going to pull, so as I can get my mob on the spot."

"A double-cross?"

"It doesn't matter to you, does it, which side you run with as long as you get your cut? And I'll pay you well."

"I'm not playing your game."

Abie dropped the mask of conciliation. "Then you'll cop it. A word from me to the slops and you'll find you're down for a stretch. Fifteen hundred that necklace is worth to the bloke that owns it, and it'll be worth three years to you. I'd think that over if I were you."

"And you'd better think over what I've said about splitting the racket. I'll come back on Thursday night for the answer."

Macrae was thinking over Abie's suggestion as he let himself out of the front door and crossed the street to Bulmer Court. He was halfway up to it, bound for bed, when he heard footsteps behind him, and then Tim Daly's heavy breathing.

"Easy on, mate. There ain't all that hurry." Macrae slowed his pace. "What'd he got to say?"

"He's sticky," Macrae replied. "Didn't want to come in."

"Damn' fool," Tim grunted.

"But I think I'll get him round."

"I don't care if you don't." Tim was thinking of the cosh he had slung under his left arm. "I know how to deal with him." He fingered the loaded rubber tube. It didn't leave no mark hardly, and them that tasted it once didn't come back for a second dose.

"Shall I tell the guv'nor?"

"I'll do that."

Macrae was relieved. At the end of the alley he said "Good night," but Tim continued to follow him until he reached Bury Square. Macrae let himself in with his latch-key, and when he got up to his room he went straight to the window.

He saw Tim Daly turn and walk back the way he had come, and cursed himself for not having slipped him. Now that his address was known he saw trouble ahead. But he had plenty of cash, and in the morning he could clear out. Where, he hadn't a notion.

He was all right here for to-night. No one could touch him. He could lock the door. They wouldn't dare to break in.

As the sudden panic subsided he suddenly felt very tired, and staggered as he walked back to the bed; even his fingers, as they tugged at his tie, lacked the strength to loose the knot. He let his hands fall between his knees.

The cigarette, down to the last half-inch, burned his lips. He spat it out and ground it under his toe. The action roused him, and he undressed, put on pyjamas, and cleaned his teeth.

Funny how doing something one did every night of one's life steadied one's nerves. It made him feel slightly virtuous. He selected a book from a pile on the floor.

The saucer on the chair was full of grey ash and stubs when Macrae at last switched out the light and turned on his side.

For two hours he slept, and then awoke to be faced once more with the problem of Abie Russ, the pearls, and Big Bill Connor. The moon was high, and its cold light shining through the torn blind lay like a silver bar across the floor.

He could see the outline of the mantelpiece, a ghostly reflection from the pier-glass over it, and could hear the noisy ticking of the alarm-clock.

He went over every point again. He'd go to Bill Connor and tell him everything; about the pearls. Connor would find a way out. He could put Tim Daly on to the job and that would settle it.

There was no need to worry. Just tell Bill Connor all about it. It was easy. What was there to bother about? He'd tell Connor. . . . But still he couldn't sleep. The streak of moonlight had moved. It fell across the chair now. He saw his clothes as he had thrown them down; his shirt, with one sleeve hanging to the floor. Damn! He hadn't folded his trousers. Still, what did it matter? He had a hundred and twenty pounds. He could buy a new suit in the morning, and silk shirts and ties and collars.

He'd go to the Burlington Arcade and really enjoy himself. Ties at half a guinea. "Quite the latest pattern, sir. Cut from a square . . . outlasts three ordinary ties. . . ." He knew the talk.

He punched his pillow until it was the right height, and snuggled down.

But even if Connor did settle with Abie Russ, that wasn't the end of it. Where would he be with Mrs. Keene? If she suspected him of stealing her necklace, that door would be shut. And he recalled once again the look on her face when he had asked her to lend him money. She wasn't ripe for a killing yet. Not by a mile.

But if he could get the pearls back to the flat, put them at the back of a drawer, and if they were found, then he could never be suspected. Yes. That was it. He would get the pearls in the morning. Put the fear of God into that little twister, Abie, and make him hand them over.

At last he was satisfied that he had found the answer to his problem, and slept.

But when he woke he realized that putting the wind up Abie Russ was not going to be so easy. The pearls were Abie's best card, and he'd stick to them.

If he could get his hands on them everything would be all right. But would it? If Abie did go to the police before he could get the pearls back into the flat! Hell! He kicked off the bedclothes and got up. Usually he lay for half an hour or more in that pleasant state when the realities of living were kept at bay by a comfortable drowsiness.

There was one thought in his mind as he shaved: Abie Russ. If he was out of it, he'd have nothing to worry about.

He dressed and went out into the Square. The tradesmen's boys, with note-books in their hands, were making their rounds for orders. He envied them. Their life was simple enough.

He tried to forget Abie, but couldn't. It was Abie who stood in the way of every solution. Sneering, condescending, oily.

It was while he was sitting at a table in the Strand Corner House that the idea came to him. The waitress had taken his order, and he was folding his paper to prop it up on the cruet.

He could kill Abie Russ.

CHAPTER EIGHT

MR. CRICK leaned back in his chair and looked down into the Court.

The morning rush was over. Advice at half a crown a time had been dispensed to a dozen assorted men with handkerchiefs knotted round their necks and women with sniffs and shawls.

A pleasant breath of wind rustled the papers on his desk, and Mr. Crick forgot the ambitions of his youth: an office with twenty clerks; junior partners to do the work.

He was thinking of nothing when he caught sight of a man coming up the Court. He had seen him yesterday, and the day before, and had wondered what his business might be.

Strangers were rare in Bulmer Court. And strangers who hung about were the object of every one's suspicions.

Peggy came into the room with some typed sheets. She put them on the desk.

"What are you looking at?" she asked.

Mr. Crick said, "Come here a minute," and pointed with his cheroot out of the window.

"What d'you mean?" Peggy had work to do, and was impatient.

"Do you see that man outside Danny's shop?"

"Yes."

Mr. Crick took a pull at his cheroot and then said: "I wonder what he's up to."

"Well, I'm sure I don't know. Will you sign these letters?"

"In a minute." Mr. Crick crossed his legs.

Peggy sighed.

Mr. Crick took no notice of the hint. "Peggy, have you ever thought how you can tell a man's profession by his walk?"

"No, of course I haven't."

"Well, neither have I till a few minutes ago, but if you think of it, there's a lot in it. Take a sailor, for instance. He's accustomed to restricted surroundings, and when he takes exercise he walks up and down."

"I wish you wouldn't tear the corners off your blotting-paper. It makes it look so untidy."

Mr. Crick pursued his idea. "A sailor always steps out with his natural length of stride. A convict, on the other hand, is accustomed to pacing round in a circle with a man three paces in front of him and another three paces behind. The result is that a man in these circumstances develops a stride shorter than the normal."

Peggy leaned her elbows on the window-sill and looked at the man outside Danny Levine's shop. He was walking up and down with short strides.

"You may be right, but I should have said he was a policeman."

"No. You're wrong there. If a policeman hasn't got to get any-where he stands in one spot. I don't know why. I suppose it must be part of the training. I've seen them at bus-stops looking for pick-pockets. They always stand with their backs to a wall, looking just like policemen."

"Then that man is a convict or a sailor." Peggy laughed.

"Yes, and I think that he has been in prison."

"Do you really?" Peggy was thrilled.

"That's funny!" Mr. Crick turned towards the open window, listening.

"What?"

"Old Lampy changed his tune just then. Did you hear? He was playing 'Roses of Picardy' and he's switched to 'Lily of Laguna.'"

The man who had been looking down the Court suddenly turned on his heel and walked quickly up the alley-way leading to the "Goat."

Two minutes later the melancholy Leith hove in sight.

"Now, there's a real policeman," Mr. Crick said.

"Yes, I know him. He's always round here at this time."

The strains of "Lily of Laguna" grew louder. "She's my Lady Love . . ." Mr. Crick tapped his toe in time to the refrain. "He plays amazingly well, that old chap. You'd think he could do better than play down here."

"That's what Mrs. Finch says. She's got a story about him that he was on the halls once earning good money. She says a woman let him down, but I think it's booze."

But Mr. Crick wasn't listening. He was humming the tune he'd heard as a boy at the old Canterbury.

"If you'll sign these letters I'll get them off."

Mr. Crick came back to the present and reached for his pen.

Tim Daly could spot a policeman in plain clothes a mile off, and when he saw Leith coming up the Court he was out of sight a split second before Leith saw him.

It wasn't that he was scared. There was nothing they could pull him for, but he didn't want to be seen anywhere near Abie's shop. It might be that he would have a job to do there one of these days.

Danny Levine peered out of the window of his shop as Leith went by, and when he had gone Danny came out.

Mrs. Finch called to him from her window. "All clear, Mr. Levine." She was laughing at him. "It was old Leith. He'll be on to you one of these days."

Lampy was playing "Roses of Picardy" again.

"Are you doing anything to-day?"

"I've finished with horses," said Mrs. Finch. "I'm going to give the dogs a run."

"Tell us what you want."

"I haven't worked it out yet." Mrs. Finch spread out the sporting edition of the *Standard* on the window-ledge.

Danny cautiously withdrew into his shop.

Piccadilly was very pleasant, and so were the dry Martinis Macrae kindly bought himself at a bar in Panton Street. As he sipped the second he ran his eye down the list of runners on the back page.

The fields were big. And he didn't like big fields, but it was the time of year when two-year-olds were running pretty true to form, and if he was careful—and, dammit, he'd got to be careful!—he could do himself some good.

The Lola colt. Tipped by eighteen papers. Forecast of starting price thirteen to eight. Johnny Cox riding. . . .

He finished his drink and got on a bus at the top of Haymarket.

Danny Levine grinned when Macrae gave him one hundred one-pound notes. "Following your luck, Captain? That's the thing to do. Now, if more people was to be what I call consistent in their investments instead of splashing 'em all over the place . . ." He licked his thumb and counted aloud. "Hundred. That's right, and I hope you brings it off again."

Macrae said he hoped so, too, and went out into the Court. He lit a cigarette and then walked to Mrs. Finch's door and rang the bell. There was no reply. He rang again.

"She's out." It was Peggy's voice; he turned on his heel. Peggy was standing inside the doorway of Mr. Crick's office. She had seen Macrae go into Danny's shop and had come down the stairs so that she could catch him as he went by.

"Jove! This is a bit of luck. I was going to ask Mrs. Finch if she could take a message to you."

"Oh." Peggy's smile was nervous, fleeting.

"I wanted you to come out with me to-night. I was thinking of having a little celebration."

"Is it your birthday?"

Macrae lied smilingly. "That's a good guess."

"I want to thank you for taking me to the pictures the other night."

"That was nothing."

"It was lovely. And the supper."

"Well, let's do it again."

"I'd like to. It'd be ever so nice, but I'd have to get back early. Mother was cross because I was so late."

Macrae stepped into the shadow of the doorway and took Peggy's hand in his. She blushed and tried to take it away. She didn't try very hard.

"When d'you finish work?"

"About five, but I'd have to go home first and tell Mother I was going out."

"Seven o'clock?"

"That'd be lovely."

"Where can we meet?"

"Wherever you say."

"All right. You be at the Southwark Tube at seven. By the book-stall." He pressed her hand and dropped it. "Seven o'clock."

He watched Peggy run up the steep flight of stairs. He'd got her going, but it wouldn't do to force the pace.

Macrae sauntered up Bulmer Court very well pleased with himself. He was thinking of Peggy.

A newsboy came running shouting: "Two-thirty winner! Two-thirty winner! . . ."

He snatched a paper. Two-thirty, Sandown. First, Comorin. Second, Flapjack. Third, Prince Regent.

He stood staring at the smudged print, refusing to believe what was printed. It couldn't be! It couldn't! He pulled the earlier edition out of his pocket. Tipped by eighteen papers. The bet he had thought was stone cold had failed him. The Lola colt couldn't have started. He'd get his money back.

But the name of the Lola colt was there in the list of starters. Slowly the realization that he had lost his money sank into his consciousness.

He folded the paper and stuffed it into a litter-basket. That was that. He'd have to think of something else. He had a few pounds left. Enough for another bet. But what was the good? He'd blow the money to-night. Take Peggy out. Do a show, supper, and a dance.

With the habit and ease born of many setbacks he thrust from him the fact of his loss. To-morrow he'd think of something.

To-morrow! It was the word which he had evoked a hundred times to help him out of a bad spot, with its promise of better things. To-morrow!

CHAPTER NINE

PEGGY WAS WAITING for him by the bookstall. She smiled shyly, and as he passed his arm within hers she pressed close to him. "I'm sorry about last night."

"That's all right."

"Bert was awfully cross at my going out with you."

Macrae laughed. "What'd he say?"

"Oh, I don't know," Peggy giggled. "But I'd keep out of his way if I was you."

"He doesn't know me."

"Mrs. Finch'll tell him."

"No, she won't. She's on my side."

"If it hadn't been for her—"

"We wouldn't have met. We must give her a night out some time. She deserves it."

They walked very close together. Macrae's arm crept round Peggy's shoulders. They did not speak for a full five minutes. They were both very happy.

At the far side of Southwark Bridge Macrae hailed a taxi, and gave the name of a restaurant in Greek Street. As he sat back in the cab Peggy snuggled up to him.

"Where are we going?"

"A little place I know. We'll feed there, and then I was thinking of the Palladium."

"I don't mind what we do."

"We might dance afterwards."

"That would be lovely, but I must be home by twelve. Mother made me promise."

"All right," Macrae replied carelessly, and at once dismissed Peggy's mother from his thoughts. He was living in the present and enjoying every minute of it.

So did Peggy until she heard a church clock strike twelve, and then she panicked. Macrae said he'd take her home in a taxi. They could stop it at the end of the street so that Mrs. Nichol would suspect nothing.

He paid the driver and when the cab was out of sight he kissed Peggy. She clung to him. This was the real thing. Love!

As their lips parted she stared at him as though she was seeing him for the first time, and then she thrust her head forward and buried her face in his shoulder. She was crying.

Macrae said: "You're a funny kid."

She raised her face to his. "I've never felt like this before." Her fingers grasped the lapels of his coat. "Sorry. I'm making a fool of myself." She dropped her hands and groped in her bag for a handkerchief. He helped her dry her eyes.

Her head was in the clouds, and a happiness she had never experienced in all her life before was wrapped around her.

Macrae walked quickly, in time with his thoughts. And as he walked his hatred for Abie Russ grew.

He was breathing quickly as he fumbled with his key for the latch; he slammed the door behind him and stumbled up the stairs.

His one consuming idea was to find the revolver that Mrs. Finch had uncovered in the cupboard of his room.

His ears were singing and his head was throbbing as he groped for the light switch. He stood quite still, trembling all over.

What had he done with the key of the cupboard? Yes, of course. It was in his pocket. He turned the key in the lock. The revolver! On the top shelf! It was too high to reach. He dragged a chair across the room, and when a leg caught in a torn corner of the rug he swore and tugged it free.

The chair rocked as he stepped on to it, and he grasped at the edge of a shelf to steady himself.

As his fingers closed round the cold steel butt of the revolver he gave a little laugh. Of course it was there. Of course. . . .

He got down off the chair and walked slowly across the room to his bed; he sat down heavily and gazed stupidly at the revolver. One shot from it and he would be clear. It wouldn't be difficult. One shot. That was all. Easy!

There wouldn't be any risk if he was careful; if no one saw him enter or leave the shop. The throbbing in his head was dying, but his hands still shook as he laid the revolver on the chair by his bed.

He got up slowly and with the step of a sick man walked over to the dressing-table and took a bottle of brandy from the top drawer. He splashed the liquor into a glass and drank it in long, sucking draughts.

He was mad! Mad! The word echoed in his brain and he laughed and drank again. He was feeling sleepy now and very, very tired.

He slept in his clothes, sprawled across the bed, and woke when it was still dark. His head was aching, his mouth dry, and he was cold.

The revolver was still lying on the chair, but he did not see it.

He undressed, put on his pyjamas, pulled the bedclothes straight, and slipped in under them. Soon he was warm and asleep.

CHAPTER TEN

MACRAE ATE NOTHING during the whole of the day. He walked to Hampstead and arrived there at one o'clock. He had three double-brandies and then wandered across the heath, smoking a chain of cigarettes, and was tired out when he struck a road. A bus was waiting by the curb. The white-coated driver was leaning against a wall talking to his conductor.

Macrae climbed on board. It was a sixpenny fare to Victoria, and when he got there he felt rested but very hungry. It was half-past five. He walked along Ebury Street to the Chelsea Hospital and down on to the Embankment. There was a tug working up the river with a string of barges in tow. The men on board seemed a million miles away, living in a different world. He envied them.

And then, in a panic, he thought of the revolver he had left in his room. If Mrs. Finch had found it! He waited impatiently for the traffic to ease up and then, seizing his chance, crossed the road and retraced his steps along the Hospital Road and turned left-handed to Sloane Square.

The Underground took him to Blackfriars, and he walked across the bridge and along Surrey Street. His pace quickened as he passed the line of shops in Fenwick Street, and he was almost running when he reached Bury Square.

His eager fingers groped under the handkerchiefs in the top drawer, and he muttered a "Thank God!" as they gripped the butt of the revolver.

It was a quarter to seven. Four hours to wait. He put the gun into a side pocket. It was bulky and heavy, but it wouldn't be noticed if he held it so that there was no sag. Abie wouldn't know what was coming to him!

And he must have gloves. He searched through two drawers before he found a pair. He stuffed them into a pocket and stood thinking for a minute. That would be all he'd need.

Then he left the room and went to a public house he knew which had a good snack bar. Two cold sausages and three double-brandies were his supper. That left him with half a crown and a few coppers, as well as his two remaining notes.

He walked to London Bridge. It was a still, dark warm night. The grinding, clanging trams, the whirr of tires on dry wood blocks, were a background to the drop-scene before him. The sky with its pin-points of light; the shadowy silhouette of Tower Bridge, the water between splashed with light from arc-lamps on the wharves.

The clock on St. Saviour's Church was striking eleven o'clock when he roused himself and with a jerk came back to the realities of the present, and its problems. His right hand strayed to the bulge on his right side.

Eleven o'clock! He must get going; Abie was expecting him!

At first he walked quickly, but when Abie's shop came in sight he slackened his pace and he began to sweat, on the palms of his hands and on his forehead. He forced himself to go on walking, but his pace became slower and doubts crowded his brain. Fear, cold fear, was not far away.

He felt for the gloves and put them on.

There was a light in the first-floor windows. That was Abie's flat. He pressed the bell and waited, his body pressed against the wall in the shadow of the portico.

Old Lampy, standing at the entrance to the Court, had his back to him. He was droning out "Red Sails in the Sunset," and as Macrae listened to the tune he did not hear the footsteps on the tiled floor of the hall within nor the click of the latch.

"Who's that?"

He turned quickly and looked into the grey-white oval of Abie's face. "Good evening."

Two seconds passed, and then Abie said:

"All right, come in."

In the light of the solitary gas-jet Macrae saw the outline of the stair-rail.

"Sorry I'm late," he muttered.

"That's all right. Go on up. You know your way."

Macrae mounted the stairs slowly. He saw Abie go to the shop door and try the handle and then turn to follow him.

From that moment Abie Russ ceased to be a human being to Eric Macrae, but was just something that was dangerous to him, and which must be eliminated.

He walked close to the wall, his feet grating on the bare wood treads; he eased the butt of the revolver half out of his pocket.

There mustn't be any hang-up. The safety catch was down; he thumbed it up. He was ready.

Abie was nervous, and Macrae smiled. If he only knew! The desire to kill overlaid every decent human trait in his being. He was no longer Captain Eric Macrae, but a killer with a soul the size of a shrivelled pea.

The love of self to the exclusion of all else had bred this obsession which had hold of him. His hands were steady and his step firm as he walked into the over-lighted room.

Abie shut the door, went over to the radio and switched it on.

"Stop that damn' thing!"

The blank, amazed expression of fear on Abie's half-turned face made Macrae laugh. He kept quite still, with his shoulders bent.

Outside in the street Lampy was still playing.

"I'm here to talk."

Still Abie made no move. He was staring at Macrae, and what he saw in his eyes took from him the power of movement and coherent speech.

He muttered something through dry lips.

Pity threatened to break down the madness of Macrae's resolution; he whipped himself back to a state of hate.

He must finish it before he weakened.

He saw nothing but Abie's face before him. The room had ceased to exist. It was as though he and Abie were standing alone in the world.

He saw Abie's hands rise before his face, and then the glint of light on the gun-barrel. He hadn't realized he had taken it from his pocket.

A horrible croak came from Abie's lips, and then a faint, "No— no—"

Macrae struck down his hands with a savage sweep of his left arm. He thrust the muzzle forward and Abie's head jerked back. His mouth opened, but no sound came.

Macrae saw only the oval of Abie's open mouth. His finger squeezed on the trigger. It seemed to him an eternity before the hammer rose and fell; there was a roar; the muzzle jerked up, and Abie sank slowly sideways to the floor, out of his vision; slowly, like a half-filled sack.

Macrae stood still for a moment, and then his legs gave way under him, and he would have fallen had he not clutched at the back of a chair.

The acrid smell of burnt cordite was in the air. It was a smell he was to remember until he died.

He looked stupidly at the muzzle of the revolver, from which a wisp of grey smoke rose and disappeared in a thin, eddying corkscrew.

It was as though he were looking at another man. He was standing outside his own body, and the merciful haze of unreality was over his eyes.

Then his eyes focused slowly on the heap on the floor at his feet. For minutes he stared at it. That purplish cloth. He'd seen it before, somewhere. His brain began to work. And back came the picture of Abie's face, contorted with terror, his hands raised in futile protection.

When the full realization came to him Macrae felt sick. He fought against it and heard himself say, "My God!" Saw himself get up and stagger to the wireless and fall across it, the palms of his hands rubbing and sliding over the cool, polished surface of the wood. He pressed his forehead to it; tried to shut out the past; to deny it.

He forced himself to stand up. It was very still in the room. In the street a car went by. He parted the curtains and looked out. There was no one in sight except old Lampy; he was still playing "Red Sails in the Sunset." Apparently he hadn't heard the shot.

He was all right and there was plenty of time, but he'd have to think and act carefully. The first thing to do was to put the revolver in Abie's hand to make it look like suicide.

And the pearls! He must get them. He knew where they were. In the shop, in the safe.

Abie would have the keys in his pocket.

Macrae had to force himself, with all the strength he could muster, to turn and face the body of Abie Russ.

A hand, dead white, lay against the dove-grey of the carpet. Quickly, breathing hard, and with panic not far away, Macrae forced the butt of the revolver under the hand and pressed the stiffening fingers round the grip.

Then, still with feverish haste, he felt for the key-chain which Abie wore, tugged at it, and pulled a bunch of keys out of the left-hand trouser pocket. He unfastened the end of the chain from a trouser-button and sat back on his heels.

So far, so good. He put a hand on a chair and pulled himself to his feet. He was still pretty bad about the legs. They were aching, trembling, and had little strength.

He looked slowly round the room and saw the whisky decanter. Why the hell hadn't he thought of that before?

He half filled the glass. God! How he needed that! He gulped and coughed as the neat spirit went down his throat. But it made him feel fine. He drank again, this time savouring it. It was good stuff, Abie's whisky. He finished the glass and refilled it. He was feeling quite different now.

There was an inch of whisky left in the decanter. He'd finish that when he'd got the pearls.

He walked to the door, opened it, and listened. There was not a sound. The gas-jet in the chandelier was burning steadily in the close, still air, giving only sufficient light to illumine the staircase and the hall below.

He walked slowly down the stairs, leaning heavily on the rail. When he reached the hall he stood for a moment listening; then he tiptoed to the shop door.

He tried two keys before he found one which turned the lock. By the light from a street lamp outside the window he saw the squat, square shape of the safe.

It was all right. There was no combination, just a simple lock and bolts worked by a handle. He turned the key and released the bolts. His fingers felt along the floor of the safe and encountered nothing but pasteboard boxes. He opened one and his fingers felt a wrist-watch. That was no good. The others held rings and one a bracelet.

Then he explored the top shelf with trembling, searching fingers. Tissue-paper rustled. He tore it apart. The pearls! His pearls!

He stuffed them into his waistcoat pocket.

Then he locked the safe and stepped out into the hall. The gas-jet bowed and flickered in the draft from the shop door and then flared up in two fangs of yellow light.

He crept to the hall door and pressed his face against the pane of the side window. Lampy was gone. He could go out. No one would see him. All he had to do was to turn the key in the lock and . . .

There was some one behind him! He dare not look! He dare not!

And yet, without realizing what he was doing, he turned slowly. There was no one there! He could hear the faint hiss of the gas-jet. That was all.

He fumbled with the spring lock and held it free while he pulled the heavy door open. Fear had hold of him and was driving him out.

Without waiting to reconnoitre the street, he stumbled out, down the two steps, and half walking and half running sped along the pavement northwards. He was out of breath when he found himself on London Bridge; he stopped and felt for his cigarette-case, and then stepped off the pavement into the embrasure in which he had stood an hour ago.

The ship was still at the wharf. A winch, protestingly, creakingly, was hauling up another hoist from her hold. It was as though he had never gone away, as though the events of the last hour were something imagined.

It couldn't have happened, he told himself, and sucked in the smoke of a cigarette gratefully. It made him feel better, steadied his nerves. He fixed his attention on the ship in a wild endeavour to deny the past. He fixed his gaze on the ship and . . .

There was some one behind him! Again cold fear gripped Macrae. Again he dared not look, and again he turned and saw—nothing.

He began to tremble and he felt sick. There was nothing there! Nothing!

For nearly an hour he stood there smoking cigarette after cigarette and staring unseeingly into the black void below.

Then he walked on blindly, his knees sagging so that he lurched and hit the stone balustrade and had to put out a hand to steady himself. Hell! He couldn't go on like this. He would be arrested for being drunk.

There was a bus-stop a hundred yards ahead. The sight of the standard with its familiar sign was oddly comforting. He stopped and leaned against it.

A bus, nearly empty, came along, and he pulled himself up the steep stairs to the top deck and sat on a seat at the back. In front of him were a man and a woman. The woman was asleep with her head on the man's shoulder. The man was trying to read a crumpled paper. As the bus pulled up at traffic lights, the woman woke, muttered something, and put her hands up to pull her hat straight. It was tilted drunkenly over her left ear.

The man said, "We're nearly home," and tried to move away and work his arms free.

Macrae would have given anything he possessed to be that man. Self-pity poured over him. If only. . .! If only . . .! If only the last hour could be sponged out! He groaned, and the man half turned his head.

Macrae coughed. The man returned to his study of the evening paper. The woman said drowsily, "What's that?"

The bus rolled on, and Macrae looked out of the window. It was taking him back the way he had come. It would pass the shop. He started to get up and looked for the bell-push.

The woman woke again to mutter, "I'm coming."

The conductor came up the stairs.

"Fares, please."

Macrae heard himself say, "Twopenny, please."

He took his ticket and rolled it up with nervous fingers. If he had wanted to he couldn't make a move now. Then as though he had been struck he stiffened. His cap! He hadn't got it on! He must have left it there. In the room!

He shut his eyes and his fingers gripped on the edge of the seat cushion. His forehead was wet and his hands were icy cold.

He forced himself to think. He'd worn it when he'd left his room in Bury Square and in the bar where he'd eaten. He must have had it on when he'd gone to Abie's; he must have left it there in the room!

He'd have to go back and get it. His initials were stamped on the leather lining. It was just the stupid sort of mistake which he had laughed at others for making.

He must go back. But as he mumbled the words he knew that he dared not return.

He dropped his cigarette and tried to stamp it out, but it had fallen in a groove in the floor. He felt for a box of matches in his pocket. His fingers touched tweed cloth. For seconds he could not realize that it was the cap. He pulled it out and unfolded it.

Tears of relief filled his eyes. He was all right. He had nothing to worry about now. He lit another cigarette and stretched out his legs, then looked out of the window. The bus was passing the pillar-box at the corner of Fenwick Street. Abie's shop was a hundred yards ahead. There was a taxi drawn up at the near-side curb.

Macrae sat tense until he saw the doorway with its pillared portico. Then he looked up, fascinated. The light was out in Abie's flat! And he had left it on! He remembered now. He should have switched it off before he left, but he hadn't and now it was out!

What could have happened? He stared down at the pavement fearfully expecting to see a policeman on guard at the street door. There was no one there. And the light was off!

Perhaps Abie wasn't dead. Only wounded, and had had the strength to put through a call for help. Perhaps the police were looking for him now!

Fear held him for a moment and then passed. His capacity for fear had gone and had left him utterly tired without the power to think.

At the next stop he got off the bus and walked through silent back streets to Bury Square. There was some brandy left in the bottle. Before he slept he was drunk.

CHAPTER ELEVEN

BEER, OLD AGE, and meek acquiescence with the blows fate had dealt him had reduced old Lampy's brain and understanding to a sodden spongelike thing. The sound of the shot which had robbed Abie Russ of life made little impression on him.

Lampy wondered vaguely what the sound meant while his fingers mechanically pressed on the keys of his accordion.

When he had come to the end of the tune he hitched up the straps on his shoulders and began to shuffle up the Court in the direction of Mrs. Finch's. She had asked him to call in for a bite of chow before he went home. Sharp eleven she had said, and he was late.

As he walked along with bent back and head thrust forward he muttered to himself, "I wonder what that was." He was thinking foggily of the sound he had heard. He'd tell Mrs. Finch and see what she thought.

He stopped at Mrs. Finch's door and knocked. He heard a chair pushed back, footsteps in the passage, and then the door was opened.

"Is it all right?" he asked, with a shy grin.

"Of course it is," Mrs. Finch replied briskly. "Bert won't be back for half an hour yet, and your supper's waiting."

Lampy slipped the strap from his shoulders and put his accordion on the floor. When he came into the front room Mrs. Finch had set a plate of stewed eels upon the table and was sawing at a loaf.

Lampy supped the juice noisily with a spoon.

Mrs. Finch, with her arms folded across her chest and her head on one side, looked at him with satisfaction.

"That'll do you a bit of good. Not half it won't. Standing out there all day." She took a step towards the table. "And I don't suppose you take a lot, do you?"

Lampy, with a laden spoon in mid-air, looked puzzled.

"I mean money. I can't think why you don't try a pitch up West. Theatre queues and that sort of thing."

Lampy put down the spoon and said, "I used to make pounds a week once. *In* the theatres. Or halls, rather. Up North."

Mrs. Finch made sympathetic clucking noises and said, "Well, fancy that, now! What happened?" She spoke with the eager interest of the professional gossip.

Lampy picked up his spoon and resumed his attack on the cooling eels. Mrs. Finch waited until he had finished before she renewed her inquiry, but Lampy replied vaguely that he managed to get along.

"Well, I calls it a shame," Mrs. Finch said, as she carried his empty plate to the sink, "with the talent you've got."

"I don't do so bad. Mr. Russ pays me regular."

"Mr. Russ! Abie Russ?"

"That's right." Lampy nodded and got up. "I heard something when I was playing to-night. Just afore I came along here." There was a puzzled frown on his face as though he were trying to recapture an elusive thought.

"Yes?" Mrs. Finch prompted. "What was it?"

"I don't know exactly. A kind of a bang."

"A bang?"

"Yes. In the street somewhere, but I didn't see nothing."

Mrs. Finch said, "Probably a car backfiring or something. Sometimes they makes a terrible noise."

"No, it wasn't that." He stood staring at the table, and then mumbled, "I don't suppose it was anything to bother about." He started to walk to the door. "Thanks for the supper. It was fine."

"I'm sure you're welcome, and if Bert's going to be out to-morrow night I'll let you know and you can come along at the same time."

She wanted to ask Lampy what Abie Russ paid him and why, but there was something about the old man's manner which stayed the question.

Lampy saw the light in Abie's flat as he reached the end of the Court.

He crossed the road and went in at the door of Danny Levine's Practice Room.

The long room was full of smoke and men drinking and talking. Danny was at the piano rattling out a tune. A can of beer stood on the top of the piano. A man was trying to follow Danny on a penny whistle, the shrill fluting rising above the buzz of talk and laughter.

It was Thursday night at Danny Levine's.

Lampy dropped his accordion to the floor, sat down on a bench, and filled his pipe. He asked a man near him the time and was told that it was close on the half-hour.

"He ought to be along any time now." Chalks O'Callaghan raised his melancholy eyes from a sketch he was making on the back of an envelope.

Lampy finished his pipe and Danny his can of beer. The talk grew less. A clock outside struck twelve in sonorous strokes. Chalks put his pencil away and yawned and grumbled, "What the hell's keeping him, anyway?"

Danny, who had come down off the platform and was standing near-by, said, "He'll be along soon." But it was clear that he was uneasy. He went back to the piano and picked out a new tune with one finger of his right hand. Some one sang the words.

At five minutes past twelve Danny kicked his stool back, put on his jacket, and left the room. He ran down the stairs, along the alleyway, and into the yard at the back of the house. He rang the bell three times.

He waited five minutes, rang again, and listened. There was no sound within the house.

Danny swore and went back up the alley and down the street a few yards. He looked up and saw the light in the windows of Abie's flat.

At first he was angry at having been kept waiting, and then vaguely alarmed. Abie had never failed them before on a Thursday night.

He went up the steps to the front door, and was feeling for the bell-push when he saw that the door was open a few inches. His fears increased. Abie always kept the door locked and bolted.

For a moment Danny thought of going back to the Room and getting some one to go with him into the house; then he changed his mind and stepped into the hall and shut the door behind him.

He called out, "Abie!" The word was swallowed up in the depths of the hall. It was like a morgue.

He walked slowly to the foot of the staircase and looked upwards.

A sliver of light showed down the side of a door on the first-floor landing, the door of Abie's room.

Perhaps he was asleep. Heartened by the thought, Danny ran up the shallow steps and knocked on the door. There was no answer. He called out "Abie!" and turned the handle. There was no one in the room. No one. "Abie!"

There was a funny smell, faint but definite. There was a glass on a table by a chair and another on the mantelpiece. Both were empty.

Then he saw a shoe lying sideways on the floor. As he took a pace sideways Danny Levine saw the body of Abie Russ—saw the black patch of blood spreading slowly, soaking into the dove-grey carpet; the smell was stronger. It was heavy and slightly sweet. He'd smelt it once round a slaughterhouse.

Danny stared at the body for half a minute, and then he looked slowly round the room—at the decanter in the open cocktail cabinet, at the radio set, at the glass on the mantelpiece.

His brain worked slowly.

He stumbled forward a pace and knelt by the body of Abie Russ. A hand outstretched lay like a dead starfish on the carpet. He touched it. The fingers were cold and stiffening. The chill of death was in them.

He listened for the sound of breathing, heard none, and got up quickly. Abie Russ was dead!

He took three quick steps across to the fireplace and opened a cupboard. His hands were trembling as they groped along a shelf and closed over a folded map. Connor would pay him for that.

He turned and looked down at the body of Abie Russ, started forward, hesitated, and then dropped on one knee. He pulled at the lapels of the coat and thrust a hand into the breast pocket and pulled out a wallet.

Now he must get out of it! The decanter caught his eye. There was half an inch of whisky in it. He splashed the liquor into a glass and drank it off. Ah! That was better. He walked quickly to the door, fumbled for the switch, and turned off the lights. Then he went out onto the landing and ran down the staircase to the hall. There he stood for a moment, trying to decide what he should do.

He must get the crowd out of it before the splits tumbled or the whole game would be spoilt. Danny Levine was thinking of his own bread and butter and not of Abie Russ. He was thinking of Tim Daly and Big Bill Connor.

He released the catch of the spring lock on the front door, pulled the door shut behind him, and stepped into the shadow of a pillar. A man was passing on the opposite side of the street. Danny waited until he had walked a hundred yards, then he had another look round. A bus was coming down the street. When it had passed he ran to the door of the Practice Room and up the stairs.

On the landing he halted, forcing the fear from his face. Chalks saw him first and said, "What did he say?"

"He—he's not coming in to-night." Danny's voice was harsh.

Chalks said, "Not coming?"

"Not to-night. He's had to go out on a job. He left a message."

"What'd it say?" Lampy asked. There was a high, querulous, complaining note in his voice.

"That you're all to clear out and not come back here till he sends word."

Excited, angry voices relayed the news. Men got up and crowded round Danny. "I can't tell you any more. You'll have to clear out."

"What about my money?"

"Yes, that's what we want—our money."

"When'll he be back?"

"I'm broke."

The man who had been playing the penny whistle began to cry. Danny swung round on him. "Shut that blinking row and get out! Get out, the lot of you!"

Slowly they went. All except old Lampy. He sat with a cold pipe between his teeth staring at the floor. His arms hung down between his knees.

Danny went to the platform and picked up his can. It was half full. He drank noisily, and banged down the lid of the piano. He was angry and very frightened. He turned and saw Lampy. "Come on. Get a move on. I'm shutting up."

Lampy got up slowly, but made no move to leave. "What's happened?" He was staring straight at Danny.

"Nothing."

"You can tell me. I won't gab."

"There's nothing to tell but what I've said." Danny put on his jacket and took a packet of cigarettes from a pocket.

His affected carelessness did not deceive old Lampy.

"Something's happened. When you came in here five minutes ago I tumbled there was something wrong."

"They've killed him."

"Killed?" Lampy breathed the word. "Are you sure?"

"Of course I am."

"When?"

"How the hell do I know?"

Lampy's lips mumbled the word "Killed" over and over again. He bent down and groped for the strap of his accordion. "Killed!"

"Yes." And then an idea came to Danny Levine. He put out his hand and gripped Lampy by the shoulder. "You were on your pitch to-night, weren't you?"

Lampy raised his eyes and met Danny's gaze. "Yes, I was. Why?"

"Did you hear anything?"

"When?"

"Any time. When you were playing."

Lampy shook his head. "I didn't hear anything," he said. And then, after a second's pause, "Yes, I did. I heard a kind of a bang. It must have come from Abie's room. I couldn't place it at the time, but now I come to think of it that's where it was."

"What time was that?"

Lampy's lower lip was trembling and he stammered in his reply. "Soon after eleven."

"Did you see anything—any one near the house?"

"No. I wasn't looking that way."

"What the hell d'you think you're paid for?"

"Well, I never thought that—"

"Oh, all right. It can't be helped now."

Danny screwed up his face in thought.

Lampy quavered, "Who was it done it?"

"I don't know. But I have an idea. There was a bloke hanging round at the beginning of the week, watching Abie's place."

"I saw a man."

"What was he like?"

"I'd know him again. He was big. A bruiser, I'd say. Breathed through his mouth."

"Tim Daly." Danny spoke the words half to himself.

Lampy said, "What's that?" and cupped a hand to his ear.

"It doesn't matter. And you'd better forget you saw anybody or heard anything. Understand?"

Lampy nodded his head slowly.

"All right. Now let's get out of here."

Lampy slung his accordion over his shoulder and shuffled to the door. Danny followed him out and locked up behind him.

"You've got to keep away from here for a spell. Got that?"

Lampy nodded.

"You don't know nothing. Forget what I've told you."

"What good'll that do? They'll find him afore very long."

Danny leaned towards the old man. "I got an idea who croaked Abie, and if I'm right he won't stop at one killing."

"You mean—"

"You know what Bert Finch got, and he hadn't done nothing. Cut him up. That's what they did. And what they've done once they can do again. Don't forget that."

Danny stood for a minute or two at the street door and watched Lampy slouch off. Then he lit a cigarette and went home. To-morrow would be soon enough to decide what line he would take.

At nine o'clock on the night on which Abie Russ was murdered, Bert Finch left the saloon bar of the "Goat," where he had spent the evening.

He went by bus and Tube to Piccadilly Circus and walked up Shaftesbury Avenue. The theatre queues were gone. A man was stacking stools on to a barrow and fastening them with a length of rope. He nodded to Bert and stopped his work to ask for a light.

"Has there been any trouble round here?" Bert asked.

The man looked puzzled, and Bert said it didn't matter and walked on. He kept close to the wall and looked behind him three times before he came to the corner of Old Compton Street.

Two men were standing talking outside a café. Bert glanced quickly at them as he passed. They didn't look at him.

At the next corner he stopped and stood looking round. Tim Daly's crowd weren't out to-night; at least, not as far as he could see. He pushed open the swing door of a bar and went in. "Double-Scotch and splash, please, miss."

The look of wary fear had gone from his eyes. He was safe here. No one at the bar took any notice of him. From outside came the sobbing notes of a fiddle. Bert sipped his drink and waited. At last the tune came to an end and the player sidled into the bar, a cap in his hand and his violin tucked under one arm.

He made his round repeating mechanically a husky, "Thank you. Thank you, gents."

Bert gave him a copper. The man did not raise his head as he said, "Thank you. All O.K. Thank you, gents."

Bert finished his drink and went out quickly, along Old Compton Street thirty yards, then he turned up Greek Street. Opposite an Italian restaurant there was a narrow alley. Bert looked behind him before he entered it. He was taking no chances, for the alley was a *cul-de-sac*.

Ahead he saw a group of men. They were standing in the entrance to a garage. He called out, "Sharky!"

A man came into the light of a street lamp and said, "You're late. We've been waiting—"

"All right," Bert interrupted, and held out his hand. "Hand it over."

"Three three six."

Bert took the money, counted it quickly, and said, "That's right."

He continued on his round. Back to Shaftesbury Avenue, past the Shaftesbury Theatre, to Lisle Street.

There he made a further collection.

At a quarter past twelve his task was finished. He took a taxi to the end of Fenwick Street and walked the last hundred yards to Abie's shop. He mounted the steps, pressed the push, heard the distant sound of the bell, and waited. Nothing happened. He tried the door. It was locked.

Then he rang again and stepped back out from under the portico. There was no light in the flat. What the hell was Abie up to? He knew he'd call at this time. He couldn't have gone to bed.

Bert rang again, and again there was no answer to the summons. He walked up and down in front of the house, and then went to the door of the Practice Room. It was locked.

He went home to bed.

CHAPTER TWELVE

At eight o'clock next morning, Bert Finch arrived at Abie's shop, to find a woman encamped on the top step.

"I can't make him hear," she complained.

"Have you rung the bell?"

"Of course I've rung the bell, and I've knocked and I've been round to the back." She sniffed and folded her arms across her flat chest.

Bert, puzzled and uneasy, stood staring up at the windows. Then he tried the door and examined the bars across the shop windows. "Last night—Well, I don't know," he muttered. "It's never happened like this before. We'll have to wait, that's all."

"You can if you like." The woman sniffed again. "But I'm going back home, and if he does come—"

"What d'you mean? If he does?"

Startled at the fierceness of his tone, the woman drew back a step. She said defensively, "He might have been run down and taken to a hospital. If I was you I'd tell the police."

The police! Like hell he'd go to the police!

"You go on home."

But the woman changed her mind. She scented a subject for gossip, and wasn't she the one that did for Mr. Russ? And if he'd been knocked down and killed, the newspapers would want to ask her questions about him. Her little brain was busy with the story she could tell. They'd want to take her photo.

"I think I'll stay. Thanks very much all the same," she replied firmly, and with the dignity of a person of importance.

"All right," Bert said casually.

He went home. Mrs. Finch asked him what was up.

"Nothing. Abie hasn't opened up yet." He picked up a week-old paper and began to read.

Mrs. Finch finished washing-up. She swept and tidied the room and then put on her bonnet. "I'm going to do some shopping."

Bert nodded without looking up. He waited until he heard the street door bang, then he took off his jacket, unbuttoned his shirt, and unstrapped a leather belt he was wearing next his skin.

The belt was heavy with coins and bulged with notes. He threw it down on his bed and sat for a time thinking and smoking. Then he got up and took the belt into the cupboard which Mrs. Finch called her kitchen. The boards under the sink were loose. The worn square of linoleum did not extend so far.

The wood was sodden with drippings from a leaky waste-pipe, and the nails which had once held down a plank drew through the wood as he prized it up.

The space below the floor was about four inches deep. He put the money-belt into the cavity and pushed it as far in as his arm could reach. Then he put the board into place, went back into the living-room, and stayed there for an hour.

A feeling of uneasiness was growing, and the desire to talk with some one at last forced him to make a move. He looked out of the window. The usual morning pilgrimage to Danny's shop had begun. He could hear the jangle of the door-bell.

He would go and see Danny.

Danny was sprawled across the counter reading the back page of the *Evening Standard*. When he looked up and saw Bert there was a curious look on his face, a fixed stare in which fear had a part.

Bert said, "What's up?" and sat on the edge of the counter.

Danny said, "Nothing," and stood up. "Why?"

"I don't know. You look funny."

"I'm all right."

"Abie's gone away."

Danny dropped his pencil on the floor, and, bending down, groped for it. "Where's he gone?" His voice was muffled.

"I don't know. I thought you might know."

Danny's face as it came up above the level of the counter was expressionless. "He never said nothing to me about going away. How d'you know he's gone?"

"The place is all shut up."

"He'll be back later on."

Bert said, "I wish to hell I knew where he is. If I don't get word soon I'll break in."

"I shouldn't do that." Danny stiffened.

"Why not?"

"Oh, I don't know. I shouldn't, that's all."

"What's biting you?"

"Nothing."

Bert stared at Danny for a moment, and then he slipped off the counter and left the shop. Danny was glad to see his back.

Lampy was hunched over his accordion. Danny stopped opposite him.

"Have you seen anything of Abie?"

Lampy replied, "Not this morning I haven't," and went on playing.

"Did you see him last night?"

"No," Lampy said, and changed from "Silver Threads Among the Gold" to "A Bachelor Gay Am I."

Bert looked down the street and saw Leith fifty yards away. Lampy had seen him first. A man who was coming down the Court turned and walked quickly away.

Leith told Bert that it was a lovely morning, and asked why he wasn't at work.

"Abie hasn't come in this morning."

Leith looked across at the shop. "That won't do trade any good. And there'll be a few wanting their dinner-money." Leith knew the complicated finances of those who lived in his manor. How they pawned clothes in the morning and redeemed them in the evening if the day's takings ran to it. They were always one jump behind, and never caught up. Thus had Abie prospered, on the pennies of the improvident.

Bert, always uneasy when within a hundred yards of a policeman, edged away. Leith saw the move.

Bert Finch interested him. So did Abie Russ and Danny Levine. He had had his eye on Danny's shop for months past.

He walked southwards along Fenwick Street. Bert watched him for a few minutes, and then said to Lampy, "That slop's got something on his mind."

"They're all that way. That's what they're paid for. Worrying about things they've no occasion to trouble with."

Bert leaned against the railings and looked across at the shop. What the hell was Abie up to? Bert was thinking of the money he had collected. If the other crowd got wind of where it was. . . The other crowd! His hand went up to feel the scar on his right cheek. It was still tender. Curse them!

Still, he could keep clear of them.

Lampy was playing "Red Sails in the Sunset." His repertoire was not extensive.

Bert wasn't thinking of anything when a man touched him on the arm. It was Tim Daly. He said, "Where's Abie?"

"I don't know."

"I've been over to his place and can't get in."

"He must have gone away."

Tim Daly looked less like a pig when he smiled, but much uglier. He was smiling now. "He knows what's best for him. Maybe that's the way of it."

Bert looked down at the pavement and did not reply.

Tim Daly turned into Bulmer Court. Bert walked to the corner and saw him go into Danny's shop.

He was frowning. He had a feeling that he'd seen the man somewhere before, but he couldn't fix him.

Danny was expecting the visit, and welcomed Tim with a nervous grin. "Come on in." He lifted a flap in the counter and kicked open the door behind him.

Tim went into the back room. Danny followed him and shut the door.

Tim sat down in a broken-springed chair before an empty fireplace. The hearth was a mess of ash and cigarette stubs.

"What's the next move?" Danny was standing with his back to Tim Daly, looking out into the back yard at an ash-bin and a pile of splintered box-wood.

"Abie'll have to come into line."

"Abie!" The cry made Tim sit up straight in his chair and turn his head towards Danny's back.

"Yes. I've explained all that before."

Danny swung round. His eyes were staring and his mouth was working. He did not speak.

Tim Daly gripped the arms of his chair and sat up straight. "What's got you?" he said. His voice was low and husky.

"I know about it. I've seen him," Danny said shrilly.

"For God's sake keep your voice down." Tim glanced at the door. "There's a slop hanging round."

"Who?"

"Leith."

"You've got a nerve," Danny said. "They'll be tumbling to it any time now."

"What the hell are you talking about?"

"Abie. Abie Russ. I went to his room last night. Just after he was shot."

"Shot!" Tim Daly repeated the word. "Shot?"

"Yes. It must have been done some time before twelve last night." Danny opened a drawer in the table and took out Abie's wallet and map. "You'd better take these."

Tim Daly stepped back and felt for the door-handle. "Where'd you get that lot?"

"From Abie's. Connor'll want them. All the stuff's there—the pitches and all that."

Tim got up. He was breathing hard, through his mouth. "All right, I'll take 'em." He stuffed the wallet and the map into an inside pocket. "I'll see you later."

He went out through the shop and down the Court. At the corner he looked for a bus. There was none in sight. He walked towards London Bridge. Before he had gone far a taxi came up behind him. He hailed it and was driven to Sammy's Club.

Tony met him at the door. "The guv'nor in yet?" Tim asked.

"No, sir." Tony concealed his interest and went on with his work of sweeping out the bar-room.

Tim ordered a double brandy-and-soda and asked for a paper. He spread it out on the bar and searched the columns. There was no mention of the death of Abie Russ. Doubts as to Danny's story struck him. But Danny had said that he'd seen the body.

Again he rustled the pages.

Tony, in answer to his demand, produced two other morning papers and a midday *News*.

Tim hadn't completed his search when he heard heavy, slow footsteps outside in the heavily carpeted passage.

Tony, polishing a glass, answered Tim's unspoken question. "That's him," he said.

Tim crushed the papers under his arm and left the bar. Big Bill Connor was taking off his hat when Tim came up with him in his room.

"Well?" The organ-like voice rumbled and the hint of a smile pulled at the corners of the pouting mouth.

Tim shut the door. He was breathing heavily. "It's about Russ. He's—he's dead."

"Dead!" Connor stood quite still, his right hand still holding his hat an inch above the desk. "Dead! Who told you that?"

"Danny Levine."

Connor dropped his hat on the table and, turning to a glass, adjusted his tie. "Did Danny kill him?" A laugh rumbled somewhere deep inside Bill Connor. He knew the kind of man Danny was. He knew that Danny couldn't have killed Abie Russ.

"I don't know. He said he found Abie dead in his room last night some time after twelve."

"How did Abie die?"

"Shot."

Connor padded to his swivel chair and sat down. "This'll make things easier; save us a lot of trouble."

"But there must be some one else trying to horn in. We'll have trouble there."

"I don't think so." Connor looked at the calendar on his desk and picked up a pen. "The man who killed Abie Russ'll have plenty to do to keep out of the way of the police. He won't bother us."

Tim Daly felt in his pocket and brought out the wallet and the map that had once belonged to Abie Russ. "Danny gave me these." He laid them on the desk.

Connor unfolded the map. "This is going to help," he said. "Abie had it well worked out." Five minutes passed before he raised his head.

"Is there anything you want me to do?" Tim asked.

"No, I don't think so." Connor rubbed his cheek up and down with a pudgy hand. Then he took a cigarette from a silver box and lit it. "It would be best if Danny was out of it. If the splits get a hold of him he'll talk."

"I can look after him.'"

"No good doing it that way." Connor took five one-pound notes from a drawer. "Give him these and tell him to go to Newcastle, get lodgings there, send me his address, and stay there till I tell him what to do."

"Why not tip him off to the splits?"

"Because he'll be useful till I get the run of this." Connor tapped the map with a forefinger. "Time enough then to put him out of the way. Get on with that right away."

Tim went to the bar. It was empty. He called out, "Tony!" and looked out of the door into the passage. "Tony!"

He opened the door of the guest-room, looked into the card-room. Tony was not about.

Tim Daly stood for half a minute thinking. Then he swore and went to the bar. A bottle of brandy was standing on the counter. He helped himself to a very generous double.

CHAPTER THIRTEEN

TONY WAS IN a call-box dialling Whitehall 1212 at the moment when Tim Daly was reporting his disappearance to Big Bill Connor.

"Put me through to Chief Inspector Thompson, quick. . . . Chief, this is Tony speaking. There's a man been killed, name Abie Russ. I don't know where."

Thompson said, "Abie Russ. All right, I've got that. Where are you calling from?"

"Leicester Square Tube."

"All right." Thompson slammed down the receiver and rang a bell. When a messenger appeared, he said, "Tell Mr. Perry I want him." He unlocked a cupboard and took out a murder-bag.

Then he flicked over the pages of a telephone directory. Richards. Roberts. Rosenheim. Rowe. Russ. A. Russ. Pawnbroker. 47 Fenwick Street. He reached for the receiver and asked for "Records."

"Inspector Thompson speaking. Do you know anything about a man Russ? Abraham. Pawnbroker. . . . All right, but get a move on."

Thompson turned, to see Perry standing by the door. "Oh, Perry, I've had a call from Tony Mascati. He said that a man called Russ has been killed. I've got the address."

A squad car took them to Abie's shop. Thompson looked at the door and barred windows and said, "We'll try the back."

The entrance to Abie's house was effected laboriously by means of a brace and bit and hack-saw, and half an hour after his arrival Thompson walked down the tiled hall. The single gas-jet in the chandelier was still burning.

Thompson tried the shop door, but it was fast. The front door was locked, but the bolts were withdrawn.

"I'll have a look upstairs. You wait here."

Perry watched Thompson climb the stairs, heard a door open, and then a cry, "Come up here."

He found Thompson standing just inside the door of the living-room of Abie's flat. He was looking at the body on the floor. "Shot through the head." He knelt and felt Abie's arm. "And I should say he's been dead some time. Twelve hours at least. Make an inventory." Thompson went out on to the landing and called down to a man below. "Take the car back to the Yard. Pick up Fielding and Hancock and send word for the surgeon to come along right away."

Then he went back into the room, walked over to the windows, and drew back the curtains. With his back to the light he surveyed the room in an attempt to get a "picture" of what had happened. There was an empty glass on the mantelpiece and another on the cocktail cabinet. Both held the dregs of a yellow liquor.

An ash-tray on a table was half-filled with squashed stubs. There was ash on the hearth; an evening paper lay on the hearth-rug. It was a late-night final edition of the previous day. The wireless set was tuned in to London Regional.

The end of a rug in front of the fireplace was rucked where Abie's feet had probably kicked it as he fell.

"There's the gun." Perry pointed with his toe to the revolver loosely clasped in Abie's left hand.

"Suicide," Thompson muttered, and went down on one knee. "I wonder." After a moment's pause he said, "Or what it's meant to look like. No scorching of the skin, or powder burns." He twisted his left wrist in an attempt to point at his right temple with his left forefinger. "How far would you say the tip of my finger is from my head?" he asked Perry.

"About four or five inches."

"I've never known a suicide to do it that way before. They usually fire through the mouth. It's the fashion nowadays."

He got up. "Make a plan of the room." Then he pulled out a pouch and filled his pipe. "It looks to me as if he'd been facing the door when he fell, and he must have been standing up. That's another reason why it doesn't look like suicide. They're nearly always sitting when they bump themselves off."

Perry nodded. "Like that bloke in the taxi last week." He was examining the window fastenings as he spoke. He lifted a sash and leaned out. "There aren't any drain-pipes within reach. If it was murder the man who did it must have come in either through the front or back door."

"And this man Russ must have known him. They apparently had a drink together."

"There are no signs of a struggle. If there had been that small table would have been knocked over."

Thompson bent down to look at the ash-tray on the table. It held the stubs of two "Gold Flake" and five "Craven A." A silver box held about fifty "Craven A." Its lid was open.

"They must have been together about ten minutes. Probably longer," Thompson said. "Long enough to smoke two cigarettes. Curious. If the killing had been intended you would have thought the murderer would have fired as soon as he came into the room. And if it was the result of a quarrel, you'd expect to see some signs of it."

"It may have been suicide," Perry suggested. "Whoever it was had the drink might have come and gone before Russ died."

"I'm not making up my mind yet," Thompson replied.

Ten minutes later the police car returned and the room was filled with men from the photography and fingerprint departments. First there was Hancock carrying an unwieldy tripod camera and a man with three flood-lights in reflectors.

Then Fielding arrived; he was carrying a suitcase.

"Get every print you can," Thompson ordered. "And photos from here and here and here." He walked to three points around the body. "Then I'll want a general view from the door as high up as you can get and another from the left-hand window."

The police surgeon arrived as the lights were being switched on and trained on the body. It was like a scene enacted on a movie set, except that the chief actor was dead.

When the photographer had done his work and had gone, the doctor got to work. First he felt the fingers holding the revolver, then he loosened their grip and threaded a short piece of string through the trigger-guard.

"Here you are, Chief. Exhibit A."

Thompson gave it to Fielding. "See if you can find anything on that, and remember it's left-hand prints we're looking for."

Fielding laid the revolver on a sheet of paper and distributed a cloud of white powder from an insufflator over the dark metal. Then he blew off the surplus and examined the result. "That's odd."

"What do you mean?"

"There's not a print on it. Smudges, that's all."

Fielding put the revolver on the table and looked at Thompson. "I don't believe he shot himself."

"I was doubtful about it, too," Thompson replied. "There's no sign of scorching. Well, you can try these two glasses, the decanter, and any other likely surface. I'm going to have a look downstairs." He turned to the doctor. "When you're ready I'd like to turn out his pockets."

"There's nothing more for me to do till I get him on the slab." The doctor tapped the dead man's skull with a pair of forceps. "The bullet's inside there." He got on to his feet.

"See what he's got on him," Thompson said to Perry.

The search of Abie's pockets revealed little of interest. There was a cigarette-case filled with "Craven A" cigarettes, some silver and coppers in the right-hand trouser pocket, and a lighter in a waistcoat pocket. On his left wrist was a square-faced wrist-watch stopped at twenty minutes past seven.

"Hasn't he got any keys?" Thompson asked.

"Not on him," Perry replied.

"Search the room. They may be hidden somewhere."

Ten minutes later Perry came out of the bedroom and said, "The only place we haven't looked in is the desk, and it's locked."

Thompson tried the roll top but couldn't move it. The drawers had no keyholes and they too could not be opened.

"We'll force it." Thompson went to the murder-bag and took out a long screw-driver and worked it into a crack alongside the lock.

The tool bent before there was a rending of wood and the lock tore from its fastening. The drawers were now free. But in none of them nor in the pigeonholes of the upper part of the desk were the keys to be found.

"We'll have to force the shop door. Get a plumber on to the job and then find out if Russ had any one working for him and bring 'em here."

Thompson had made a cursory examination of the shop and had found nothing of importance or interest when Perry came in with Bert Finch.

"I've got a man who says he worked for Russ."

Thompson pushed his hat on the back of his head and had a look at Bert.

"Where did you find him?" he asked Perry.

"In a public house across the road."

"Hold your head up," Thompson ordered sharply.

Bert looked up slowly. There was a look of sullen obstinacy in his eyes.

"What d'you know about this?"

"About what?"

"Abie Russ being killed."

"Killed!" There was no doubt that Bert was surprised. "Killed! When?"

"That's what I thought you might be able to tell me. Sit down."

"I'd sooner stand."

"All right." Thompson took out his pipe and picked at the dottle with a match. "Why didn't you come to work this morning?"

"I did, but I couldn't get in. The front door was locked."

"Hadn't you got a key?"

"No."

"Did you ring the bell?"

"No, I didn't. You see, there was Mrs. Ridge, her that does for Abie. She was on the step and she said she'd rung and knocked and hadn't got no answer."

"And you took her word for it?"

"That's right."

"What did you do after that?"

"Hung about for a bit and then went home."

"Where's that?"

"Bulmer Court. Across the road."

"Lodgings?"

"No. I live with my mother."

"How long have you been working for Russ?"

"Two years."

"What are your duties?"

"Help in the shop."

"Do you have anything to do with the books?"

"If I'm on my own I enter up the pledge-book. That's it over there." Bert pointed to a ledger lying on a desk.

"We'll check up on the stock later." Thompson knocked out his pipe and took a pouch from his pocket. "Do you know if Russ had any enemies?"

There was a pause of seconds before Bert answered. "No. No, I'm sure he hadn't." His tone was eager. A shade too eager, Thompson thought. Bert went on: "Of course, I didn't know a lot about him. I never saw him out of working hours. I was always finished at six or soon after."

"He lived upstairs alone?"

"Yes. That's right. Mrs. Ridge came in by the day. She'd cook his breakfast and then come back later to do the cleaning."

"I've got her outside," Perry said, and Thompson nodded.

"What time did you leave last night?"

"Six o'clock."

"Where was Russ at that time?"

"Here in the shop. He came out into the hall with me and I heard him shoot the bolts."

"Oh! Did he always do that?"

"Yes. He was very particular about locking everything up."

"And was that the last time you saw him?"

"Yes. But I—"

"Go on," Thompson urged.

"I wasn't going to say nothing."

"Yes, you were. Let's have it."

"I never saw Abie Russ after I left at six o'clock, and that's the gospel truth. So help me."

Thompson accepted the statement with a nod and said: "Do you know where Russ kept his keys?"

"In his pocket."

"What about the safe?"

"He had the key of that. I never had nothing to do with it."

"What is kept in it?"

"Jewellery, I think. He always handled that sort of stuff himself. I don't know nothing about it."

Thompson went over to the pledge-book and opened it. "Come over here a minute and tell me which are your entries."

Bert pointed to a line of unformed, spidery writing. "That's mine." He turned back a page. "And this one and these two."

Thompson noted that the amounts advanced were small. All were under ten shillings.

"There's nothing much here." He turned and looked at the safe. "I wonder what the blazes has happened to the keys."

"I don't know nothing about the safe."

"Yes, you said that before. You can wait outside." He said to Perry: "I'll see this woman, Mrs. Ridge."

Mrs. Ridge's day had come. She had always wanted to be in a "case"; to be questioned by the police, to give interviews to reporters and have her photo in the papers.

She started off: "Well, I knew as there was something up as soon as I saw the house. And as a matter of fact I had a funny feeling the minute I got up, and I said to my old man, I said—"

"Your name's Ridge, isn't it?"

Thompson looked a very ordinary sort of a man. She'd seen lots like him before and that little blighter with him. . . .

"I asked you if your name was Ridge."

"Yes. That's my name." Mrs. Ridge was offended.

"You work for Mr. Russ by the day?"

"Yes." She wanted to tell her story her own way. How Mr. Russ had looked the last time she'd seen him, how she'd cooked his breakfast, and what he ate, but somehow she couldn't get started.

"What were your hours?"

"Well, I come in the morning about half-past seven and get his breakfast ready."

"And then you go home and come back later to clean the place?"

The man seemed to know all about it without her saying a word. She said, "Yes," disappointedly.

"What time do you usually get back here?"

"Round about ten. I does the rooms and cooks his dinner and waits till he's finished. Then I washes up and goes home."

"Do you come back after that?"

"No, I'm finished then."

"Did Mr. Russ have any visitors?"

"Not that I knows of."

"What does he do about his supper?"

"Sometimes he cooks it himself and leaves me to wash up when I come in the morning. Other times he goes out for it."

"What happened last night?"

"I don't know. I haven't been upstairs yet."

"Has he ever said anything to you about being afraid of any one?"

"No." Mrs. Ridge shook her head slowly. She would dearly have loved to have been able to give a more exciting answer.

"Do you want to ask her anything?" Thompson said to Perry.

"Yes, there is one point I'd like to clear up."

"Go ahead."

"Mrs. Ridge, I believe Bert Finch came to the house early this morning."

"Yes, he did. I was outside and I told him how I couldn't make Mr. Russ hear and he said that Mr. Russ must have gone away as he hadn't seen him the night before."

"Can you remember his exact words?"

"Well, no, I don't think I can, but as near as I can say, he said he was along late last night and didn't get no answer when he rang the bell then."

"Just speak a bit slower, if you don't mind, Mrs. Ridge. I want to get this down." Thompson had an open notebook on his knee and a pencil in his hand. "Let me have it again, but start at the beginning. You were standing outside the door of this shop. What time would that be?"

"Round about eight. I was wondering what was best for me to do, when Bert Finch came along. I said that I couldn't get no answer, and he said, 'Well, I'm not surprised, because he wasn't in when I looked him up late last night.'"

"Are you sure he used these words, 'late last night'?"

"I'll take my dying oath that that was what he said."

"Did he say anything more about that visit?"

"No. I told him that I'd rung and knocked and hadn't got no answer, and he said then it wouldn't be no good us waiting and told me to go home."

Thompson dismissed Mrs. Ridge and had Bert brought back. As Bert came slowly into the room he stepped up to him and said: "I want the truth out of you."

Bert fell back half a pace. Thompson followed him. "You told me that the last time you saw Abie Russ was when you went off duty at six o'clock. That's right, isn't it?"

Bert's lower lip quivered and he put a hand up to his face. He didn't look at Thompson.

"You were here at this shop late last night."

"Yes, I was, but I didn't go in. I just—"

"I don't care about that. You were round here last night late. What time was it?"

"After twelve."

"What did you want with Russ at that time of night?"

"I wanted to see him about a friend of mine who wanted to get his suit out. He'd got the offer of a job, and—"

"What's his name? This friend of yours."

"I'm not going to tell you that." Bert had come to the end of his lie.

"Because he doesn't exist." Thompson was grim.

Bert stared at the bottom button of Thompson's waistcoat. It was doing its duty well.

"Now, come on, Finch, and tell me all about it." Thompson's manner changed. He put a hand on Bert's shoulder. "You've got nothing to be afraid of as long as you tell the truth."

"I didn't come back into the shop after I'd left at six o'clock."

"But you tried to."

"Yes. I tried, but Abie wasn't in then."

"Why did you think that?"

"Well, he didn't answer the bell and there wasn't a light in his room."

"Perhaps he'd gone to bed," Thompson suggested.

Bert did not reply.

"That's a possibility, isn't it?"

Bert said slowly, "Yes, I suppose it is."

"But you didn't think of it at the time?"

"No, I suppose I didn't."

"Well, let's get back to the time you left at six o'clock. Was any one about then?"

"How d'you mean?"

"Any customers in the shop?"

"No. I told you Abie bolted the door after I'd gone out."

"Did you see any one outside in the street? Any one that knew you?"

"Yes. Old Lampy. I spoke to him."

"Who's Lampy?"

"He works a pitch opposite at the end of Bulmer Court."

"What did you say to him?"

"Nothing much. I might have said it was a fine night."

"Where did you go after that?"

"To the 'Goat.'"

"Did you meet any one there?"

"Danny Levine; and my mother came in later."

"Who was behind the bar?"

"We call him Tom. I don't know what his other name is."

"How long did you stay at the 'Goat'?"

"I don't know. An hour or two maybe."

"And after that?"

"I took a walk around and met the bloke I told you about. He asked me to go and see Abie for him and see if he could get his suit out of soak. I said I would."

"Where did you meet this man?"

"Shaftesbury Avenue."

"What were you doing up there?"

"Nothing. Just taking a walk to pass the time."

"You weren't doing anything of the sort. You were with Abie Russ; up in his room. He let you in."

Colour flooded Bert's sallow cheeks. "I wasn't! I tell you I wasn't—"

"All right. Take it easy." Thompson felt in his pocket. "Have you got a cigarette on you?"

Bert produced a packet of Player's.

Thompson took one. "Do you always smoke these?"

"Yes."

"All right. That's all I want with you now. You can wait outside."

When the door had shut behind Bert, Thompson put the cigarette in his pocket and brought out his pipe.

"What do you think of him?" he asked Perry.

"I thought he was a twister at first. His looks are against him; but a lot of what he said sounded like the truth."

"Yes. All except about that friend of his who wanted to get a suit out of pawn."

The door opened and Leith came in looking like a Scotsman who has lost a sixpence down the drain.

"The D.D.I. told me to report to you," he said to Thompson, who smiled.

"Cheer up, Leith. It's only a suicide, or maybe a murder. We don't know yet."

"Murder, eh?" Leith's eyebrows lifted a fraction of an inch. "That'll be a nice change."

"Well, it's been a change for Russ all right."

"How was it done?"

"Shot with a revolver."

"Have you fixed the time?"

"Not exactly. It was probably done some time last night."

"Then the best thing I can do is to find out if any one heard the shot." Leith jerked his head in the direction of the window. "There's old Lampy. I'll have a go at him first."

"What about the houses opposite?"

"There's no one living in them; not for a hundred yards each way. They're going to be pulled down next week."

"Do you know Danny Levine?"

"Yes, I know Danny. He's got a paper-shop in Bulmer Court. I've had my eye on him for a month past."

"Why?"

"Betting. From what I can make out he's in a fair way of business. Works in with an office in the West End."

"On the level?"

"No. All cash bets. The D.D.I. knows all about it and wants to make a raid, but Danny's fly as the devil. I've never been able to catch any one going into his shop for betting, but I know there's a crowd that does."

"I'll go along with you. We'll pay him a visit," Thompson said, and then turned to Perry. "Get some one to open that safe and check up all the pledges with the book entries."

CHAPTER FOURTEEN

LAMPY WAS DRONING out a tune as Thompson and Leith crossed the road. He saw them leave the shop but did not look up as they approached.

Leith tapped the top of his accordion with his knuckles, and Lampy stopped playing with a wheezy whine.

"Where were you last night?"

Lampy's lips moved for a second or two before any sound came from them. Thompson noticed that his right hand was shaking.

"Last night?" Lampy muttered. "I was here for a time."

"Till when?"

"About eleven o'clock."

"Where did you go then?"

"To Mrs. Finch's. She had some supper for me. Eels."

"That's the mother of Bert Finch," Leith explained to Thompson. "She lives in the Court."

Thompson said, "Yes, I see," and asked Lampy: "How long were you over your supper?"

"I couldn't say. It might have been half an hour. I didn't stop after I'd finished because Mrs. Finch was expecting Bert home, and Bert don't like me going to his place."

"So you didn't see him?"

"Yes, I saw him. When I was on my way home, going along Fenwick Street. There was a cab come along and stopped and Bert Finch got out."

"Whereabouts?"

"Near the post-office."

"Was he alone?"

"I didn't see nobody with him."

"Where did he go after he'd left the taxi?"

"Along the street the way I'd come."

"That would take him to the pawnshop?"

"That's where he was going."

"How'd you know that?"

"I seen him go up the steps."

"Did he go in?"

"I suppose he did."

"Where were you at this time?" Thompson asked.

"Opposite the post-office at the corner."

"What time would that be?"

"It's difficult to say exactly," Lampy mumbled.

"Well, you told me you went to Mrs. Finch's at about eleven and you stayed there half an hour."

"Yes, that's right."

"Then you saw Bert Finch in Fenwick Street at about half-past eleven."

"That's about when it would be," Lampy agreed. "Some time about then."

"How long were you playing last night?"

"I started at ten o'clock."

"Where were you before that?"

"In the 'Goat.'"

"Was Bert Finch there at any time?"

"Yes, but I couldn't say when. I didn't take much notice of him." It was clear that Lampy was not a friend of Bert's. "His ma was there, too."

"And Danny Levine?"

"I dunno. He may have been."

"Did you hear anything out of the ordinary when you were playing between ten and eleven?"

A startled look chased across Lampy's face. Then he said quickly, "No, I never heard nothing."

"Are you sure about that? You didn't hear a shot fired?"

"A shot? No, of course I didn't." Lampy's fingers were nervously clutching at the strap of his accordion. "I never heard no shot."

Thompson was looking thoughtful as he walked on up the Court.

Mrs. Finch was having a sit-me-down after her morning's shopping when Leith knocked on her door. When she opened it he said, "This is Chief Inspector Thompson. He wants to have a word with you."

Mrs. Finch's eyes opened very wide and she gave a little gasp.

"That's all right," Thompson said. "Nothing to be worried about."

Mrs. Finch clutched her chest and managed to say, "Just wait a minute till I get the place cleared up a bit."

But Thompson said that that didn't matter and followed her into the room. He sat down in the chair Mrs. Finch offered him and put his hat on the table.

"You had company to supper last night, I hear?"

"Company!" Mrs. Finch had recovered her voice, and the noise she made almost startled Thompson. "Lampy was here, if that's what you mean. You see, I'm sorry for the old blighter, standing out there all day, and when Bert ain't here, I sometimes has him in for a bit of a feed, and last night he come in at—now, let me see when it was. . ." Mrs. Finch struck an attitude of deep thought, a finger on her lips and her head bent back so far that she was apparently searching the ceiling for the elusive figure.

"Would it be about eleven o'clock?" Thompson prompted.

"Eleven o'clock." Mrs. Finch's head jerked back and a forefinger was outstretched towards Thompson. "Eleven o'clock. That's just about when he did come, because you see—"

"You were expecting Bert back and you didn't want him to find Lampy here and that's why you noticed the time?"

"Now, how did you know that?"

"It doesn't matter."

Mrs. Finch went on staring at Thompson in amazed surprise. If she had been asked she would no doubt have said that she thought the London policeman was wonderful. Magic. That's what it was, she thought, and felt very uncomfortable. Not, of course, that she had anything to hide, but still. . .

"When did Bert get home?"

"Bert! Oh, yes, he came in after twelve. Twenty past it might have been; not much more than that."

"Did he tell you where he'd been?"

"No; and I didn't ask him. It would have been a waste of breath if I had. He said it was late for me to be up, and I said that I'd had some mending to do for Captain Macrae, and that's what had kept me up."

"Captain Macrae?"

"Yes, he's a gent I does for. Lives in Bury Square, he does. Not far from here and he is a real gent. He's got a trouser-press; and uses it, too."

Thompson hid a smile. That was a test for a gentleman he hadn't heard before. He himself never used a trouser-press.

"Does Bert go out much in the evenings?"

"Every night."

"He's got a girl?"

"Yes, but he doesn't take her out except on Saturdays."

"What's her name?"

"Peggy Nichol. She works for Mr. Crick." She walked to the window and pointed across the Court. "That's his office there. He's a solicitor."

"Where does she live?"

Mrs. Finch gave Thompson Peggy's address.

As he was writing it down Leith came up to where he was sitting. He had something in his hand. He held it up.

"Is this yours?"

"What's that?" Mrs. Finch withdrew her attention from Thompson and stared at the jewel-case.

"Oh, that?" she said weakly.

Thompson looked up. "Where'd you find that?"

"On the mantelpiece. Behind the clock." Leith opened the case and ran a finger over the satin lining. It made a faint rasping noise. "It's new."

Thompson took the case from Leith and examined it. He noted the name of a well-known jeweller printed inside the lid. "Where did this come from?"

Mrs. Finch lost her head and lied. "I've never seen it before."

"Sure about that?"

"Yes, of course I am." Her hands were clutching tightly on the folds of her skirt.

"Then I suppose it belongs to Bert."

"No, it's not his."

"Then how did it get behind the clock? It isn't Lampy's, is it?"

Mrs. Finch made a noise that was meant to be a scornful laugh. "Lampy!"

"Better have a look round," Thompson said to Leith over his shoulder. "You don't mind, do you, Mrs. Finch?"

"Mind what?"

"It looks as though there'd been a necklace in this case. We'd like to find it."

"There's no necklace here."

"It may have been put away somewhere by the same person who hid this case behind the clock." Thompson got up. "Go ahead, Leith."

The search proceeded methodically. First every cupboard was examined. Then the chairs, the drawers in the table, and the chest in the back room.

Thompson walked round the sides of both rooms, treading heavily as he did so. He was looking for a loose board. He found several, and searched the floor below them before he came to the place under the sink. He called out, "Leith! Come here a minute!"

Leith found him lying on his side on the floor with one arm out of sight. The money-belt which Bert had hidden was by his side. "Look what I've got."

"Anything else?"

"I don't think so." Thompson withdrew his arm and shone a torch into the opening. "No. That's the lot." He got up and carried the belt into the front room. "Ever seen this before?" he asked Mrs. Finch.

"What is it?"

Thompson made no reply, but stretched the belt on the table, opened the first pocket, and pulled out a flat wad of one-pound notes.

When the belt was empty there was a good pile of money on the table.

"Well, I never!"

"Nice little lot, isn't it?" Thompson said, and leaned against the wall.

"I don't know nothing about it. I'm an honest woman, and so is Bert, and if I was to fall dead this very minute—"

"Be quiet!"

Mrs. Finch's protestations died in a complaining whine.

"If your son didn't hide that stuff, who did?"

"I don't know, I'm sure."

"Do you have any visitors?"

"Only Lampy."

"Any one else?"

"No; and Bert never brings any one in neither, but this hasn't nothing to do with him. He's straight, and even though it is his own mother that says it, it's the truth. He's been working for Abie Russ for forty-five bob a week for close on a year, and before that he had a job in the New Cut. He was there since he left school and no one's ever had a word to say against him. You can ask Mr. Russ and he'll tell you the same, and—"

"Mr. Russ is dead."

Mrs. Finch, her mouth half-open as though to speak, stared stupidly at Thompson. She put up a hand to clear a straggling hair from her eyes.

"I never knew that." She spoke in a whisper.

"Neither did I till an hour ago."

"What happened?"

"I don't know."

"Is that—is that why you're here?"

"Yes."

"Where's Bert?"

"I expect he's at the police station by now."

Mrs. Finch came at Thompson in a fury of passion. He caught her wrists and held her off. Leith pinned her arms to her sides.

"There's no need to get excited. He's not under arrest. We only want him to tell us where he was last night."

The fight went out of Mrs. Finch.

Thompson said to Leith, "All right. Let her go." He took Mrs. Finch by the arm and pushed her into a chair.

"Did you see Bert last night?"

"Yes, he was with me here."

"At what time?"

"He came back for his supper at six o'clock and after that I went with him to the 'Goat.' He turned in soon after nine."

"But just a few minutes ago you said that Bert came in after midnight. And old Lampy says that Bert wasn't here when you gave him supper at eleven."

"Bert was in this house from six o'clock last night until he went to work this morning, except for the time he and me was at the 'Goat.'"

"That's what you say now."

"Yes, and it's the truth. You ask Bert."

"I've had a word with him, and he doesn't say anything about having had supper with you or going to bed at nine."

"Well, that's what he did do."

"If Bert didn't bring the money here, who did?"

"I don't know. And if I did I wouldn't tell you. I'm not saying anything more."

"All right. But if you change your mind let me know. Come on, Leith, we'll go and see Danny Levine."

Mrs. Finch sat quite still for a long time after Thompson and Leith had gone. She tried to think, but couldn't. Abie Russ was dead! Bert had been taken by the police. She felt very tired.

Then she remembered Mr. Crick. He was a lawyer. He would know what to do. She got up and went into the kitchen for her bag. It was on the gas-stove where she'd left it. Eagerly she took out her purse and counted the coins it held. Fifteen and six. That would be enough to go on with. Mr. Crick didn't charge a lot.

She found Peggy alone in the outer office typing a letter.

"Good morning, Mrs. Finch," Peggy said brightly. And then: "Whatever's the matter? You're looking terrible."

"It's Bert. He's been took and I've got to see Mr. Crick right away."

"Bert! What for?"

"Mr. Russ is dead. And they think Bert did it. They didn't say as much, but I know. He's at the police station."

"Wait here." Peggy was gone but a minute. When she came back she said: "Mr. Crick'll see you."

Peggy opened the door of Mr. Crick's room. Mrs. Finch sidled in and sat on the edge of a chair.

"Well, what's your trouble?" Mr. Crick barked.

Mrs. Finch told her story incoherently, but Mr. Crick was patient, and when she had run down he put his questions.

"Did you know anything about the money?"

"No. I swear I don't. I'd never seen it before."

"And the jewel case?"

"It was mine."

Mr. Crick took his cheroot from his mouth and leaned forward. "It was yours? Where'd you get it?"

"At a place where I work."

"Was it empty then?"

"Yes, and I didn't think there was anything wrong in taking it. It isn't as if it's worth anything."

"Well, I don't suppose it matters one way or another. It's the money we've got to think about. I'll see Bert and find out what he's got to say about it."

Mr. Crick sat staring at the blotter for a couple of minutes. When he looked up he seemed quite surprised to see Mrs. Finch still sitting opposite him. "Well, if there's nothing else you've got to say . . ." he hinted.

Mrs. Finch said she didn't think she'd forgotten anything and left the room.

Before she had reached the bottom of the stairs Peggy was in Mr. Crick's room. There were tears in her eyes.

"What's happened?"

"Abie Russ is dead."

"Yes, I know that—Mrs. Finch told me—but what about Bert?"

"The police have got him down at the station."

"Oh!" Peggy looked quickly away. Her hand went to her mouth, and she began to cry.

Mr. Crick felt acutely uncomfortable. "It's no use worrying until we find out what's happened. It may have been an accident—or suicide." His tone was unconvincing.

"You don't believe that?"

Mr. Crick recalled the man who had been seen watching Abie's shop on the night of his visit there on the Monday. Abie had been scared. And then there was the man he had seen from his window walking up and down outside Danny Levine's shop.

Mr. Crick put his cheroot in the saucer and did a thing he had never done before. He took a girl's hand in his. "I'm a lawyer and I don't believe anything I hear unless the person who tells me swears an affidavit. And sometimes I don't believe him even then." Mr. Crick struck a match and relit his cheroot, and as he tossed the match out of the window he said: "I suppose you've made it up with Bert—that quarrel you had with him?"

"No. And I never shall."

"There's some one else?"

"Yes."

"How long is it you've been going with Bert?"

"Five years. I'll tell you what happened." Peggy dabbed at her eyes and sniffed. "Bert wouldn't take me out except on Saturdays."

"Why not?"

"That was the trouble. He wouldn't tell me. All he said was that he had a job to do every night except Saturday. I asked him what it was, but he wouldn't say, and I said, 'Well, if that is the way of it, I'm finished with you,' and—"

"And then you met some one else who would take you out? Who is he?"

"Captain Macrae."

"Where did you meet him?"

"Mrs. Finch introduced us. She said that he'd seen me and had asked her if she could arrange it so that we could meet, and she did."

"Mrs. Finch?"

"Yes, she works for him."

"I see. Well, now I'm going to see Bert and find out what it's all about."

"You'll come back here afterwards?"

Mr. Crick pulled himself to his feet, and buttoned his coat. "Yes. About three, I expect."

Peggy turned away. "All right."

Mr. Crick squeezed between the desk and the wall. "Now, what have you done with my hat?"

Peggy gave it to him.

Mr. Crick took a bus to the police station and asked to see the sergeant on duty.

"You've got a client of mine here," he said, and put his card on the sergeant's desk.

The sergeant knew Mr. Crick. "And not the first," he replied. "You want to see him, I suppose?"

"That's the idea," said Mr. Crick, and felt for his cigar-case. Then he remembered where he was. "Has any charge been made?"

"Yes. With being in possession of money, well knowing it to have been stolen."

"Oh, I see. You're holding him on that till you make up your mind."

"We found twenty-two pounds hidden in his room."

"How was it made up?"

The sergeant slipped off his stool, opened a safe, and took out a bulky envelope. He emptied its contents on his desk.

Mr. Crick looked relieved. The notes were old and dirty. There were no fivers among them.

"Has he said anything?"

"Yes, we took a statement from him."

Mr. Crick said "Damn" under his breath as he put out a hand to take the file from the sergeant.

"You haven't wasted much time," he said, as he ran his eye down the first sheet. When he had finished reading he asked if he could see Bert Finch.

The sergeant told the jailer to fetch Bert and showed Mr. Crick into a bare lime-washed room. There was a white pine table, six hard chairs, and a strong smell of carbolic.

Bert shuffled into the room. He was wearing felt slippers and had no tie.

"Well, what have you been up to?"

Bert tried to smile.

"Now, sit down and tell me all about it."

Bert waited till the jailer had gone and then he started forward in his chair and gripped Mr. Crick by the arm. "They think I killed Abie. Killed him." His mouth worked and he began to cry.

For two hours he had stood up to the police questioning without weakening, but the moment that he was alone with one who had come to help him his reserve cracked.

"You believe me, Mr. Crick? You do, don't you? Why should I kill Abie? They said it was because I wanted money. They found some in my room. But if I wanted to steal from Abie I could have done it any time. I had no reason to kill him."

"Where did that money come from?"

"You know, Mr. Crick, that I collect the busker takings every night. Well, last night I did it same as usual, and I went to the shop to give it to Abie, but I couldn't get in. I rang, but there wasn't no answer."

"I suppose you were alone?"

"Yes, of course. I took a taxi to the corner by the post-office and walked the last bit."

"And after that?"

"I went straight home."

"You didn't go back and have another try?"

"No, I'd had enough of it. I'd been on my feet since nine o'clock, and I was pretty near done in."

"Why did you tell the police you came to the shop at all?"

"They knew about it."

"Oh, they did, did they?" Mr. Crick leaned back and rubbed his chin. "Who d'you think saw you?"

"I don't know. I wasn't taking any notice."

"And what about the jewel-case? Where did that come from?"

"I don't know. They showed it me, but I swear I've never seen it before."

"All right." Mr. Crick took a note-book from his pocket, laid it open on the table, and pulled up his chair. "I want you to run through what you did last night. From the time you left the shop. Don't miss anything out."

"We ought to be able to get you an alibi out of that," Mr. Crick said, when Bert had finished.

"I was wondering if I ought to have told them about it."

"You'll land yourself in trouble for certain if you do. Don't say anything at present. I'll consider the matter and let you know to-morrow." Mr. Crick put his note-book away and got up. "And if there's anything you want, let me know."

"I'm sure it's very good of you to take all this trouble," Bert said.

He looked like a dog that had been beaten for something and didn't understand why.

Mr. Crick said he must be going, and went.

Peggy was looking anxiously out of the window when Mr. Crick returned to the office. She ran down the stairs and met him at the street door.

"How is he? What did he say?"

"He's all right. You've nothing to worry about. They've got him on a receiving charge."

"Then it's not about Russ?"

"No. Not yet."

Mr. Crick took a half crown from his pocket. "I dare say Bert could do with a good supper; you know what he likes."

CHAPTER FIFTEEN

Now I want to see this man Levine," Thompson said to Leith as they left Mrs. Finch's front door.

"That's his place," Leith replied, and walked towards Danny's shop. He tried the handle, but the door was locked. Then he pressed his face against the glass. "It looks like he's out."

"There's a card in the window." Thompson read it aloud. "Back at two."

"He's usually around at this time of day," was Leith's comment. "Shall I wait for him?"

"No, we'll go back and see if Perry's got any news." Fielding was bending over a table in the living-room of Abie's flat when Thompson came in. He looked up when the door opened.

"Have you found anything?" Thompson asked.

"I've got two sets of dabs off one of the glasses. The dead man's and some one else's, and the way I figure it out is that Russ either had a couple of drinks or took his time about one. The second man only held the glass once."

"And what about the other?"

"The man who handled it wore gloves." Fielding picked up a cotton thread. "I found that caught on a screw-head in the door-handle."

Thompson took an envelope from the murder-bag and put the thread into it.

"So it looks as though there were two men besides Russ in this room."

Fielding agreed. Then he pointed to the wireless set. "Abie Russ worked the knobs of that and the man with gloves laid his hands on the top of it."

He walked across the room and picked up a two-foot square of three-ply wood. On one side of it was a portrait of Lloyd George. That was apparent from the upper part of the head; the face was almost obliterated.

"Oil," Fielding said. "And here's another that's caught it a bit worse."

"Where'd you find these?"

"Standing against the wall over by the window. There's dabs all over 'em as far as I can see, but I haven't had time to work 'em up yet."

"Well, we've got plenty of stuff to get on with."

Thompson looked at one corner of the room. "Hullo! Where does that lead to?"

There was an opening in the wall.

Fielding said: "Perry found that."

A section of the panelling was swung inwards. A passage, ten feet long, led to a door which was ajar.

Thompson reached it in three quick strides. "Well, I'm blowed!"

He stood for a moment looking round Danny Levine's Practice Room. Then he walked to the piano and turned over a pile of tattered music sheets. Beside them was a glass with the dregs of beer in it; cigarette-butts littered the floor, and the smell of stale smoke was in the air.

Thompson made a circuit of the room and tried the door at the far end. It was locked. Then he went back to the flat and examined the oil-soaked pictures. "I'd give something to know why they're here," he muttered, and began to fill his pipe. As he was lighting it Perry came running up the stairs.

"I say, Chief. I've found the driver who brought Bert Finch here last night."

"Good." Thompson pressed down the glowing tobacco with a match-box and blew out a cloud of smoke. "What has he got to say?"

"I haven't asked him anything yet. I thought I'd leave the questioning to you."

"Righto. I'll see him now."

"He's downstairs in the hall."

The taximan's story was soon told. He had picked up Bert Finch in St. Martin's Lane, near the Coliseum, and had driven him to the post-office in Fenwick Street.

"Was he alone?" Thompson asked.

"Yes, sir."

"Did he seem nervous at all?"

The taximan thought for a moment, and then said: "He was all right as far as I could see, but I did notice that he looked up and down the street before he got into the cab, and he spoke very quick."

"Can you remember what he said?"

"Well, as near as I can call to mind, he told me to take him to London Bridge and then to carry straight on till he told me where to stop."

"Did he say he was in a hurry?"

"No, sir. Nothing like that. When we got a bit past the Unicorn Packing Works he knocked on the glass and I drew in to the side and stopped."

"Was that anywhere near here?"

"Yes, sir. About a hundred yards down the street. Near the post-office."

"What time was it?"

"Round about half-past twelve."

When the man had gone, Thompson said:

"Now let's see how the times work out. That old beggar with the accordion gives us the first lead. He left Mrs. Finch's to go home at half-past eleven and he saw Bert Finch get out of a taxi outside the post-office."

"But the driver of the cab put the time much later than that," Perry objected. "He said it was half-past twelve."

"That doesn't fit," Thompson agreed. "And I'd sooner trust the cabby than old Lampy. But, at the same time, Mrs. Finch said it was half-past eleven when he left her house."

Perry walked over to the window and looked out. "He's still there. Shall I get him back?"

"Yes. Let's see if we can clear up this point."

Lampy shuffled into the room slowly, fearfully.

"It's all right. The body's not here," Thompson assured him. "Sit down." He pointed to a chair with the toe of his shoe. And as Lampy hesitated, he said, "What the hell's the matter with you? Sit down."

Lampy took an uneasy seat and his right hand rose to claw at his face.

Thompson got up and took his pipe from his mouth. "Now, I want to know what you were doing between half-past eleven and half-past twelve last night."

"Last night?" Lampy quavered.

"Yes. Where did you go after you left Mrs. Finch?"

"Home. Same as I told you."

"North along Fenwick Street?"

"Yes, that's right."

"Past the post-office?"

"Yes."

"And you saw Bert Finch getting out of a taxi?"

"That's what I said."

"Yes, I know that. And it's true enough. Bert did come down in a taxi. But not at half-past eleven."

"Well, I couldn't say to a minute when it was, but it must have been round about then."

"No, it wasn't. It was at half-past twelve. Where were you between then and half-past eleven?"

Old Lampy's finger-nails rasped on the stubble on his cheek and his eyes looked first to the right and then to the left, like those of one who lies.

"Come on. Let's have it. What were you up to?"

A ghost of a frightened smile spread over old Lampy's face. "I went along to see Danny Levine."

"Why didn't you tell me that before?"

"I didn't think it mattered."

"Where was Danny?" Thompson shot out the question.

"In his room. Where he always is at that time."

"You mean in his shop?"

"No. In the place next door to here."

"Through there?" Thompson pointed to the open space in the wall.

Lampy turned and said, "Yes."

"And what was Danny Levine doing there?"

"His usual. Playing the pianner. He teaches us blokes tunes at a tanner a time."

Remembering the size of the room, the chairs and benches, and cigarette-stubs and ash on the floor, Thompson said: "There was a crowd there?"

"Quite a few," Lampy mumbled.

"And they'd come there to learn tunes from Danny Levine?"

There was relief on Lampy's face as he answered, "Yes, that's right."

"How long did you stay there?"

"I can't say exactly."

"An hour?"

"May have been. You see, we was waiting for—" Lampy suddenly stopped talking and the light of fear was in his eyes.

Thompson put a hand under his chin and jerked his head up. "Out with it! Who were you waiting for?"

"Let me alone!" Lampy's voice was high-pitched and unnatural, like that of a frightened child.

"Who were you waiting for?"

"We weren't waiting for nobody."

"Yes, you were. Who was it?"

Lampy's weak resolve gave way before the force of Thompson's demand.

"Abie." The name came in a whisper.

"Abie Russ?"

"Yes."

Thompson dropped his hand and drew back. He had won.

"He always came along of a night-time to the room," Lampy said.

"Why?"

"To give us our money."

"Did he turn up last night?"

"I didn't see him."

"When did you leave?"

"I don't rightly know, but it was after twelve."

"Did you get your money?"

"No."

"What were you to be paid for?"

"Playing."

"How much?"

"Half a dollar and a can. Sometimes it was a bit more, not a lot."

"What was the idea?"

Lampy looked stupid.

"Why should Abie pay you half a dollar?"

"Because—because . . ."

"Go on."

"Well, I don't suppose there's any harm in saying it now. He's gone, and that's the finish." Lampy's eyes shyly sought Thompson's. "You won't hold it against me, guv'nor?"

"Not if I can help it."

"Well, it's like this. Danny Levine ran a book at his shop up the Court. I was the billow."

"He means he was the lookout," Leith said, and looked as though he had at last found the answer to a difficult problem.

"That's right. I was looking out for Danny. When a split happened along I played a particular tune. It was 'Lily of Laguna.'"

"And to think I never tumbled to that!" Leith's tone was bitter.

"But there isn't any betting at night," Thompson said.

"I was looking out for Abie then. He was scared."

"What of?"

"There's been a bloke hanging around, and Abie figured he wasn't after no good, so that's why I stopped around till eleven o'clock, to give him the office."

"And was there anybody outside Abie's shop last night?"

"No, guv'nor. Not when I went off."

"Are you sure about that?"

"Yes. I had a good look up and down the street."

"And you went to the Practice Room after you left Mrs. Finch?"

"Yes."

"And Danny Levine was there?"

Lampy nodded.

"Was he expecting Abie Russ, too?"

"Yes, and when Abie didn't come we all went home."

Thompson went over to the wall and picked up the oil-soaked picture of Mr. Lloyd George. He held it so that the light from the window fell on it. "Have you ever seen this before?"

Lampy shrank back in his chair.

"Well?"

"Yes, Chalks did it."

"Who is Chalks?"

"Chalks O'Callaghan. A bloke that worked for Abie. Doing daubs."

"Where does he live?"

"I dunno."

"Where did you see this before?"

"In the room. Through there."

"Do you know how it got spoiled?"

"No. I don't know nothing about it."

"Was Chalks in the room last night?"

"Yes, he was. I spoke to him."

"Did he say anything about this picture?"

"I didn't hear him say nothing."

"All right, you can go."

When Lampy had gone, Thompson looked across at Perry, who was standing with his back to the mantelpiece and his feet in the grate. "Can you make any sense out of all that?"

"I think we ought to pick up this bookmaker bloke, Danny Levine. He might help."

"Yes, I'd like to have a look inside that shop of his."

"You won't find anything there, if I know Danny." Leith looked his most lugubrious. "He's as fly as a crate of monkeys. I've been keeping an eye on him ever since Christmas."

Mrs. Finch, on watch at her front window, saw Thompson coming up the Court.

"Back again. I wonder what he wants this time," she muttered under her breath. "Anyway, I won't say nothing. I won't answer any of his questions, and if he as much as—"

The soliloquy ended abruptly as Thompson halted in front of Danny's shop door. He rattled the handle and then signed to one of the party, who produced a bunch of keys. Mrs. Finch could see first one tried and then another. Her excitement rose. Things was moving, and no mistake. The rozzers breaking into Danny's shop! She leaned so far out of her window that only her toes touched the floor.

They'd have to bust in the door if they couldn't find a key to fit the lock. And what if Danny was to come along at that very minute? She looked up at the Court and then back to Danny's shop. The door had been opened. She saw Thompson go in, and after him a bloke she didn't know, and then Leith.

Thompson walked through to the back room. "Be careful what you touch until Fielding has had a go here," he ordered.

A cupboard door was open and he looked inside. It was empty except for two mugs, a brown tea-pot with a broken spout, and a paper packet containing tea.

The grate was half-full of burnt paper, which had been crushed to tiny fragments. "We shan't be able to get anything out of that lot," Thompson said. He pointed to the floor and said to Perry, "Pick up all these cigarette-ends and see if you can find out what makes they are." Then he touched Leith on the arm. "Get Fielding. And tell him to bring his bag with him."

When Fielding arrived Thompson went out into the back yard with Perry.

"This is a funny business," he said as he picked at the ash in his pipe with a match. "What was Abie's game, do you think?"

"I suppose he was a fence."

"No, that won't work. There was a crowd of men in that room, and they were to be paid by Russ."

"Bookmaking racket perhaps. And they were the scouts."

"Maybe it was. And the money you found in Finch's room was part of the takings from some other district."

The window of Danny's back room was raised and Fielding put out his head. "I've found something interesting. Come and have a look."

When Thompson entered the room Fielding pointed to a thumb-print on the table. It had been dusted with a fine grey powder and every line and whorl was clear to the naked eye. "The man who made that handled one of the glasses in the room over the pawnshop."

"Which one?" Thompson asked.

"The glass that Abie Russ drank out of. He used it after Abie did."

Thompson turned to Perry. "Send out a description of Danny Levine. Quick as you can."

"The prints on the glass were good," Fielding continued when Perry had gone. "Both sets. Of course, there was a bit of overlapping, as Russ used his right hand and the other man his left."

"Right hand!" Thompson looked at Fielding. "Are you sure about that?"

"Yes, no doubt about it."

Thompson knocked out his pipe and put it in his pocket. "I'm going back to Abie's flat," he announced. "You carry on here."

A man was kneeling before the safe in Abie's shop. He was wearing an eye-shield and in his hands was an oxy-acetylene blow-lamp. Two cylinders of gas stood by his elbow.

The roar of the lamp drowned the sound of Thompson's entry. He bent and touched the man, who looked round and then turned off the taps.

"I'm just about through. Give me another five minutes."

"O.K. Go ahead."

When the door swung open Thompson opened the pledge-book and with Leith's assistance he checked the contents of the safe.

When the tally was complete, Thompson said: "Well, there's nothing missing from there."

Perry came in to report that he'd put out a call for Danny Levine.

"Good. He won't get far."

Perry looked at the safe. "Anything missing?" he asked.

"No. All present and correct. It looks as though that empty jewel-case in Finch's room hadn't anything to do with this business. If its contents had been taken as a pledge, there should be an entry in the book."

"That depends on what advance was made," Perry replied. "If it was more than ten pounds, there wouldn't be any need to enter it up."

"Yes, of course. I'd forgotten. But that doesn't help us."

"Russ might have made a note of it somewhere." Perry opened a drawer of the desk and pulled out a handful of papers. But there was no record of any transaction among them nor anywhere else in the shop.

"And he'd no papers in his pockets," Thompson said when the search was complete. "We'll have to leave the jewel-case out of our calculations for the time being. The man who killed Russ was either Bert Finch or Danny Levine."

"Killed Russ! But it was suicide!"

"Like hell it was. Abie Russ was right-handed. The gun was in his left hand, and there was no scorching of the skin. Suicide won't work."

"Bert Finch had a motive; that money hidden under the floor in his room, and he was seen near the shop at half-past twelve."

"Yes, he's a likely one. But I wouldn't be surprised if Danny Levine had a hand in it, too; otherwise why should he have cleared out?"

At half-past two that afternoon a patrolling constable found a man huddled in a doorway in a street which runs from the Princes Theatre to Long Acre.

It was Tony Mascati. And he wasn't asleep and he wasn't drunk.

He moaned when the constable pulled at a handful of his coat and his head fell slackly forward on his chest.

An ambulance carried him swiftly to the casualty ward of the Walbrook Hospital, and there he was laid upon a high table and his clothes were removed.

Concussion. Broken: three ribs and jaw. A message was flashed to New Scotland Yard and for two hours police cars cruised in the vicinity. Their bag was a dozen of those "known to the police," but questioning failed to pin the assault to any one of them. Tony Mascati, with his jaw set and with bandages round his ribs, was laid in a bed. He lay there as still and almost as silent as a corpse for an hour.

On a chair by his bed sat a constable with his helmet on the floor by his feet; on a table was an open note-book and a pencil.

At intervals a nurse would stop by the bed and look inquiring. The constable would shake his head and perhaps yawn and wonder how long he would have to sit there on that very hard chair.

An hour passed. Outside a clock struck four. The constable achieved an uneasy sleep for five minutes, and then jerked himself awake. The head of the sick man rolled sideways on the pillow and his eyelids quivered. He drew in his breath and expelled it in a thin whining sound.

The constable cleared his throat and said: "Feeling better?"

"It—was—Tim—"

"What's that?"

"Tim. Tim Daly done it."

A pencil bore down heavily on a page of the note-book.

"Anything else?"

But Tony Mascati did not hear the words.

"Tim Daly!" Thompson repeated the name as it came to him over the wire. "Did Tony say where he hung out?"

"No."

Thompson put down the receiver and said to Perry: "Tony Mascati's been beaten up. He was the man who told me that Abie Russ had been killed."

"He spoke out of turn."

"Yes, and now we've got to find Tim Daly. Get through to the Information Room and see if they can help us."

Five minutes later Perry said: "Sammy's Club, Brennan Street."

"All right. Let's go."

CHAPTER SIXTEEN

A QUARTER OF an hour later Thompson tried the door of Sammy's Club. It was locked. He pressed a bell-push and listened. He could hear two men talking inside. He rang again.

"Hullo, Tim."

Tim Daly stared at Thompson for a second and then he tried to shut the door. A number nine boot stopped that.

"You can't come in."

"Like hell I can't."

"Where's your warrant?"

Thompson lowered his shoulder and shoved. Tim Daly staggered back against the wall of the passage. Then he recovered himself and tried to run, but Thompson caught him by one arm; Perry held the other.

Thompson grinned. "This isn't the way to treat distinguished visitors, Tim. You ought to know better than that."

"You've no right in here. This is a club."

Tim Daly was breathing heavily through his mouth.

"Put the cuffs on him and keep him here while I have a look round," Thompson said to Perry. He opened a door and looked into the bar. It was empty. So was the con room.

He walked down the passage and flung open the door at the end. A light was burning on the broad desk. The curtains were drawn over the windows.

A pen lay on the blotter. Thompson picked it up. The ink in the nib was wet. He drew back the curtains and looked down into a yard. There were three men there. Two police officers and Big Bill Connor.

Thompson put his head out and called: "Bring him up here."

Bill Connor was sulky and silent as he was pushed into the room. Thompson slammed down the window-sash and turned a key in the lock of the door.

Connor was staring at the carpet.

"Well, now, this is a surprise. I didn't know you and Tim had teamed up."

Thompson's gaze was straying round the room as he spoke. He knew Bill Connor and his capacity for silence.

"Nice place. Nice furniture." He walked round the desk and tried the top drawer. It was locked. "Frisk him."

The two plain-clothes men emptied Connor's pockets and laid the contents before Thompson. A gold cigarette-case. A gold light-er. A silk handkerchief. A bunch of keys. Two wallets, and some silver and copper coins.

Thompson picked up one of the wallets. It was stuffed with notes and there were three visiting-cards in it. "M. Jerome," he read. "That's a nice name you've picked. Better than Connor. Sounds a lot better."

Bill Connor kept his head bent down and did not speak.

Thompson opened the other wallet and took from it a folded map. "London and Environs" was its title. It was sprinkled with dots and crosses drawn in red ink.

They were thick in Piccadilly, Shaftesbury Avenue, and the Strand.

Thompson was frowning as he refolded it. There was a book of stamps half-used and an envelope in another pocket. *A. Russ, 47 Fenwick Street, Southwark.*

He held it out. "Where did you get this?"

Bill Connor raised his heavy head.

"Find out. I'm not talking."

Thompson turned the envelope over. The back of it was covered with pencil writing. It meant nothing to Thompson, and he laid it on one side and turned out the remainder of the contents of the wallets. There was another envelope addressed to A. Russ, a receipt for the payment of rates, and two bills made out in the same name.

Thompson opened the door and called out to Perry: "I've got Bill Connor in here. Take him along to Howard Street. And Tim Daly, too. Keep 'em there till I come."

Thompson saw the police car drive off, and then he went back into Bill Connor's room and searched it methodically. Two piles of papers grew on the desk: one related to the business of the club and was of no immediate interest. The other consisted of odd scraps of paper, envelopes, and the covers of cigarette-packets. Each bore scribbled words. One read: *Old Compton and Greek. Busker.* Another: *Embankment, Charing X. Dauber.*

Thompson read every one, and when he had finished there was the light of understanding in his eyes.

He was tying up the bundle when the phone-bell rang.

It was Perry calling from Howard Street police station. "There's a man here called Crick. He says he thinks he can give some useful information about the Abie Russ killing."

"Who is he?"

"A solicitor. Got an office in Bulmer Court."

"I'll come right along. Have either of the other two said anything yet?"

"No."

"We've got Tim Daly's dabs at the Yard, and Bill Connor's. Tell Fielding to get hold of them and compare 'em with those he got at Abie's flat and in Danny Levine's shop."

Perry said, "O.K.," and Thompson rang off.

The charge-room was thick with the smoke and scent of one of Mr. Crick's cheroots. The owner was seated uncomfortably on a hard chair reading an evening paper.

When Thompson came in, Perry, who was writing at a table, got up. "This is Mr. Crick."

"You've got some news for us?" Thompson said as he shook hands.

"It may not be any use," Mr. Crick replied. "But I thought I ought to tell you that two days ago—that'd be Wednesday—I saw a suspicious character hanging round Bulmer Court. When I first saw him he was outside Levine's shop."

"What do you mean, suspicious?"

"He'd been in prison."

"Why did you think that?"

"The way he walked."

"Anything else about him?"

"No."

"Well, what did he look like?"

Mr. Crick gave a very faithful description of Tim Daly, and finished up, "He was a man of the bruiser type."

Thompson exchanged a glance with Perry. "We'd better have a parade right away."

Seven passers-by were brought in by the sergeant and stood in a row in the yard at the back of the station. Tim Daly was brought into the charge-room.

Thompson said to him: "In connection with the death of Abraham Russ, I propose to place you for identification by Mr. Crick, who saw you in Bulmer Court on Wednesday of this week. Have you any objection?"

"I don't know anything about Abie Russ."

"Do you object to being put up for identification?"

"You can do what you blooming well like, but I don't know anything about Russ. Never heard of him."

"All right. Take him out."

Perry touched him on the arm. "Come along." When they got out into the yard Perry asked: "Where do you want to stand?"

Tim elbowed his way between two men and the line bent and spread out.

Mr. Crick walked up the line, and when he came to Tim Daly he touched him and said, "This is the man I saw in Bulmer Court on Wednesday."

When Mr. Crick had gone and Tim Daly was back in his cell, Thompson untied the bundle of papers he had found in Connor's room and spread them out on the table in the charge-room.

"Abie Russ was working a racket," he said.

"A racket!"

"Yes. There's hundreds of 'em going on all the time. Why you don't hear about them is simply because the men who run them don't use guns. A broken bottle, a knife, or the toe of a steel-shod boot do the trick without any noise, and the bloke that gets it doesn't squeal for fear he'll get a worse dose.

"Now, just think a minute. You've stood in a theatre queue and seen the entertainers come along and do their stuff. Each turn lasts about five minutes. As soon as one fellow has finished there's another waiting to take his place. That isn't chance. It's all worked out.

"And the men who stand outside tea-shops with trays of matches. They pay for their pitches. And so do pavement artists and men who play cornets outside pubs. Coffee stall-keepers have to pay protection money.

"You can call it a racket or a union—it comes to the same thing in the end."

Thompson spread out the pile of papers on the table. "This is what I think happened. Bill Connor and Abie Russ were in the same game. They quarrelled, and—"

"Connor killed Russ?"

"No, he didn't do it himself; he probably got Tim Daly to fire the shot."

"Then one of them'll talk."

"I don't know. Connor's clever enough to know when to keep his trap shut. And Tim Daly's cunning."

"What about Bert Finch?"

"I don't know." Thompson picked up one of the wallets he'd found on Bill Connor. "That belonged to Abie Russ." He took the envelope with the pencilled entries on it and gave it to Perry. "Does that make sense to you?"

Perry walked to the window and examined the writing carefully. After a minute or two he said: "I think it's something to do with jewellery. I'm pretty sure that that word at the top means 'carat.'"

"We'll make sure. I'll get a jeweller to examine it."

Mr. White, who kept a shop near the post-office in Fenwick Street, took one look at the envelope and said: "I know what this is about. Just wait a minute." He pushed his glasses on to his forehead and disappeared into a room at the back of his shop.

It wasn't long before he was back with a folded paper in his hand. He spread it out on the scarred glass top of a show-case. Thompson read the description of the pearl necklace which had been stolen from Mrs. Keene. "Are you sure you're not mistaken?"

Mr. White said he was quite sure. "A hundred and ten. There's the figure there at the top. And here are the weights."

"But there's only about twenty-five on the envelope."

"And that's what's on this notice, too, if you care to count 'em. Every fourth bead's been weighed, which is customary in the case of a long string like this one. The figures tally near enough."

When they were out in the street Thompson said: "Well, I wonder if this is going to help us. It's quite a different line."

"Russ might have got rid of the pearls before he was murdered."

"Yes. But what about that empty case we found at the Finches' place?"

"Yes, I know. And the twenty-two pounds in notes," Perry added. "We know Bert Finch was at Abie's shop last night and we've only his word for it that he didn't go in. It's quite likely that he killed Abie for the cash he had about the place."

"And while he was rifling the safe, he found the pearls and took them as well?"

"Yes, and later on got the wind up and hid them somewhere."

"In that case I'd have expected to find them under the floor with the money," Thompson said.

"There's another reason why Bert Finch killed Russ. They knew each other. If Finch came to the shop Russ would let him in, but he surely would never have admitted Tim Daly if he was in with a rival crowd."

"Then how did Abie's wallet get into the possession of Bill Connor? Can you tell me that? And how did Connor know that Abie was dead before we knew ourselves? Who told him?"

"I don't know. We might have another go at Bert Finch."

"And here's another thing. If Lampy was telling the truth, he and Danny Levine were expecting Abie Russ to come to the Practice Room before midnight. Abie never turned up there, and half an hour after that Lampy saw Bert Finch get out of the taxi by the post-office. Finch might have been speaking the truth when he said that he didn't go into the shop last night."

"If that were so, then some one else killed Abie, probably before midnight."

As they turned into the police station Thompson said: "I don't think I've ever had such a damn' puzzling case." He looked at the circular. "Call up the Yard and get all the particulars you can about the theft of this necklace. You never know, we might get a line to work on that way."

When Mrs. Finch left Mr. Crick's office she went straight to Bury Square. There was one thought in her mind. She must get money so that she could help Bert. He'd acted funny the past month or so, and she'd been mad at him because he wouldn't talk; wouldn't tell her things, and was angry when she questioned him. When he'd fought with Peggy she'd been glad and had welcomed the chance to introduce her to Captain Macrae. She wasn't so sure now that she'd done right. The Captain was out of Peggy's class, and maybe if Bert had married he'd have changed and got more sociable; more like he used to be.

But the little troubles of the past were as nothing now. All that mattered was to get money to pay Mr. Crick. She didn't know how much he'd want, but lawyers charged a lot. Every one said so. Maybe the Captain would help her.

It was only a couple of days ago he'd given her a pound note, and it wasn't for anything she'd done, because he'd paid up all he owed before that.

Her pace grew quicker as she neared Bury Square, and she was almost running when she turned the corner. There he was! Ahead of her. That was a bit of luck. And he hadn't half got a lot of papers under his arm. He was holding one up and was reading it as he walked up the steps.

"Captain!"

Macrae stopped and looked round.

"I'm glad I caught you. Do you mind if I come up and have a word?"

"Of course not." Macrae tried to make his voice sound ordinary. He opened the door and they went up the stairs side by side.

"It's Bert. He's got into a bit of a mess, and I came along to see if you could help me. You're always so kind."

"What's the trouble?"

"Well, it's nothing much, and then it's a lot, if you know what I mean."

Macrae did not know what she meant, but asked no questions. They were quite unnecessary. The brook flowed on.

"The police came to my place and asked me where Bert was last night, and I didn't know and I said I didn't know, and then they searched everywhere and found a lot of money."

"Money?"

"Yes, there was ever so much. Pound notes and silver. They took it away with them and they've took Bert."

"What for?"

"They didn't say, but it's got to do with Abie Russ. He's been murdered."

"No, he hasn't. It was suicide." Macrae's voice was harsh. "Who told you it was murder? The police?"

"No, they just said he was dead, but it must have been murder. Why else should they take Bert and ask me all them questions? Mrs. Ridge said that there was blood all over the walls, and—"

"What did you tell them?" Macrae asked suddenly.

"Nothing. I never said a word hardly. Only that Bert had been in the house all last night and he couldn't have done it."

Macrae lit a cigarette and began to walk up and down the room.

"I'm sorry if I've caused you any trouble," went on Mrs. Finch, "but what I was wondering was if you could let me have a pound or two."

Macrae felt in his pocket and took out two crumpled notes and a few shillings in silver. It was all the money he possessed. He gave Mrs. Finch one of the notes.

She thanked him effusively, and then said: "You see, the lawyers are going to cost me a lot of money. I'm getting that Mr. Crick—"

"Crick?"

"Yes, he's the bloke Peggy works for. They say he's very clever, and I'm sure it's very kind of you, Captain, to give me this money. I'll pay it back as soon as ever I can."

Mrs. Finch talked herself out of the room.

When she had gone, Macrae kicked the door shut. First he swore and then he laughed. It was damn' funny. Damn' funny. He'd given a pound to the defence fund of a man suspected of a murder he himself had committed.

The wicker chair creaked as he sat back in it.

Bert Finch accused of the murder! He hadn't thought of that. What would he do if Bert were convicted? He drove the thought from his mind. Mrs. Finch had probably got it all wrong. Why should the police suspect her son? Besides, he'd fixed it so that it looked as though Abie had committed suicide. He'd put the gun in Abie's hand.

They couldn't get Finch for it. And there was nothing in the papers. He picked the first one off the pile he'd brought in. It was the one he'd read. He threw it aside and picked up another. Nothing there. He tried the next.

Hell! Yes. Here it was in the Stop Press. "The Southwark Murder. Man detained." That was all. A man detained!

He took the string of pearls from his pocket. Mrs. Keene was due back to-night. He must go to her flat and hide them there. And Abie's keys. What a damn' fool he'd been to carry them around! If they were found on him! He went cold at the thought. But what the hell was the good of getting into a panic?

He got out of the chair and lit a cigarette. He'd done all right so far, and there wasn't a dog's chance anything could happen now. All the same, the sooner he was rid of the pearls the better; and the keys—he could chuck them away anywhere.

Mrs. Keene wouldn't be back before six. He took out the letter he had received that morning. Yes. Half-past five at Paddington.

Hours to wait.

But first he'd have lunch; a damn' good lunch. He took his money from his pocket, looked at it, and laughed. Down to his last quid, but what the hell! He'd get the run of his teeth from Mrs. Keene and the usual fees. A guinea for a dinner-dance. Oh, he'd manage all right.

After lunch he returned to Bury Square and sat and read and smoked till four o'clock. Then he got up and went out. He took a route which led him, far from Bulmer Court, to Blackfriars Bridge.

He felt in his pocket. The pearls were still there; quite safe. Once he'd got rid of them he would be absolutely clear. And the keys. He'd been waiting his chance to throw them away ever since he'd left his room, but there had always been some one near.

He bought an evening paper in the Strand and stopped to read it. The announcement he'd read before in the Stop Press was now on the front page. There was nothing new except two lines. "It has not yet been definitely established that the death of Abraham Russ was due to foul play. There are grounds for the belief that he committed suicide."

Ah! That was better. All this talk of Bert Finch being suspected of murder must be wrong. And he hadn't left any clues for the police to pick up. He was sure of that. He'd worn gloves all the time. Abie's own prints would be on the pistol-grip.

Macrae was beginning to feel as pleased with himself as though he had done a really fine bit of work, instead of having committed the foulest crime in the Calendar.

His own complete conceit allowed no thoughts of pity for the man who had died to gain a foothold in his mind. And the madness which had seized him twenty-four hours ago continued. Since Abie Russ had died at his hand he could no longer stand back and look with horror on himself.

Perhaps it was merciful that this was so.

While he was waiting for a bus he saw a litter-basket on a lamppost. He slipped Abie's bunch of keys into a fold of his paper and thrust it into the basket.

Then he jumped on to a bus and rode to Piccadilly Circus and walked up Shaftesbury Avenue to the club. There was a knot of loafers on the pavement outside the street door, and as he turned to go in one of them called out: "It's no good, mister. The rozzers have shut it up."

"When?"

"Not long ago."

As Macrae started to walk away a man followed him. "They've took the boss," he croaked. "And Tim as well. You better keep away from here else it'll be your turn next."

Macrae gave him a shilling.

He walked to Cambridge Circus and down Charing Cross Road to a news theatre. There was a Mickey Mouse film being shown; a man in the next seat was laughing with his head thrown back and was beating on his knees with his hands.

Macrae wanted to laugh, too, but he couldn't. He tried to concentrate on the dancing figures on the screen, but they meant nothing to him. When people laughed he hated them with all the nervous energy of an overwrought man. He stood it for a quarter of an hour and then went out and walked to the National Gallery, and here for a time he found peace. He sat on a cushioned seat and looked at the vista of polished wood floors framed in diminishing doorways; attendants moving like clockwork figures running down; a woman with a hand under her up-tilted chin gazing at the portrait of Mrs. Siddons. Frith's Derby Day. He'd never seen it before and got up to have a closer look.

"Quite amazing," he muttered to himself, and almost wept a tear at the figure of the tumbler's child looking wistfully at a hamper which surely must have been supplied by Mr. Fortnum, or possibly by Mr. Mason.

An attendant padded towards Macrae.

"We'll be closing shortly, sir. In five minutes."

It was five and twenty to six when Macrae came out into the sunlight, and for a moment he stood looking across Trafalgar Square, at the fountains falling in silver cascades and the pigeons fatly waddling in search of crumbs.

It was a view of London he'd never seen before. He'd always been too busy thinking of himself.

No time for a bus. He felt in his pocket. Fifteen shillings left. He hailed a taxi.

CHAPTER SEVENTEEN

OUR MR. BRODERICK, employee of the firm of Devon and Forbes, Assessors, was as dry an old stick as could be found within a half-mile radius of Temple Bar.

His work consisted of the examination of claims brought against insurance companies, and in his time he had saved them very large sums of money.

He was all the more valuable to the clients of his firm because he never gossiped, and except for such innocent phrases as, "I am now going to lunch. I will return at two o'clock," and "I am now going home," he seldom gave evidence that he even possessed vocal cords.

On Thursday afternoon, the day on which Abie Russ died, the papers relating to the claim of Mrs. Keene were sent to the office of Devon and Forbes, and were put on Mr. Broderick's desk.

He read them carefully, and then as carefully he picked up a pen and dipped it in the ink. He intended to write the words, "Appears to be genuine," and to add a spidery signature, when he changed his mind and dried the nib.

He read the papers again, searching this time for something which would confirm the vague suspicion that had arisen in his mind. He found none. Mrs. Keene's "history" gave no hint that she might be a party to fraud. Lucy Maddox's life also appeared to have been blameless, and she was not "walking out" with a young man.

Reason bade Mr. Broderick approve the payment of the claim, but instinct stayed his hand.

His only weakness, if one excepts his passion for buying books which he seldom read, was attending entertainments at which young ladies made startling disappearances from trunks. The disappearance of Mrs. Keene's pearl necklace was quite as startling, because there was not one shred of evidence which showed how or whence it had gone.

Mr. Broderick put the papers in a drawer and locked it. Then he put on his floppy black felt hat and informed the office boy that he was now going home.

As he meandered through Lincoln's Inn Fields his brain was busy with the problem, and before he reached Kingsway he came to the conclusion that Maddox might well have been mistaken in thinking that she had put the pearls into the jewel-case in London, and had carried them to Longwood House, in the county of Berkshire.

Mr. Broderick knew women; not by personal contact, because that would have made him feel acutely uncomfortable, but by their rambling, illogical statements and letters. That a woman was incapable of telling the truth was his firm belief; not because as a class they were dishonest, but simply because they were incapable of concentration. Their minds too much resembled the flight of a restless bird.

Having decided that further investigation was required before Mrs. Keene was paid the value of her necklace, Mr. Broderick directed his course northwards to a favourite book-browsing ground near the British Museum.

Next morning, while chipping a lightly boiled egg, he decided to report to the senior partner that he proposed to make inquiries. A telegram was sent to Mrs. Keene asking her to return to Town at her earliest convenience, as it was desired to make an examination of her flat.

Mrs. Keene was annoyed, because she was expecting a cheque for fifteen hundred pounds, and after the trouble she had with the local police she considered that she deserved it.

She drafted several petulant wires before she decided on a compromise. She would send Maddox to receive, and if necessary entertain, the representative of Messrs. Devon and Forbes. She would follow by a later train.

At eleven o'clock on Friday morning Mr. Broderick rang the bell of Mrs. Keene's flat and was admitted by Lucy Maddox in her outdoor clothes.

He said: "Good morning, madam."

Lucy Maddox explained that she was not Mrs. Keene, but her maid, and added that her mistress would not return until after midday.

Mr. Broderick was pleased. He could handle maids and still their talk. Mistresses were different.

"I would like to have a look around, if I may," he said, and proceeded to search every room with the method of an experienced police officer.

The pearls were not in the flat.

"Now I would like you to tell me exactly what you did when you packed the jewel-case," he said to Maddox.

She told her story for the fifth time.

Mr. Broderick asked questions.

"Did you keep a list of the jewellery?" "Are you not mistaken in saying . . ." "Is it not possible that you might have . . ."

Patient probing rewarded Mr. Broderick; Lucy Maddox, who was becoming tearful, admitted that she really could not remember having placed the necklace in the jewel-case.

Mr. Broderick was satisfied, and, after assuring Maddox that he did not suspect her of having stolen the pearls, went to a tea-shop for lunch and a game of dominoes.

Had he been twenty years younger, no doubt he would have rung up his office and passed on the information he had obtained. But that was not Mr. Broderick's way. He spent an hour over his lunch. He walked without haste to Lincoln's Inn and sat down at his desk to write his report. The last few lines read: "I am of the opinion that the matter should be referred to the police authorities and their assistance requested to trace the theft of the necklace from the flat of their owner."

Before a call could be put through to New Scotland Yard the phone-bell rang and Chief Inspector Thompson asked if he might be supplied with information relating to the loss of Mrs. Keene's necklace. The senior partner replied by reading portions of Mr. Broderick's report, and a meeting was arranged for six o'clock that evening at Mrs. Keene's flat.

The porter at the block of flats saluted Macrae as he got out of his taxi. "Mrs. Keene has been asking for you, sir."

"Asking for me? But she's not due back till six."

"She arrived shortly after one o'clock, sir. She had to come back to see the police."

"What about?"

"Her pearls. They were stolen."

"Yes, I heard about that. But they were taken when she was in the country."

"That was what was thought at first, sir, but I understand now that they may have been taken from the flat before she left Town."

Macrae said, "But that's nonsense," and ran up the stairs.

The maid let him in. "Madam is in the lounge, sir. She's expecting you."

Macrae gave her his hat and adjusted his tie in the hall mirror, then he put on his most charming smile; acting a part at short notice was Macrae's strong suit.

Mrs. Keene was sitting on the chesterfield with her feet on one arm. "Eric, my dear, I've been aching for you. You don't know what I've been through since I've been away."

"The police? They can be a damn' nuisance, I know." He gave her hand just the right pressure and drew up a chair.

"They're coming this evening, at six."

"But the porter told me the police had been here this morning."

"No, that was Mr. Broderick. Get me a drink and I'll tell you all about it."

Macrae poured out two very generous double-whiskies, added splashes of soda, and gave a glass to Mrs. Keene.

"Scotland's only real use," she said, and drank. "Now I'll tell you about Mr. Broderick. He's reduced poor Maddox to absolute pulp, and if there's one thing that really drives me mad it's a woman crying when she's doing my hair."

"And you say the police are coming here to-night?"

"Yes, they rang up about ten minutes ago; said it was frightfully important and could I see them. I had to say I would."

Macrae got up and finished his drink. "Well, I'm awfully sorry, but I've got to dash away."

"Eric, you can't! I was counting on you to support me."

"I've promised to meet a bloke about a business matter. But it shouldn't take long."

"Oh, well, it can't be helped. Come back as soon as ever you can and we'll go to the San Fresca."

"I'd love to," Macrae said, and it was nothing less than the truth. The chance of earning a guinea was just what he wanted at that moment.

He stepped into the hall. There was no sign of the maid. He listened at the bedroom door for a moment and turned the handle. The room was empty. He darted across to the dressing-table, opened the top drawer, and slipped the pearls down by the side of a pile of handkerchiefs.

When he walked out into the street he really felt that everything was all right. He had got rid of the keys and the pearls. Now he could go ahead and bleed Mrs. Keene.

Across the street was the public house. That was fine. He could have a drink there and watch the door of the flats. When the police had gone he would go and change into tails and then come back and take her out.

Mr. Broderick arrived at Mrs. Keene's flat a few minutes before Thompson got there. He waited in the hall, sitting uncomfortably on a chair which was never meant to be sat on.

When Thompson arrived he introduced himself, and the detective said: "I'm very glad you're here, Mr. Broderick. I've heard about your report."

Mr. Broderick bowed primly.

The maid was about to open the door of the lounge, when Thompson stopped her. "I want a word with you."

"Yes, sir?"

"You told this gentleman that it is possible that you did not take the pearls out of their case and put them in the jewel-case."

"Yes, sir. But I can't really remember clear. There was a lot of them. Rings and brooches and so on."

"Yes, of course. I understand." Thompson took from his pocket the case which had been found in Mrs. Finch's room. "Have you ever seen this before?" He opened the lid.

Maddox, her hands clasped before her, bent her head to read the name written on the lining. "That's just like the one the necklace was in, sir, but there's no way of telling if it's the same one or not; if we had the necklace I would soon know."

"Yes, so would I." Thompson handed the case to Mr. Broderick. "That fits the description all right."

Mr. Broderick made a noise which clearly indicated that an empty case was but an empty case to him. He wanted the pearls.

"Well, shall we go in?" Thompson said.

Mrs. Keene put on her very best party manner for Thompson and Mr. Broderick. She was dignified. She was gracious; but she was still very common.

"Good evening, Inspector." Two fingers were Thompson's share of her hand.

Mr. Broderick kept well away and bowed.

"I'm sorry to trouble you, Mrs. Keene, but we've made rather an interesting discovery with regard to that pearl necklace of yours. It was pawned. We know where and we have the case."

"So that all that remains is to find the pearls," said Mr. Broderick. He was looking at the ceiling when Thompson turned towards him.

Mrs. Keene laughed in a most cultured manner.

"I'd like to see where you kept them, if you don't mind, Mrs. Keene."

"Certainly." She led the way to her bedroom. "They were in that drawer." She pulled it out.

"Do you think we could have the maid in?"

Mrs. Keene rang the bell.

When Maddox appeared, Thompson said to her, "I want you to show me what you did when you packed the jewellery."

"Well, sir, all the cases were in that drawer, and I took them out and opened them and—"

"All right. Put the cases in the drawer."

"Very well, sir."

"They are kept in a safe now," Mrs. Keene said, and gave Maddox a key.

"Do you mind if I take this stuff out of the drawer?" Thompson asked.

"Not at all. Do just as you wish."

Thompson put his fingers round a stack of handkerchiefs, and as he did so he said, "Hullo! What have we got here?"

Mr. Broderick, who hitherto had taken no interest in the proceedings, adjusted his pince-nez and took a step towards the dressing-table.

Thompson held up a string of pearls.

Mr. Broderick said, "Dear me!"

Mrs. Keene looked a question at Maddox.

Maddox gave a squawk and said, "Well, I never!"

It was Thompson's turn to speak. He handed the string to Mr. Broderick.

"Can you identify them?"

Mr. Broderick ran the beads through his fingers, examined the diamond clasp, and said, "Not definitely, but these are real pearls. Mrs. Keene might be able to help us."

He handed over the necklace.

"This is mine."

"The one you lost?" Thompson asked.

"Yes, of course. I only had one string."

"Then I wonder if you would be so kind as to give me a short statement in writing to that effect?" Mr. Broderick was determined that the proper formalities should be observed.

He obtained his discharge and was about to leave, when he remembered something. He drew Thompson to one side and whispered to him, "I searched this flat this morning and I didn't find the pearls."

"Did you look in the drawer?"

"I did." Mr. Broderick put Mrs. Keene's note in his breast pocket. "Just a conjuring trick," he said, and turned towards the door.

Thompson said something which may have been, "Conjuring trick he damned."

He stood for a moment thinking, then he said to Mrs. Keene: "What do you know about this?"

"I? I know nothing." Then the import of the question reached her brain. "Are you suggesting that I stole my own pearls?" The affected tone had gone. This was the real Mrs. Keene. A very angry Mrs. Keene.

"I'm not suggesting anything. I'm asking you a question." Thompson's tone was unpleasant.

"And I've given you my answer."

"Now, now, Mrs. Keene, there's no need to get excited. If I was rude, please forgive me." Thompson smiled. Like Macrae, he, too, would have made a good actor, which perhaps was the reason why he was a good detective.

Mrs. Keene held her pose of an insulted woman, and insulted in her own house, too!

"I've got a very difficult job to do and I've been at it all day. That must be my excuse," Thompson continued. "I have reason to believe that the theft of your pearls may be connected with the death of a man."

Mrs. Keene said, "What?" in a whisper. She was standing very still with one hand half-raised to her face.

Thompson avoided her gaze. "If I knew who took these pearls and pawned them, and then put them back in the drawer of your dressing-table, I'd feel I was getting somewhere near the man who killed Abie Russ."

"Then I wish I could help you. But I can't. I know nothing. I've been away, and if the pearls were left behind they must have been stolen then."

"There's no evidence that any one broke into the flat. All the keys have been accounted for. I didn't handle this case myself, but I've had a talk with the man who did. He says that your maid—"

"Maddox! She's been with me for fifteen years. I would trust her with anything."

"We've checked up on her and have ruled her out as a suspect."

"There's no one else."

"Visitors?"

"None of them could have done a thing like this. Stolen my pearls! Really, Inspector, I think that it's a little absurd to suppose that my own mother or sister—"

"All right, we'll leave your mother and sister out of it. Who else have you invited here?"

"Now, let me see. There's Fred Murray, my sister's husband; he's a stockbroker. And a very old school friend of mine, a Miss Pelly; she comes down for a week every summer. She's a school-teacher in Middlesbrough. I used to live there when my husband was alive. I think that's all."

There was a lack of decision in Mrs. Keene's voice which prompted Thompson to ask, "Are you quite sure?"

There was a silence of nearly a minute before Mrs. Keene answered: "I know a Captain Macrae slightly. But I don't think you need bother about him. I'm perfectly sure that he knows nothing about my pearls."

"How long have you known him?"

"Oh, I don't really know. Not very long."

"A month?"

"No, longer than that. I met him first when I came back from Switzerland in March."

"How did you make his acquaintance?"

"At a sherry party my sister gave. She introduced us."

"And since that time how often have you seen him?"

"I couldn't say exactly. Perhaps a dozen times."

"He was a friend of yours?"

Colour rose in Mrs. Keene's cheeks. "Yes, I suppose he was." She paused uncomfortably. "I pay Captain Macrae for taking me out. There! That's an admission for a woman to make." She laughed harshly.

"Nothing wrong in that. It's done every day," Thompson assured her.

"Yes, I dare say, but still it's not a thing one talks about. I haven't even told my sister."

"Can you give me Macrae's address?"

"Yes, I've got it written down somewhere. Excuse me a minute." Mrs. Keene went to her desk.

He had heard that name before. Macrae? Captain Macrae? Now, when the devil was it? He had talked with so many people that day. Macrae! It was no good. He'd ask Perry and Leith. Maybe they would remember.

Mrs. Keene came rustling back with a small black notebook in her hand. "The address is 6 Bury Square. I think it's somewhere in Southwark."

"Thank you very much. Now, when did you last see Macrae?"

"Only a few minutes ago." She looked at the clock. "He had gone only a short time before you arrived."

"Has he got a key to the flat?"

"No."

"What did you talk about?"

"I can't really remember." Mrs. Keene was tired of answering questions.

"Did you tell him I was coming here this evening?"

"Yes, I think I did."

"Did he say anything?"

"No."

"But he left the flat?"

"Yes, he said he had a business appointment, but would be back in time to take me out to dinner. We're going to the San Fresca."

Thompson got up and opened the door of the bedroom. "I want to get an idea of the layout of this flat. Where does that door go to?"

"That is the bathroom."

"And the other?"

"Into the hall."

Thompson came back into the lounge. "Did Macrae let himself out?"

"I think so."

"You didn't ring for the maid?"

"No."

"Would you mind doing so now? There's just one question I'd like to ask her."

When Maddox came in, Thompson said: "Did you see Captain Macrae when he left this evening?"

"No, sir."

"Thank you. That's all I want to know."

Maddox withdrew.

"I'm afraid I'm being a very great nuisance, Mrs. Keene, but I haven't finished yet."

"Then please help yourself to a drink, and give me one, too. Whisky-and-soda."

Thompson gave her a glass and sat on the arm of a chair. "Now I want you to go back to the time you left for your visit to the country. Did Macrae come here at any time on that day?"

"Yes, he was here when I was leaving. I was sitting in this room and he came in and we talked for a little while."

"Where was your maid?"

"After she let him in she went to my bedroom to finish packing."

"And then?"

"Well, we had lunch, and when we got back Maddox said she was ready, and Captain Macrae came down with us and saw us into the taxi."

"Did you lock up the flat?"

"Yes."

"Sure?"

"Positive. I remember trying the door to see if it was properly locked."

"Then Macrae didn't go to the station with you?"

"No."

"Have you by any chance got a photograph of him?"

"Yes, there is one somewhere." Mrs. Keene went into her bedroom and returned a minute or two later with a silver frame. She gave it to Thompson.

"Do you mind if I borrow it?"

"You'll let me have it back?"

"Of course. To-morrow."

Thompson finished his drink and got up.

"I'm very much obliged to you, Mrs. Keene, for your patience. But before I go I want you to promise me that you will say nothing to Captain Macrae about our talk this evening."

"I'll try not to. But it may be rather difficult. He'll be sure to ask me what happened."

"Then tell him that I was making an examination of the flat and came to the conclusion that the theft of the pearls was an outside job."

"Shall I tell him that they've been found?"

"No. Don't say anything about that."

"Very well, Inspector. Good night."

Thompson met the porter in the hall. "Do you know Captain Macrae?" he asked.

"Yes, sir. He's a friend of Mrs. Keene's."

"Did you see him here on Monday? The day Mrs. Keene went to the country."

"Yes, sir. He was about then. He said I ought to back the Mayfly filly. Of course I didn't."

"She won?"

"A hundred to eight."

"Did Captain Macrae leave with Mrs. Keene?"

"Yes, I think he did. I didn't see him after she'd gone."

"You were on duty in the hall here?"

"That's right, sir, I was. Of course, I had plenty to do, checking parcels and letters and running the lift, so it wouldn't be right to say I was in the hall all the time."

"What did you do after Mrs. Keene left?"

"Well, I couldn't rightly say, sir."

"Where do you keep the letters?"

"In my room behind the lift."

"So you might have gone in there?"

"Yes, I might have," the porter agreed.

"And if any one had entered the building at that time, you wouldn't have seen him?"

"That's right, sir."

"By the way, what time did Macrae arrive this evening?"

"Half-past five. I told him that Mrs. Keene was expecting him."

"And what did he say to that?"

"He seemed surprised, sir. I told him that the lady had come back early to see you about the loss of her necklace."

"Do you remember what he said?"

"I think it was something about her not being expected before six o'clock."

"And what happened then?"

"He went up to Mrs. Keene's flat."

"I see. I'm much obliged to you. By the way, have you got a key to the flat?"

"Yes, sir."

"I'd like to borrow it."

"Well, sir—" the porter spoke doubtfully.

"I'll give it you back to-morrow."

A shilling stilled further protests.

When Thompson and Perry had gone, the porter muttered half aloud: "I wonder what the Captain's been up to?" Then his thoughts turned to the Mayfly filly and the money he'd lost by not backing her. He soon forgot all about Captain Eric Macrae.

CHAPTER EIGHTEEN

MACRAE HAD LOWERED a pint of beer and several Scotches by the time he saw Thompson leave the block of flats. He waited until Thompson was out of sight and then took a taxi to Bury Square. He was feeling very pleased with himself, and ran up the stairs two at a time. The last loose end had been tied up. He was rid of the keys, the pearls, and Abie Russ. He could now get back to his old job.

There was a line of light under the door. He stopped on the landing and for a moment fear gripped his heart. Then he forced himself to open the door. It was probably Mrs. Finch clearing up. He walked in with a swagger.

It was Peggy. She was standing by the mantelpiece with a photograph in her hand. She turned, and in the half-light, with her mass of rebellious black hair, she looked very attractive.

"Peggy!"

"I'm sorry. I know I oughtn't to have come, but—"

"That's all right." He walked quickly to her and put an arm round her shoulder. "What are you looking at?"

Peggy pointed to the photograph she had put down on the table. It was the one of a long low house with a little boy holding a pony before the door.

"That was me at the age of ten." Macrae's lips parted in a half-smile. For a second or two he went back in his mind twenty-nine years. He remembered the day when it was taken and the job he'd had catching the pony, butter-fat and wild from the effect of a month at grass; the walnut tree on the lawn. The nuts had always been soft and bitter, but with the obstinacy of youth he had eaten them and kidded himself they were good.

He put the photograph back on the mantelpiece with its face to the wall.

"Now what can I do for you?"

"Nothing. I only wanted to see you, that's all."

Macrae looked at his watch. "Well, I'm awfully sorry, but I've got to go out in about ten minutes."

Damn the girl! What was she after? He opened a drawer and took out a stiff shirt. It had been worn once but would have to do again. He had no other.

"Have you heard about Mr. Russ?"

Macrae became quite still, and he did not turn his head as he answered, "Yes, why?"

"The police think that Bert did it." There was a break in Peggy's voice.

"Bert? Bert Finch?"

Macrae laid the shirt over the back of a chair.

"Yes. He's a friend of mine."

"I say, I'm awfully sorry, and if there's anything I can do—"

"No. There's nothing. But—well, I just wanted to talk to some one. It's been rather a shock."

Macrae's remedy for other people's shocks was money. He produced a ten-shilling note and put it in Peggy's hand. "Buy yourself something with that to-morrow, and don't worry about Bert. He didn't kill Russ. It was suicide."

Peggy, with the note crushed in her hand, turned and ran from the room. At the street door she fumbled for her handkerchief, for she was crying.

A plain-clothes officer keeping observation on Mortlake Mansions saw Macrae arrive and, ten minutes later, drive away in a taxi with Mrs. Keene. He was close enough to hear Macrae say, "the San Fresca." Then he went to a call-box and dialled Whitehall 1212.

Thompson was waiting for the call. When he put down the receiver he said to Perry, "That was Sims. They've gone to the San Fresca." He picked up his hat. "Come on."

"To Bury Square?"

"Yes. But we'll look up Mrs. Finch first."

"Why?"

"I've just remembered that when I was questioning her this morning she said that she worked for Macrae."

They drove to the end of Bulmer Court and walked to Mrs. Finch's door. That lady put her head out of her window when she heard the bell and said, "Oh, it's you, is it? What's the trouble now?"

"Come on. Open up," Thompson said sharply. "I want a word with you, and I haven't all night to waste."

When Mrs. Finch opened the door her lips were pressed together in a thin line. She wasn't going to answer no more questions, whatever they said. She'd been a fool to have talked the way she did, but that wasn't going to happen again.

As Mrs. Finch lifted the latch Thompson pushed the door wide open and walked in. Mrs. Finch followed slowly. Just like the police! Coming busting in as if they owned the place.

"You work for a Captain Macrae, don't you?" was Thompson's first question.

"Well, if I do, that ain't a crime, is it?"

"You told me you did this morning."

"I may have said it and I may not. I can't remember."

"Don't be stupid."

"All right, then. I do work for Captain Macrae. What about it?"

"Have you got a key of his flat?"

"Oh, that's the game, is it? Well, let me tell you, Mr. Blooming Policeman, that if I have got a key, which I don't say I have, you're not going to get it. Captain Macrae's a gentleman, and what d'you think he'd say if I was to let you into his room when he wasn't there? It wouldn't be right." Mrs. Finch looked very virtuous. She added, "And I'd lose my job."

"You needn't worry about that. We'll look after you if there's any trouble."

"Me looked after by a copper! The idea! I can look after myself. Thanks very much."

"Yes, I dare say you can, but what about that son of yours?"

"What's that?"

"Now listen to me. You're a sensible woman and you want to help Bert, don't you?"

The ice of Mrs. Finch's resolution showed signs of cracking.

"Of course I'd do anything to help Bert, but I don't see what you're getting at."

"You don't believe that Bert killed Abie Russ. Of course you don't. And I've got an idea that you may be right."

"Is that the truth or are you just saying it?" Mrs. Finch unfolded her arms and put her hands on the table. "Because if you are—"

"We haven't charged Bert with murder, have we?"

"No, that's right. But it doesn't mean to say that you won't to-morrow."

"Look here, Mrs. Finch. Abie Russ has been murdered, and I mean to get the man who did it."

"But the Captain told me that Abie had killed hisself."

Thompson's eyes were half closed when he asked: "When did he say that?"

"This morning. Not long after you'd been gone from here. I told him Bert had been took, and he said I wasn't to worry 'cause it was suicide."

"Where did you see Macrae?"

"In his room."

"All right. Now let me have the key."

"You won't tell the Captain it was me that gave it you?"

"No, of course not."

"Well, I don't know, I'm sure, what's best." Mrs. Finch went into the kitchen and came back with her bag. "What'll he say if he finds you there?"

"He won't be back till late."

"All right, then. Here you are. How long'll you be?"

Thompson put the key in his pocket. "Not more than an hour, I expect."

"I'll wait for you."

Mrs. Finch watched Thompson and Perry disappear up the Court; then she looked across at the house opposite. There was a light in Mr. Crick's room and she could see him sitting at his desk. "I'll go over and see Mr. Crick. That's what I'll do," she said to herself. "He ought to know what's going on."

She climbed the steep stairway to the office and knocked timidly on the door of Peggy's room. There was no reply. She knocked again louder.

There was a sound of movement in the room next door and Mr. Crick came out.

"Who are you?" he asked, peering at Mrs. Finch; it was dark in the passage.

"It's me—Mrs. Finch. Oh, Mr. Crick, the police have been in again and they've gone to see the Captain. They made me give 'em the key of his room, and I knew as how I oughtn't to do it, and—"

"Come in and sit down." Mr. Crick held the door open. He was looking very tired.

When Mrs. Finch was settled and he had lighted a fresh cheroot he said, "Who is the Captain? And what do the police want with him?"

"It's Captain Macrae. He lives in Bury Square, and I does for him. He's a friend of Peggy's, too."

"Oh, yes, she told me something about him to-day. You introduced them, didn't you?"

"Yes, and I wish I hadn't now. I only did it because I thought it would make Bert a bit jealous. He hasn't been treating Peggy right for some time past, and though he is my own son, I don't think it's fair on Peggy keeping her hanging on like this all this time. He's making good money and he could get spliced to-morrow if he wanted to."

"But what's the trouble?"

"Peggy's fallen for the Captain. That's what."

"Can he afford to marry her?"

"I don't know whether he can or whether he can't, but that's not what I'm worrying about. She's gone on him."

"Why do you think that?"

"She went to see him to-night. I don't know what passed, but when she come back with the key I could see she'd been crying. I asked her what was the matter, but she said it was nothing and went away."

"I'd like to tell Captain Macrae what I think of him."

"He's all right really. He gave me a pound to help Bert, and it's not the first time, either, he's give me money when I wanted it."

"That's an easy way to salve your conscience," said Mr. Crick. "It's the way you treat people that really counts."

"Money buys things," argued Mrs. Finch. "And things is what you wants to keep you cheery." She was thinking of beer, pigs' trotters, and eels.

"Have you told the police the truth about that jewel-case?"

"No, I haven't."

"Where did you find it?"

"Like I said before, where I works."

"Where's that?"

"At the Captain's place. In Bury Square."

"You'd better tell the police. If you like, I'll come with you."

Mr. Crick arranged the papers on his desk into a neat pile.

He looked at the marble clock, which still said twenty minutes to seven, and yawned.

Mrs. Finch got up and said, "I needn't trouble you, Mr. Crick. The inspector that's got the key of the Captain's room is bringing it back and I'll see him then."

Mrs. Finch found no one waiting by her door. She went into her front room and sat in the dark. She had plenty to think about.

Thompson unlocked the door of Macrae's room and switched on the light.

He stood for a minute taking in every detail. The divan bed. The linoleum on the floor. The white pine chest-of-drawers. The crazy wicker chair.

He walked over to the mantelpiece to have a closer look at a framed group. It was of a team of cadets at the Royal Military College, Sandhurst. August, 1917. He looked for Macrae's name, but did not find it.

Then he brought out the photograph of Macrae which he'd borrowed from Mrs. Keene. He compared it with each of the men in the group in turn.

Half-way along the second row he muttered, "That's like him," and then aloud: "Perry, can you see any resemblance between these two?"

"You mean this fellow with the moustache?"

"Yes. His name appears to be Cartwright."

"They're certainly alike, but I wouldn't like to bet on it."

Thompson was making a further comparison when Perry moved over to the cupboard.

He tried the door. It was unlocked. "Gosh! Look at this junk."

Thompson joined him. "War relics. What damn' awful things to keep!" He reached up and took down a Uhlan's helmet. It was thick with dust. He said to Perry, "You go through the chest-of-drawers while I have a look at this lot." He selected a chair which looked as though it might stand his weight and stood on it.

Perry was busy with the second drawer when Thompson got down off the chair. He had something in his left hand.

"Exhibit A," he said.

Perry looked up. "What's that?"

"An opened package of .45 cartridges."

Perry picked up one. "Service revolver ammunition," he said.

Thompson nodded. "There are about five or six missing." He folded the paper round the remaining cartridges and slipped the string in place to hold them.

"It was a .45 nickel bullet that was dug out of Abie's skull," Perry said.

"It is a common type."

"Macrae visited Mrs. Keene's flat between the time Broderick searched it and you found the pearls."

"Yes, we've got something to ask Captain Macrae. He'll make suspect number four. Bert Finch, one; Danny Levine, two; and Tim Daly, three. Quite a bunch. Which do you back?"

"Tim Daly. He's got a record."

"Murderers don't always have records. In fact they're quite often ordinary sort of people up to the time they kill. And that's what makes 'em so damn' hard to catch." Thompson saw a coat on the back of a chair. He ran through the pockets and brought out a pair of dirty white string gloves. "What do you think of these?"

Perry took one in his hands and examined it under the light. "I don't think I've ever seen a pair like this before."

"I haven't either," Thompson said. "We'll take 'em along with us, and I'd like to check up this bloke's dabs." He looked round the room. There was a small silver cigarette-box on the mantelpiece. "This may give us what we want." He held it up to the light. "It's a long time since it's been cleaned."

Perry moved a photograph, saw a saucer, and said, "Hullo! What's this?"

Thompson touched the greasy black liquid it contained with the tip of a finger. "Paint or some sort of varnish stain. That's what it looks like," he said. Then he took out his note-book. "It would be a good thing if we could dig up Macrae's past history."

Perry picked up the frame holding the photograph of the country house. He took out the back. "The name of the photographer is J. Simpson, of Shrewsbury."

"Anything else?"

Perry put back the photograph and took a book out of a shelf hanging above the bed. "E. Cartwright, 1915," he read. He looked at the fly-leaves of the remainder of the books and said, "No addresses in any of them. Any use looking in the cupboard?"

"There are some boots there. Have a look and see if there's a maker's name on them."

Perry pulled out one of a pair of patent-leather half-Wellingtons. They were cracked and there were deep wrinkles over the instep.

"Charles Peabody, St. James's." He looked at the others. "They're all the same."

Thompson looked at his watch. "Time we were moving," he said, and stood for a moment looking round the room. "I don't think we've missed anything."

Mrs. Finch started up in her chair when she heard the sound of footsteps in the Court. She looked out of the window. Yes, that was them all right. Thompson's bulk could not be easily mistaken.

She opened the door. Thompson gave her the key and thanked her for the loan of it. He was about to walk on, when she said: "There's something I wanted to talk to you about, Inspector."

"Yes?"

"That case that was found behind the clock in my room."

"What about it?"

"I told you I didn't know where it had come from, but Mr. Crick says that I ought to tell the truth about it."

"Mr. Crick? Oh, yes. Well, what have you got to say?"

"It was me that put that case behind the clock, and I'll tell you how I come to get it."

"Did Bert know?"

"No. I swear he didn't."

"All right. Go ahead."

"It was on Tuesday. I was giving the Captain's room a proper turn-out and I found it in the chair under the cushion. I opened it up, and when I found there wasn't nothing in it I puts it in me bag to take home. And that's all there is to it."

"Why didn't you tell me this before?"

"Well, you put the wind up me, asking questions that fierce that I didn't know what to say; and what with Bert took and all, I says to myself, 'Maria,' I says, 'the best thing you can do is to say you never saw it nowhere before, and you don't know how it got behind that there clock.' But when I told Mr. Crick he said—"

"Yes, you told me what he said."

"It wasn't as if it was worth anything, and I knew the Captain wouldn't mind me having it. Why, that very evening he gave me a quid. He'd got a whole lot of notes. He must have struck it lucky that day."

"This was on Tuesday night?"

"That's right. And he didn't owe half what he give me."

"I may have to ask you some questions about that some other time. But I've got a job on at the moment. Good night."

Thompson drove to the Yard and went straight to the laboratory, where Fielding was at work. He put the cigarette-box on the bench and said, "See if you can get anything off that."

Fielding dusted grey powder over the surface of the box, fanned off the surplus with a folded newspaper, and then studied the result through a magnifying-glass. "There's two good prints and one doubtful. Whose do you think they are?"

"They may have been made by the man who was in Abie Russ's room somewhere round the time he was killed."

Fielding opened a cupboard and took out a foolscap envelope. "These are enlargements of the prints on the glasses." He looked at the cigarette-box again and then back to the photographs. Two minutes later he said, "No luck."

Thompson produced the pair of string gloves he had found in a pocket of the coat in Macrae's room. "What d'you make of these?"

Fielding put his hand in one of them and flexed his fingers. "They're used for riding, aren't they?"

"I don't know."

Fielding made a cut with a pair of scissors, drew out a thread, and laid it on the bench. Then he picked up a seed-envelope and took from it another thread. "That's the one you found on the door-knob in Russ's room."

"Do you think they're the same?" Thompson asked.

"I'll tell you in a minute." Fielding laid the threads side by side on a glass slide and slid it into a microscope. When he had focused the eye-lens he said to Thompson, "You have a look."

"I can't see any difference."

"Nor can I. These aren't threads that are used much. In fact I have an idea that they're made especially for this type of glove. They're laid like yams in a hawser-laid rope, with a left-hand twist. That's what gives the grip on wet reins."

Thompson turned to Perry. "It's time we picked up Macrae. We'll go to the San Fresca now."

Thompson told the driver of the police car to go to Woolworth's in the Strand.

CHAPTER NINETEEN

When the car drew up, Thompson jumped out. "Wait here," he told the driver, and walked to the San Fresca. A man standing opposite the doors came up to him and said, "He's inside."

Thompson said, "I shan't want you again to-night," and went into the hotel.

A page-boy led him to a position from which he could look down into the restaurant. Macrae was sitting back in his chair, laughing. He was holding a cigar in his hand. The woman opposite was talking volubly. There was a bottle of champagne in an ice-bucket by Macrae's right side.

Thompson stood there for some time, then he went back to the vestibule and out into the street. Perry was waiting for him.

"Have you spotted him?"

"Yes," Thompson replied. "He's having the hell of a time with Mrs. Keene. She's all over him. The damn' fool!"

"What d'you make of him?"

"Smooth. A damn' sight too smooth."

Macrae seldom got drunk, and he wasn't drunk to-night, in spite of the fact that he had nearly a bottle of champagne on board. He was living in the present and drinking to forget the past. It seemed a long time ago. A hand touched his shoulder. A gentle pressure. He swung round in his chair. There was no one there. Three feet away at a table against the wall a man was sitting with a girl. Their heads were close together.

Must have been his imagination. He lifted his glass and drank.

"Eric, you're not listening. I was telling you about Monica. She said . . ."

He fought to keep his attention on what she was saying. But who the hell was this woman Monica?

". . . Well, I told her that I wouldn't stand for that sort of thing, and Jim—he was that boy I met at Longwood . . ."

Again the touch on his shoulder. He wouldn't look round. He wouldn't!

The pressure increased. He could feel fingers digging into his flesh. He sat upright and looked quickly over his shoulder. Some damn' fool trying to be funny. But there was no one there. The couple who had been sitting at the next table had gone.

Mrs. Keene had stopped talking for a moment and was fitting a cigarette into her holder. He struck a match, and as he looked at the flame burning steadily in the still air he thought, "I'm at the San Fresca. I'm sitting at a table with Mrs. Keene. There's nothing to be afraid of. I'm imagining things, that's all. Nerves."

A waiter refilled his glass. Macrae ordered brandy and then said to Mrs. Keene: "What did the police want?"

She answered unwillingly. "Oh, they only wanted to know where I kept the necklace."

"But it was stolen while you were at Longwood. Why should the people in Town worry?"

"I don't know. Shall we dance?"

"Let's wait till the next. I can't do a rhumba, and I want to know what happened."

"Eric, please don't be tiresome. I want to forget all about the necklace." Mrs. Keene squashed out her cigarette. "You're not looking well. Shall we go home?"

"No, of course not. I'm absolutely O.K. Let's dance."

Out on the crowded floor, with the drugging rhythm of a slow fox trot beating in his brain, Macrae snatched a few minutes of relief.

When the music stopped Mrs. Keene said, "I insist on going home at once. You're dead tired, and I've had enough, too."

Thompson saw them come out into the street and sent Perry for the police car. "He'll be taking the woman home. We'll pick him up at the flat."

Macrae had seen Mrs. Keene into the lift at Mortlake Mansions and was walking down the steps to the street when Thompson and Perry approached him.

Thompson said: "We are police officers. Are you Captain Eric Macrae?"

Macrae replied, "Yes," without thinking, and then asked, "What the blazes do you want? And how do I know you're a police officer?"

Thompson produced his warrant card. "I am making inquiries into the theft of a pearl necklace, the property of a Mrs. Keene. I believe you are a friend of that lady?"

"Yes, I know her, but I don't know anything about her pearls."

"Would you mind coming to the station with me? There are a few questions I'd like to ask you."

Macrae said: "Of course not. It won't take long, will it? I'm about ready for bed."

"No, I don't think so," Thompson said. "There are just one or two points I want to check up on and I think you may be able to help me."

Perry opened the rear door of the police car and got in. Thompson signed to Macrae to follow and got in himself. "Howard Street," he said to the driver.

During the drive Macrae sat quite motionless. He tried to think, to argue with himself, to recollect his movements on the night that Abie Russ died. Even in the supreme privacy of his own mind he would not admit the words "kill" nor "murder."

Abie Russ had died, and he had deserved to die. He clung to that phrase and repeated it over and over again in his brain. Abie had deserved to die.

He had left no fingerprints. No one had seen him enter or leave the shop. No one even knew that he had had dealings with Abie, except Bill Connor, and he wouldn't let him down.

He tried to forecast the questions he would be asked; where was he on the evening of the twenty-first? He'd say he was at the club.

That would be his alibi. And there was Tim Daly. He would swear anything. That part of it was all right.

All he'd got to do was to keep his head; deny that he'd ever known Abie Russ or had ever been to the shop.

He leaned forward and looked out of the side window. They were at Hyde Park Corner. He could see the gates into the Park.

There was a bus keeping pace with the car on the other side. It was nearly empty. A man was reading a paper, which was jerking up and down. A child was standing on a seat with its nose pressed flat against the glass.

Macrae hated children, but at that moment he would very gladly have acted as the custodian of the stickiest-fingered baby, even as far as Ham Common.

The traffic thinned and the police car drew ahead of the bus, past the driver, sitting high up, crouched over the wheel; down into the dip of the Green Park and up to the Ritz. He'd dined there once. But that was a very long time ago.

The car turned right-handed into St. James's. He caught a glimpse of a red-coated sentry outside the Palace. It wasn't far now. He had got to have it clear in his mind, the story he was going to tell. They hadn't mentioned the name of Abie Russ, but he knew that was what they wanted him for. He knew it. His hand, as it raised his cigarette to his mouth, was cold; it was shaking and his palm was moist. God! He'd have to take a pull at himself.

At last the drive ended. The car drew up and Perry got out. He walked close beside Macrae up three steps under a blue-glass shaded lantern into a square hall.

The uniformed man at the door followed them in and saluted Thompson. "I'll tell the sergeant," he said, and disappeared through a doorway.

The sergeant came into the hall. He wasn't wearing his cap, and Macrae thought that he didn't look like a real policeman.

"Charge?" he asked Thompson, who replied, "No. Interrogation."

The sergeant asked them to follow him and led the way to a small room at the end of a long passage. A stair led up from the centre of the floor to a hatch in the ceiling. The trap-door was shut.

"I hope you don't mind using this place," the sergeant said. "But we're sorting out a crowd of drunk and disorderlys in the charge-room."

"This is all right," Thompson said. "You needn't wait."

The sergeant took three chairs from the wall and placed them at the table, then he switched on another light and left the room.

"Sit down," Thompson ordered, and took a chair on the opposite side of the table. Perry sat beside him.

"I suppose you've heard all about the theft of Mrs. Keene's pearl necklace?" Thompson asked.

"Yes, she told me it had been taken."

"Have you got a key to Mrs. Keene's flat?" Perry asked.

Macrae turned his head quickly and said, "No. The maid always let me in."

"You remember the day Mrs. Keene went away?"

"Yes. It was last Monday. I was there when she left."

"Did you see any one loitering near the flat or on the stairs?"

"No."

"Did you go to the flat at any time when Mrs. Keene was away?"

"No. Of course I didn't."

"So to-day was the first time you visited the flat since she went on her visit to the country?"

"Yes; I had a letter from her saying that she would be returning to-day at about six o'clock."

"But you arrived at Mortlake Mansions at half-past five. Is that correct?" Thompson put the question.

"I'm not sure about the exact time, but I thought it was nearer six."

"The porter says that he saw you at the flats at half-past five this evening. Is that right?"

"I don't know what time it was exactly."

"So you intended to get there before Mrs. Keene arrived?"

"No, I didn't."

"I suggest to you that you did."

"That's not true."

"And that you meant to return the pearl necklace to Mrs. Keene's flat before she came back."

Macrae made a poor attempt at a laugh. "That's absurd. I was with Mrs. Keene all the time I was in the flat, and besides, I never touched the pearls. Why should I?"

"Perhaps you were hard up."

"I wasn't."

"You had a fairly large sum in your possession on Monday night. Where did it come from?"

"Betting."

"Who's your bookmaker?"

"Look here, I'm not answering any more questions. If I chose to back a horse that isn't any of your business."

"It would be better for you if you answered my question."

Macrae thought for a minute and then said: "Danny Levine."

"You knew Danny Levine?"

"Yes."

"Do you know where he is now?"

"No."

"Do you know where he lives?"

"No."

"Where did you see him when you made that bet?"

"At his shop in Bulmer Court."

Perry leaned forward across the table: "The pearls were found in Mrs. Keene's flat this evening; after you had been there."

"I don't know anything about that."

"You put them into the drawer in Mrs. Keene's room."

"No, I didn't."

"When you left the flat at about six o'clock this evening you let yourself out. That's correct, isn't it?"

"I don't remember. I think the maid was somewhere about."

"She says that she did not see you leave."

"I can't remember if I saw her or not."

"Let us assume she didn't see you go, and that she was in her own room at that time; it would then have been possible for you to have put the pearls into the drawer where they were found."

Macrae looked down at the table. He did not speak.

"That is a possible explanation, isn't it?"

"Possible, yes," Macrae mumbled. "But I didn't do it, and you can't—"

He stopped suddenly.

Thompson said, "Go on."

"I wasn't going to say anything."

Thompson stood up and moved round the table until he was close to Macrae. "Oh, yes, you were," he accused. He put a hand on Macrae's shoulder and forced him to turn towards him. "You think that you're going to get away with this, but you're not. You stole the pearls from Mrs. Keene's bedroom on Monday. The day she went to Longwood."

Macrae tried to get up, but Thompson pushed him back into his chair. "That's the truth, isn't it?"

"Oh, for God's sake leave me alone!" Macrae cried. "How can I think if you keep on like this?" There was a nervous break in his voice.

"Why do you want to think if you're telling the truth?"

Perry closed in on the other side. "You paid Bill Connor forty pounds last Monday."

"No, I didn't."

Perry opened an account book and laid it on the table. "This was found in Bill Connor's room at Sammy's Club. Just have a look at this entry."

Macrae read the words, "Received from E. Macrae, £40," and a date.

"Do you remember now?"

"Yes. I'd forgotten about that."

"Like hell you had," Thompson thought, and then said aloud: "Now, look here, Macrae. It'll be better for you if you'll tell us all about it and clear the whole thing up. Mrs. Keene has got the neck-lace back and the underwriters aren't interested any longer."

"I'm not talking. You can do what you damn' well please."

"That's not going to do you any good. You take my advice and tell the truth. It'll have to come out in the long run, but if you put us to a lot of trouble you can't expect us to make it easy for you. That's sense, isn't it?"

Macrae put his hand in his breast pocket and brought out a cig-arette-case.

"Put that away. You can't smoke here."

"And you can't keep me. If you're going to make a charge why don't you get on with it?"

"Plenty of time for that later. The night's young." Thompson slipped off the table and walked to the door. He signed to Perry to join him. "Get hold of the jailer and tell him to come in here and keep an eye on Macrae. We'll leave him alone for a bit."

Thompson went down the passage and into the charge-room. The drunks were gone and the sergeant was sitting at his desk reading an evening paper. He looked up as Thompson came into the room, and said, "Have you finished with him?"

"No, not yet. He's sticky. What about Connor and Daly? Have they said anything?"

"No, and you'll have a job with Connor. He's not the sort that talks. Nor Tim Daly neither. Do you want to see them?"

"No, I'll wait till I've finished with Macrae, and that's going to take some time. Do you think you can get me some tea or cocoa or something?"

Thompson read the sergeant's paper while the sergeant put a kettle on a gas-ring and took cups and a tea-pot out of a cupboard.

When the tea was made he threw the paper aside. "We've got to find out where Macrae got the money to pay Bill Connor. If we can bust that story about getting it from Danny Levine there's a chance we might get him to open up."

"And admit he popped the pearls?" Perry said.

"Yes. With Abie Russ."

"Bert Finch may help us there.'"

"That's an idea. If we can crack Macrae's story I think he'll go with a run and maybe make a statement."

"He's not the sort that can hold out for long if we keep at him."

Thompson agreed, and dropped a lump of sugar into his cup.

Macrae, in the back room alone with the jailer, sat staring at a knot in the table. He'd done all right so far. They were trying to bluff him into making a confession, but he'd never do that. He'd read often enough in the papers that well-worn phrase: "I took him in custody and charged him. I cautioned him and later he made a statement."

Why did the damn' fools make statements? If every accused man were dumb there wouldn't be many convictions. Field had signed his own death warrant that way; by talking.

He looked at the jailer, a red-faced man in constable's uniform who was staring at the toes of his boots. He said to him, "Where does that stairway go to?"

"Up to the dock. We're under the police court. You're not to talk."

Macrae stared at the stairway with morbid curiosity. He thought, "I wonder what it's like going up there?" and tried to picture the scene above when the Court was sitting. He'd been summoned once for not having a collar on his dog; but he couldn't remember much about it except an officious usher, and the magistrate, a snuffy little man with a bald head, who hardly listened to what he said. The case had been dismissed on payment of one shilling costs.

The jailer made unpleasant noises and shifted his gaze to the light over the table. He was apparently one of those fortunate men who could do nothing and not be bored; he looked just stupid.

What was going on outside? Macrae moved in his chair and looked at the door. It said nothing as eloquently as only a closed door can do. It was the essence of negation. He wondered vaguely where he'd heard that phrase before.

What were they talking about? That big bull of a man who could be so damned nasty one minute and pleasant the next. And the other one. Perry. Macrae couldn't forget the way they had looked at him, dispassionately, probing. Like hospital surgeons might regard a public-ward patient. Just another case. Another problem to solve. But a surgeon could cut you up. The police couldn't open up your brain and read the thoughts that were within.

What was that quotation? "Speech is given man so that he can hide his thoughts." Something like that. And that other saying that we are but islands shouting lies to each other across a sea of misunderstanding.

But life wasn't like that. It was damn' difficult to hide one's thoughts. Far easier to say what was in one's mind. Especially when you were tired. Why not tell them everything and get it over? They would let him rest then.

It would be funny to see the face of the judge when he said, "Yes, I did it and I'm glad I did. I'm glad. I'm glad." He was beginning to feel drowsy. Hell! He roused himself. They would be coming back soon and he must be ready to meet the attack.

What would it be? Were they going to question him about Abie Russ? Yes, that was it. They thought that he had killed Abie. They hadn't said anything about it yet, but that was what they were after. This business about the pearls was only a lead up to the real questioning.

His brain was steady now. Clear and cool. He thought out every move. They'd ask him first where he had been on the night that Abie had died. That was easy. He'd say he'd been at the club. Connor would back him up. But he'd been through all that in the taxi. What else was there they might ask? Had he known Russ? Of course he hadn't. He didn't even know where Abie lived.

Oh, it would be all right. As long as he didn't get tired and let them lead him into a trap. But he was tired. He shouldn't have had that brandy.

The jailer yawned and crossed his legs.

Macrae looked at his watch. It was twenty minutes to one. Curse them! Why didn't they come and get on with it?

Perhaps they were going to let him go. And then—God! There it was again. That grasp on his shoulder.

Macrae was glad to see Thompson come into the room.

Thompson put the palms of his hands flat on the table.

"You know Abie Russ, don't you?"

Though he had been preparing for just such a question as this, Macrae was not ready. He said, "Yes," and then "No," quickly. "No, I don't know him. Who is he?"

"You read the papers, don't you?"

"Yes, sometimes."

"Abie Russ was killed last night in his flat. Surely you heard about it?"

Macrae tried to simulate dawning understanding.

"Yes, of course I know about that. When you mentioned his name I knew it was familiar and I thought I must have met him somewhere."

"Where were you last night?"

"At Sammy's Club."

"Oh, that's interesting. You're a member, I suppose?"

"Yes, but I don't go there a lot."

"But you were there last night?"

"Yes. From about ten o'clock till after midnight."

"Who was there?"

"Two or three fellows I know. I can't quite think of their names at the moment."

"Anyway, you were at the club. We'll go into the details later."

"There was one man I know who saw me. His name's Connor."

"Any one else?"

"I'm pretty sure Tim Daly was there. Yes, I know he was. Either of them'll speak for me."

"I'm sure they will," Thompson said drily. "Where did you go after you left the club?"

"Home."

"Bury Square?"

"Yes. How did you know that?"

Thompson ignored the question. "Did you walk back or take a bus or what?"

"I went by Tube. There's a station close to the Square."

"So you didn't go anywhere near Russ's shop that night."

"No, of course not."

"Then you know where it is?"

"I think I passed it once. It's somewhere near Bulmer Court."

"You've been into the shop; now, haven't you?" Thompson was quietly persuasive.

Macrae tried to think. When he had taken the pearls to Abie there had been some one else in the shop. Some one who might identify him. Perhaps it would be safer to tell the truth.

"Yes. As a matter of fact I did go to Russ's shop once. I was broke and tried to raise something on my links."

"What advance did you get?"

"Nothing. Russ only offered thirty bob."

"What day was that?"

"I don't know. Last week some time."

"Was it on Monday?"

"It may have been."

"Try and think. It's rather important."

"I can't remember."

"You wouldn't object if I brought along the man who worked in the shop. If he saw you he might be able to help us in fixing the day."

Macrae said, "No. I don't mind."

Thompson stood back from the table and whispered to Perry, who then left the room. He came back a few minutes later and said: "They're bringing him along now."

Bert Finch had been asleep, and he raised a hand to shade his eyes from the bright light in the room. Thompson took him by the arm and led him up to the table. He pointed to Macrae and asked: "Have you seen this man before?"

Bert lowered his hand and screwed up his eyes as he looked at Macrae. Then he said: "He's like a bloke that came into the shop last Monday."

"How do you know it was Monday?" Thompson asked.

"Because Monday's our busy day, and I was busy getting the books entered up when this bloke came in and knocked on the desk."

"What did he say?"

"He asked to see the boss. So I called out to Abie, who was at the back of the shop checking over a lot of clothes, and he came along and then I went on with my work."

"Did you hear anything of the conversation between Abie and this man?"

"No. I didn't listen."

"Did this man pledge anything?"

"He must have done, 'cause Abie went to the safe near where I was standing and took out a lot of notes. I couldn't say how many there was."

"What did Abie do with the notes?"

"He took them to the counter opposite where this bloke was standing, and I wondered at the time what the pledge was."

"Did you see anything pass between Abie and this man?"

"No, I couldn't from where I was. And that's all I know."

"Did you look in the pledge-book at any time to find out what Abie had advanced the money on?"

"No. I wasn't interested."

"How much money do you think Abie took from the safe?"

"I couldn't say that. But it was a tidy sum. It must have been. The bundle of notes was as thick as my three fingers very nearly."

Thompson looked at Macrae. "Do you want to ask any questions?"

"No. But I'd like to say that this man is mistaken. I never received any money from Abie Russ, and I never pawned anything at his shop."

Thompson touched Perry on the arm. "All right. I've finished with Finch." The jailer led Bert away, and Thompson returned to his position opposite Macrae.

"That doesn't make it too good for you," he said.

"That man was lying. I've never seen him before."

"That's your answer, is it? All right, we'll leave it at that for the time being. Now I want to ask you about another matter. You were in the Army at one time, weren't you?"

Macrae flushed. "Yes. I resigned my commission soon after the war."

"And I suppose when you were serving you owned a revolver."

Macrae felt for the side of his chair and clutched it tightly. His body was quite rigid. His lips were dry. He tried to think, but could not. His brain felt numb.

"Come along. There's nothing to be worried about. I suppose every serving-officer in war time had a revolver issued to him. You must have had one."

"Yes. I suppose I did," Macrae heard himself say.

"And ammunition, too?"

"Yes. But it was all returned when I left my regiment."

"Quite sure about that?"

"I don't remember exactly. It's a long time ago."

"But your recollection is that you returned your revolver and ammunition?"

"Yes."

"You kept some mementoes of the war though, didn't you?"

Macrae relaxed. Thank God, they were off the subject of the revolver. He sat slackly in his chair.

"I brought a few things back, but I don't know what happened to them."

"There's quite a collection in your room at Bury Square," Thompson said in a conversational tone. "In a cupboard."

Cupboard! So they knew! They knew! They were playing with him and leading him on. His breath was coming quickly as though he had been running. His hands were spread on the table, and as they moved his nails made a rasping sound on the rough wood.

"I don't know what's in the cupboard. I locked it up years ago and have never opened it since."

"Was there a revolver and ammunition there?"

"No, I'm positive there wasn't."

"You're sure about that, yet you've just told me you don't know what was in the cupboard."

Macrae did not speak.

"Then I'll tell you." Thompson sat on the table and leaned on one elbow. Macrae stared at the notice on the wall. "There are a number of pairs of boots on the floor level, and some uniform tunics hanging up. On the first shelf there is a pile of trench maps, a German soldier's helmet, one or two sword bayonets, and a few fragments of shells. On the top shelf there are more maps, some khaki knitted scarves, a Balaclava helmet, and . . ." Thompson felt in his pocket and brought out a small parcel tied with coarse white string. "And this. Have a look at it."

Macrae was still staring blankly at the wall. Thompson pushed the parcel so that it touched his right hand.

"I want you to tell me if this is your property."

Macrae looked down without moving his head. He said at once: "No."

"It came out of the cupboard in your room."

"No, it didn't."

"Now, that's absurd." Thompson sat upright. "I found it there myself."

"I've never seen this parcel before. I swear that."

"It was found in your room, in the cupboard, on the top shelf."

"Then some one must have put it there."

Thompson picked at the knot and took off the string. Two cartridges rolled out on to the table. The nickel-steel bullets were bright.

There was no expression in Macrae's eyes as he looked at them. He was utterly exhausted. All he wanted was to be allowed to sleep, to stretch out his legs. "I want to go to bed," he said. His voice was flat.

"Would you care to make a statement first? Maybe you'd sleep better if you did; ease your mind."

"No."

"Just an account of your movements last night from six o'clock onwards. It needn't take you long. You can dictate it."

"No."

"All right. Have it your own way."

"What are you going to do with me?" Macrae spoke hoarsely, urgently.

"I'm afraid you'll have to stay here for the night. I can send for anything you want."

"I'd like pyjamas and a razor and something to read."

Thompson tore a leaf out of his note-book and handed it with a pencil to Macrae. "Make out a list."

When Macrae had finished writing he said: "I'd like to see a solicitor."

"I'll arrange that. Who d'you want?"

Macrae remembered that Peggy Nichol had told him that she worked for a solicitor. "I've forgotten his name, but he's got an office in Bulmer Court."

"All right, we'll find him for you," Thompson said, and told the jailer to take Macrae to a cell. Then he went along the passage to the charge-room. "Sergeant, do you know a solicitor in Bulmer Court?"

The sergeant smiled, despite the fact that it was after 2 A.M. "Crick has an office there. He's the only one I know."

"What's he like?"

"He's the fellow who came in to tell you about Tim Daly. He's got quite a big police-court practice."

"Macrae wants to see him."

"Crick's all right, but—"

"But what?"

"He had some connection with Abie Russ. I've never been able to find out what it was."

"What do you know?"

"That Crick has been known to visit Abie Russ."

"Who told you?"

"Leith. He saw Crick go into the house last Monday."

"Monday seems to have been a busy day," Thompson muttered. And then aloud he asked: "What time of day was it?"

"About nine in the evening."

"I wonder where he comes into the picture?" Thompson said to Perry. "We'll have a word with Mr. Crick before we turn him over to Macrae."

"I've got his phone number," the sergeant said. "Shall I get through?"

Thompson nodded. "But before you do that, let's have the stuff you took off Macrae."

The sergeant unlocked a drawer. "It's all in here. A bunch of keys, a wallet, watch, three-and-ninepence in small change, and a—"

"All right. You get on to Crick." Thompson pulled the drawer out and carried it to a table. He took a key from his pocket. It was the one he had borrowed from the porter at Mortlake Mansions. "Damn' fool!" he said under his breath.

Perry said: "What?"

"I've found a match for the key of Mrs. Keene's flat on Macrae's ring. He lied when he said he hadn't got one."

"He lied about that packet of revolver ammunition."

"Yes." Thompson got up and ran his fingers through his hair. "If we could only start him talking, I feel we'd get somewhere."

"Or find out where the gun came from."

"Not much hope there if it was a war time issue."

"I say! Look at this!" Perry exclaimed.

"Where'd you find it?"

"Among the stuff that was taken off Macrae."

Thompson took a length of knotted string from Perry. There was a tab on it, and scrawled on the tab the word "Pearls," and the figures "110."

"Which pocket did you find this in?" Thompson asked the sergeant.

The sergeant consulted a list. "Right-hand trouser."

"Well, that cooks Macrae's goose as far as the pearls are concerned," Thompson said. He pointed to the tab. "That was probably written by Abie Russ. We'll check the writing to make sure."

Thompson tossed the string back into the drawer, stretched his arms, and yawned. "Hell! I'm sleepy." He went out into the street.

The driver of the police car was dozing over the wheel. He looked up sleepily.

Thompson gave him the list Macrae had made out and the key. "Go to 6 Bury Square, first floor front, and get this lot."

CHAPTER TWENTY

WHEN THOMPSON came back into the charge-room the sergeant was talking to Mr. Crick on the phone. "Yes, I think you ought to come along right away. . . . It's about the theft of a pearl necklace. . . . No, he hasn't been charged yet. . . . All right. . . . 'By."

Thompson said: "I want to see Connor."

The sergeant slipped off his stool, opened the passage door, and called out to the jailer.

It took some time to wake Bill Connor, and when he was on his feet he was cross. He looked gross and dirty. He wasn't wearing a collar and his hair was tousled.

"'Evening, Bill. Sorry to drag you out at this time of the morning. Take a seat."

"Now, look here, Mr. Thompson, what's the big idea?" Connor's voice boomed huskily. "I haven't done anything you can pull me for, and when I come up to-morrow I'm having a swell mouthpiece, and if I don't get costs out of your crowd, then I'm a Dutchman, and what's more I'm going to issue a writ for false imprisonment and—"

"All right, Bill, I know how it goes. But just listen to me for a minute. You know a man called Eric Macrae, don't you?"

Connor's face was wiped clean of expression before he said: "I may do. What of it?"

"Did you see him last night?"

"I don't know."

"Then you didn't see him. Where were you?"

"At the club."

"And Macrae wasn't there?"

"Is that what you want me to say?"

"I'm asking you a plain question. Was Macrae at your club last night?"

Connor pouted his thick lips and said: "Yes, Captain Macrae was there."

"At what time?"

"Till we shut up."

"What time was that?"

"Two or three o'clock. I don't know exactly when it was, but I saw him myself, and—"

"Like hell you did! You were in the room at the back except when you went out for dinner at half-past eight. You came back at ten and went to your room and stayed there."

There was anger in Connor's eyes.

"Who said that?"

"Never mind."

"Tony Mascati?"

Thompson didn't speak.

"Tim said he was a nark."

"And so he beat him up. Stupid thing to do."

"I don't know what Tim did, and I don't damn' well care."

"You're going to care. Quite a lot. But there's something else I've got to ask you."

Connor stiffened, and a look of crafty caution came over his face. "Well, what is it?"

"What do you know about the death of Abie Russ?"

"Abie Russ? Never heard of the man."

"Oh, yes, you have, and you knew he was dead an hour before you should have known."

"Who is Russ, anyway?"

"A pawnbroker who was shot through the head some time last night. A statement was issued by the Press Bureau at noon. It appeared in the stop press of the early editions of the evening papers. Tim Daly told you he was dead at eleven o'clock."

Connor laughed.

"How did Tim Daly know that Russ had been killed?"

"I don't know."

"Yes, you do."

"Mr. Thompson, I do not know one thing about this man Russ. How he lived or how he died. I was in my room at the club on Thursday night till late."

"You know who killed Abie Russ."

Connor's heavy head moved slowly from side to side. "You are quite wrong. I know—nothing." He yawned and looked round the room.

"What do you know about Macrae?"

"Nothing."

"He used your club."

"He came there, yes; but I do not know his business."

"He paid you forty pounds on Monday night. What was that for?"

"Card debts. He played a lot."

"How did he get the money?"

"I didn't ask him. Why should I? He paid; that was enough."

"How long had he owed it you?"

"A week, I think. I cannot remember."

"Who killed Abie Russ?"

"I have told you. I do not know."

"Who do you think killed him?"

"I have no idea."

"His death concerned you?"

"No. It did not."

"Then why should Daly have told you about it?"

"I do not know why he told me."

"You knew Abie Russ?"

"No, I didn't."

"He was working a racket."

"Well?"

"And you were on the same game."

"I do not understand."

Thompson leaned back in his chair and took a map off a side table. He unfolded it and held it up. "You've seen this before, haven't you?"

"No."

"It was found in your room at the club."

"Some one must have put it there."

"And this." Thompson took a wallet from his pocket and put it down before Connor. "It belonged to Abie Russ. I got it out of a drawer in your desk."

Connor drew in his breath sharply, and his sagging shoulders stiffened.

"Would you like to tell me how it got into that drawer?" Thompson said.

Connor stared at the wallet for a minute in silence, then he said: "Tim gave it to me. On Friday morning. When he told me Abie Russ was dead." His voice rose an octave. "I don't know how he got it. He didn't tell me. I know nothing about it. Ask Tim Daly."

"You did know Abie Russ?"

"Yes, I knew him." Connor's voice was now low and husky, and his eyes looked first to the right and then to the left. Then he continued speaking quickly: "But I don't know what happened to him. I was in my room all the night, and—"

"You've said all that before," Thompson said sharply. "Let's forget that bit." He pulled his chair up to the table and leaned on his elbows, his chin cupped in his hands.

"You were either working or going to work the street racket. That's right, isn't it?"

"I was thinking about it."

"Abie Russ was doing the same thing?"

"Yes, I believe he was."

"You were trying to chisel in?"

"No, Mr. Thompson. I'll tell you how it was. Abie had more territory than he could handle, and I was going to take a bit of it and pay him a share of the takings."

"Did you go and see Abie, or did he come to you?"

"I never saw him."

"That doesn't make sense. You made a deal with him—"

"We didn't meet. I sent a man to talk to him."

"Who was that?"

"Captain Macrae."

"Did he go to Russ's flat?"

"Yes. On Tuesday."

"And what was the result?"

"Abie agreed to my suggestion. I was satisfied, and I thought everything was going to be all right."

"So Macrae was working for you?"

"Only that once."

"And you're sure you didn't send him to see Abie on Thursday night?"

"I never saw Macrae on Thursday."

"But you told me a little while back that Macrae was at the club all Thursday night."

Seconds passed, and then Connor said: "Oh, Thursday. I forgot. Yes, that's right. What I said the first time is true. Macrae was in the club that night."

"You've got plenty to do getting yourself out of trouble without bothering about Macrae. And besides, that sort of alibi's not going to do him any good. What value do you think a jury would put on it? You'd be cross-examined as to character. Your record would come out; your dealings with Russ and Tim Daly; and I'd tell them I'd found Abie's wallet in your room. Think that over."

Thompson leaned back in his chair and looked at the ceiling.

Connor moved uneasily in his chair. "Yes, I see what you mean, Mr. Thompson."

"All right, then. Let's have the truth. You don't know where Macrae was on Thursday night?"

"Yes. That's right."

"Did Macrae carry a gun?"

"I don't know. I shouldn't have thought he did."

"So it comes to this. You made a bargain with Abie Russ through Macrae?"

"Yes."

"Then Abie conveniently died."

Connor wetted his lips.

"And that left the field clear for you?"

"Mr. Thompson, you know me. You know I never work the strong-arm stuff. I've pulled a few jobs in my time, but I've never done anything like this. What would be the sense in it? It'd be bound to lead to a load of trouble and spoil the whole game."

"Right. Then tell me the truth. How did Tim Daly know Abie had been killed?"

"I don't know. Tim just came into my room and said that Abie had been shot."

"And gave you Abie's wallet?"

"Yes."

"Did you ask him how he got hold of it?"

"Yes, but he wouldn't say."

"Looks as if Tim did the shooting, doesn't it?"

"He hasn't got a gun."

"You can't say that for certain."

"I know Tim Daly. And so do you, Mr. Thompson. Shooting's right off his line."

"It was." Thompson looked straight at Connor. "But there was nothing to stop him making a start. If either Tim Daly or Macrae killed Abie Russ you'll have a lot of explaining to do."

"They didn't do it, Mr. Thompson."

"All right. I think I've got your story. You can go and turn in."

When Connor had gone, Perry said: "It looks pretty clear. It's Tim Daly or Macrae."

"Yes, maybe. But we haven't a scrap of evidence to prove that Daly was in Abie's room at the time of the killing. We didn't find any of his dabs on the glasses or on the furniture."

"Gloves."

"Yes. But that doesn't help. We'll have him in and see what we can get out of him."

Tim Daly came into the room and looked suspiciously round with his pig-eyes. He knew Thompson, but gave no sign of recognition. The jailer led him up to the table.

"Well, Tim, what did you want to hitch up with Connor for?"

"What's that?" Tim's brain was working even more slowly than usual.

"You're heading for trouble. You told me when you came out you were going to get a job."

"So I did." The ghost of a grin came over Tim's face.

"Yes, with Bill Connor. You're a damn' fool. Connor'd drop you like a hot spud if there was any trouble and leave you to hold the bag."

"He pays regular. That's what counts with me."

"Money's not going to help you now."

"I haven't done nothing. I'll take my dying oath on that, Mr. Thompson."

"What were you doing in Bulmer Court on Wednesday?"

"I was seeing Danny Levine."

"Why?"

"He's a pal of mine. I came over to have a yarn with him."

"Where is he now?"

"Who?"

"Danny Levine." Thompson was patient.

"I dunno."

"Have you seen him since Wednesday?"

"No. I haven't been over this side at all."

"Danny Levine worked for Abie Russ."

"He may have done. I dunno."

"You knew that all right. And you knew that Bill Connor was trying to get in on Abie's racket."

Tim laughed. "I tell you, me and Danny was pals, that's all. I sometimes had a bet with him, but I didn't know nothing about him being hitched up with Abie Russ."

"You knew Abie Russ?"

"I'd seen him once or twice. That's all."

"You knew him by sight?"

"Yes."

"Who killed him?"

"How should I know?"

"Who do you think killed him?"

"I dunno."

"You told Bill Connor at eleven o'clock on Friday morning that Abie was dead. How did you know that?"

"I never said anything of the sort. The first I knew of Abie being shot was seeing it in the papers."

"When?"

"I dunno."

"Connor says you did tell him about the murder. And he says you gave him Abie's wallet at the same time. How did you get hold of it?"

Tim stared at the floor for a minute. When he looked up, Thompson caught his eye.

"Let's have it."

"It was given to me."

"By whom?"

"Danny Levine."

"Did he say how he got it?"

"No."

"He just gave you the wallet, and told you that Abie Russ was dead?"

"Yes."

"What were his words?"

"Just that Abie had been killed. And that it was Bert Finch that done it, seeing that he worked for Abie."

"Where did this talk take place?"

"In Danny's shop."

"What time?"

"Friday morning, about ten o'clock."

"But you've told me already that you hadn't seen Danny Levine since Wednesday."

"I must have made a mistake in the day."

Thompson did not pursue the subject.

"Did Captain Macrae kill Russ?"

"No, he didn't do it." Tim spoke with contempt.

"What had Connor got to do with Abie Russ?"

"Nothing, guv'nor," was Tim's quick denial. "He didn't know nothing about Abie. I'll swear that."

"That's curious, because he told me he'd had dealings with Russ, and that Macrae was acting for him."

"I don't know nothing about that."

"Were you in the club on Thursday night?"

"Yes. I was there from about half-past eight until we shut up. That would be about half-past one."

"Did you see Macrae there?"

"No."

"Could he have been in the club without your meeting him?"

"I don't think so."

"All right. You can go."

"Hullo, Danny." Leith, who had been standing in a doorway at the end of Bulmer Court, stepped out of the shadows and gripped Danny's right arm. "Where are you off to?"

"Mrs. Finch's."

"The Chief wants a word with you."

"With me?"

"Yes. Where've you been?" Leith loosed his grip on Danny's arm and ran his hands over his body, feeling every pocket.

"What's the idea?"

"You'll know soon enough. Come on, let's get going."

Thompson was coming out of the police station when Leith and Danny Levine walked up the steps.

"Who've you got there?" Thompson asked.

"Danny Levine."

"Where'd you find him?"

"In Bulmer Court."

Thompson told Perry to cancel the call for Levine and followed Leith into the charge-room.

Danny looked more than ever like a monkey dressed up as a gymnastic instructor. He was wearing a grey sweater with a high roll collar; a threadbare coat was buttoned tightly across his chest and a cloth cap was pulled down over his eyes.

"Let's have a look at you." Thompson put a hand on Danny's shoulder and spun him round until he faced the light. Leith took off his cap.

Danny looked as though he were going to cry.

"Give him a chair," Thompson said. Danny collapsed on it. His hands were rubbing up and down his trousers and he was biting his lower lip to keep it from trembling.

"Easy meat," Thompson thought. Then aloud he said, "When did you first know Abie Russ was dead?"

Seconds passed before Danny could speak. He who had been so ready with his tongue in teaching songs at six-pence a time, quick at a back answer, and ready to argue the point on any subject, mumbled, "I was meaning to—to—come and tell you about it, but I was scared—"

"And ran away. Why?"

"I must have lost my head."

Thompson gave him a cigarette and struck a match. "What happened on Thursday night?"

"Thursday night?" Danny passed a trembling hand across his face. "I went to the room as usual. The boys were there waiting."

"For Abie Russ?"

"Yes."

"All right. Go on."

"Well, I stopped there for a time. And after a bit I got sort of worried and I thought I'd go and see—and see if he was coming or not."

"What time was this?"

"Getting on for midnight it would be."

"When were you expecting Abie?"

"Half-past eleven. That was his regular time. He wasn't often more than a few minutes late."

"Was Lampy about when you went to look for Abie?"

"Yes, he was in the room. I went to the back door in the yard and rang. I waited for a bit and rang again. There wasn't no answer, so I went round the front. The door was open."

"Wide?"

"No. Only an inch or two. I went in and up the stairs. There was a light in Abie's room. I could see it through the crack. I opened the door and saw him lying there with a gun in his hand."

"Sure about that?"

"Yes."

"All right. What did you do next?"

"I cleared out quick as I could."

"You didn't touch anything in the room?"

"I had a drink—that was all—and—"

"Just tell me exactly what you did."

"There was a glass on a table. I put some whisky in it and drank it off. If I hadn't I wouldn't have got out of the place."

"And after that?"

"I went back to the room and told the crowd to clear out. Then I locked up and went home."

"Where's that?"

"At the back of my shop in the Court."

"Did you see Bert Finch at any time?"

"No."

"Or Tim Daly?"

"Not till the next morning. He came in and I told him what had happened."

"Did you give him anything?"

Danny stared at Thompson for a moment, and then said, "Yes. How did you know that?"

"It was a wallet, wasn't it?"

"Yes."

"One that had belonged to Abie Russ?"

"Yes."

"And a map?"

"Yes."

Thompson almost laughed at Danny's look of blank amazement. "I've had a word with Tim Daly and Connor."

"They've been talking?" Danny muttered. He stared at the table, but saw nothing.

"Why didn't you go to the police when you found that Abie had been killed?"

"I thought I'd better keep out of it. I didn't want a lot of trouble."

"Why did you wait till the next morning before you ran away?"

"I wouldn't have gone then if it hadn't been for Tim. He came back to the shop after about an hour and gave me a fiver and said I was to clear out. 'You take a train north,' he said. 'Newcastle. And lie up there. Send me your address and I'll tell you when you can come back.'"

"Why did you come back?"

"Well, I didn't go away really. Only as far as King's Cross. I saw a couple of splits at the ticket-office so I gave up that idea. I took a room in Hoxton and I tried to sleep, but I couldn't. I was worrying about what was happening. When it got late I thought I'd go and see Mrs. Finch and see if she knew anything, and that's how I'm here."

"Did Tim Daly come and see you on Wednesday?"

"Tuesday or Wednesday. I can't remember which day it was."

"What did he want?"

"He just came for a yarn. That was all."

"You worked for Abie Russ, didn't you?"

"I helped him in the evenings."

"Working the racket?"

Danny's mouth fell open. His fingers were clutching at the edge of the table.

"Racket?" He whispered the word. "I don't know nothing about no racket. I just—"

"Oh, come off it. You knew all about Abie's game. That's why you took his wallet and the map and gave them to Tim Daly. You were double-crossing Abie."

"No, I wasn't. I'd never do a thing like that."

"But you did give Abie's map to Tim Daly?"

"Yes, but that was after I knew Abie had been killed. There wasn't no harm in doing it then."

"Now tell me about Abie's racket."

And Danny Levine explained the details of the organization built up by Abie Russ. How miserable old men were forced to pay for the privilege of standing in the streets for twelve hours a day holding a tray of match-boxes, or for sitting cross-legged on the pavement with a "show of daubs." How the men who performed before theatre queues had to contribute a quarter of their takings. Coffee-stall proprietors paid so that their property might remain intact. Street bookmakers were supplied with scouts at a fixed rate. . . .

"Bert Finch collected from the buskers round about Shaftesbury Avenue. Every night he'd go off about eight and come to the shop with the takings."

"What time did he get back?"

"Never much before half-past twelve."

"Just one more question. Did Captain Macrae have a bet with you on Monday?"

"Not on Monday."

"On any day this week?"

"Yes. On Tuesday. He won eighty quid, but he lost a century the next day. He had a hundred quid on the Lola colt to win. And it didn't finish in the first three."

"Are you sure that losing bet was made on Wednesday?"

"Of course I am."

When Danny Levine had been taken away, Thompson filled his pipe. "Gosh! What a racket! That man Russ must have been netting a packet. It's put another piece of jigsaw in place."

"How do you mean?"

"It explains where Bert Finch got that wad of money from, and it partly corroborates his story about the time he got to the shop. Danny Levine saw Abie dead at midnight. And according to the taxi-driver, Finch didn't get there till half an hour after that, which according to Levine, was his usual time."

"Yes, it may let out Bert Finch, but it doesn't help us much in the case against Macrae."

"Tim Daly has busted his alibi, and Tony Mascati'll probably be able to give evidence on that point, too. He was on duty at the club and he'll know if Macrae was there on Thursday night, and besides that Macrae's been proved to be a liar. He said he had only visited Abie to try and pawn his links and had failed. I think it's pretty clear now that he did soak something, probably the pearls, otherwise Abie wouldn't have given him the pile of money Finch saw him take from the safe. Connor says that he sent Macrae to Abie two days ago. Macrae never said anything about that visit."

"Yes, but even if he's proved to be a liar it doesn't mean to say he's a murderer."

"I know that, but think of all we've got against him. First of all there's the tab with Abie's writing on it. That came off a parcel containing the pearls. Then there's the thread on the door-handle of Abie's room. That thread came from the gloves we found in Macrae's room in Bury Square. He was broke and owed Bill Connor forty pounds. He paid that sum on Monday after his first visit to Abie Russ. He had a key of Mrs. Keene's flat. An empty jewel-case was found in his room by Mrs. Finch. And lastly, when Mrs. Finch told him that Russ had been killed he said that it was suicide. Why did he say that unless he'd been in Abie's room? And there's that business of the bet he had with Danny Levine. He lied about it."

"Yes, I've been thinking about that," said Perry. "Why should he have tried to raise money with Abie Russ if he'd already got the money he wanted by a bet earlier in the day?"

"I'd missed that. He isn't being very clever." Thompson picked up Macrae's cigarette-case and opened it. "Gold Flake. And there were two stubs of Gold Flake cigarettes in Abie's room."

"All circumstantial evidence," Perry objected.

Thompson took out his pocket-book and produced a newspaper cutting. "Listen to this. It's a report of the summing-up of the late Mr. Justice Avory in the Allaway case:

"If you find a number of circumstances, all deposed to by independent witnesses, witnesses independent of each other deposing to facts which, when fitted together like pieces of a puzzle, produce one picture, and that picture represents the prisoner's guilt, then a conclusion founded on such evidence is much more safe and reliable than a conclusion founded upon the evidence of one person who swore he saw the crime committed. It has been expressed another way, that circumstances cannot lie. . . ."

"No one saw Macrae actually enter the shop, and no one heard the shot fired," Perry said.

"That's the part which hardly ever is proved in a murder trial. I mean proved by direct evidence, but in spite of that quite a lot of murderers are hanged. All the same, if we could trace the gun to him I'd feel a lot happier. Thank God we don't have to establish a 'motive.'" Thompson, who had been sitting with his chair tilted back against the wall, let it come forward on to its four legs and got up.

"When Macrae has had twenty-four hours to think things over I'll have another talk with him, and then . . ."

"And then what?"

"He'll make a statement that'll cross the t's and dot the i's."

CHAPTER TWENTY-ONE

THE BUSES had stopped running on the route which passed Mr. Crick's house when the phone-bell rang and he was summoned to Howard Street police station. As he walked through the deserted streets he wondered what hopeless case he was going to be asked to handle this time. He had long given up hope that one day he would be engaged in a case that would make his name.

He did not walk quickly, and the questioning of Danny Levine had been completed by the time he mounted the steps and passed in under the blue light. The constable on duty saluted him. They were old enemies.

"Got the Yard inside," the policeman said.

"The Russ case?"

"Must be. Thompson's here. And Perry; from the Central Office."

Mr. Crick stood for a moment in the door of the charge-room looking round. The sergeant saw him and said, "Come along in, Mr. Crick. You know Mr. Thompson."

"Good evening." Thompson held out his hand. "Macrae'll be glad to see you. He's a bit wrought up."

"Captain Macrae?"

"That's what he calls himself," Thompson replied.

"What's the charge?"

"Haven't made one yet. Time enough in the morning."

"Can you give me some idea?"

Thompson hesitated for a moment and then said: "Theft of a pearl necklace."

"Oh," said Mr. Crick. "I thought . . ."

"Yes?" Thompson prompted. "What were you going to say?"

"Nothing," said Mr. Crick quickly, and asked if he might see Macrae.

The sergeant looked a question at Thompson, who nodded.

"I'll take you along, Mr. Crick," the sergeant said. "You can talk with him in the waiting-room."

Mr. Crick was watching the door as it opened. Macrae came in. He was smiling, and held out his hand. "I'm awfully sorry to drag you out at this time of night."

"That's all right. I understand."

Mr. Crick brought a chair up to the table. Macrae waited until the jailer went out of the room and then the mask fell.

"You will help me, won't you? I can't pay you a lot, but there's no one else I can go to, and . . ." The words ceased and his lips puckered.

Mr. Crick pushed him into the chair and then turned away. "You've got to take a pull on yourself. If you don't I can't help you. Have you made a statement?"

"No. They wanted me to, but I refused."

"That's something to the good." Mr. Crick sat down facing Macrae. "What's it all about?"

"A pearl necklace that belonged to a friend of mine. They think I stole it."

"Who did it belong to?"

"Mrs. Keene."

Mr. Crick produced a note-book and pencil and wrote the name. "Why do they think you took it?"

"Because I was a friend of hers. I was at her flat the day it was stolen."

"When was that?"

"Monday."

"Did you take it?"

"No, of course I didn't. I knew nothing about it having gone till I saw a report in the paper." Macrae told of Mrs. Keene's trip to the country; of his visit to the flat that evening; and of the dinner at the San Fresca.

"Anything else?"

"I paid a bill of forty pounds on Monday night. They think I got the money by pawning the necklace."

"Did you tell 'em that?"

"No."

"Where did you get the money?"

"Betting."

"Who with?"

"Danny Levine."

"As far as you know, have the police any evidence which could connect you with the theft of this necklace?"

"No."

Mr. Crick frowned. "Are you sure you've told me everything?"

Macrae was looking at the floor when he answered. "Well, there was something else. I went to Abie's shop on Monday to pawn my cuff-links. He wouldn't offer me enough, so I came away."

"Abie Russ!" Mr. Crick said softly. "So you knew him?"

"No. That was the first time I'd ever seen him."

"And the only time?"

"Yes."

Mr. Crick sat staring at Macrae for a minute or two. Then he got out of his chair, walked round the table, and put a hand on Macrae's shoulder.

Macrae began to cry. "They think I killed Abie Russ! They think I killed him! Killed him! But I didn't! I swear I didn't!"

"Oh, so that's the real trouble," Mr. Crick muttered to himself. He walked to the end of the room and stood staring blankly at the wall. Then he turned back to Macrae. "Why should the police think you killed Russ?" Macrae dabbed at his eyes with a wadded handkerchief and sat up straight in his chair. "They asked me a lot of questions about whether I knew Abie and what I'd been doing on Thursday night."

"What did you tell them?"

"That I'd been at Sammy's Club."

"Is that your alibi?"

"Yes."

"Did any one see you there?"

"Yes. Tim Daly and Bill Connor."

"You'd better let me have their addresses. I'll get their statements before the police get on to them."

"I don't know where they live, but you can find them at the club."

"I'll look 'em up." Mr. Crick picked up his hat. "Now, if you remember anything you haven't told me, write it down. Don't make any statement. Don't answer any more questions, and try to get some sleep."

But Macrae did not sleep. The confidence in his ability to outwit the police, which so far had kept fear at arm's length, had been sapped by the events of the last few hours.

And now he was shut up like an animal. He had often tried to imagine what it would be like. The reality was very different from what he had imagined it to be.

When he had undressed and put on pyjamas he lay down on the bed and stared at the ceiling. He was tired, but sleep was far away. He could hear a man snoring in the next cell. Lucky devil! If only he could forget even for a short hour!

He did not think of Abie Russ. He suffered no remorse; his thoughts, his hopes, and his fears were for himself and himself alone.

But the tremendous conceit which had kept him going, and by virtue of which he had convinced himself that the police could never touch him, had begun to crumble under the rain of questions put by Thompson.

Again and again had a finger been laid on the weak points of his story. He remembered Thompson's words after Bert had identified him. "That doesn't make it too good for you."

He had been proved a liar, and the shock to his own pride was almost as great as the fear of what might happen in the future.

If only they'd tell him what they were going to do, it would be something. They were probably discussing him now, testing every word he had spoken.

He felt as helpless as a patient on an operating table.

There were footsteps in the stone passage outside; he could hear a shutter being drawn back and then closed again. It was the jailer going rounds. He was at the next cell. Three shuffling steps and a square of light showed in the door; and then two eyes looking at him.

"All right?"

"Yes, thanks."

The shutter slid across and he was alone again. Utterly alone. He turned on his right side and pulled up the blanket. Coarse hairs tickled his chin. He shut his eyes and tried to conjure up the daydream which had often helped him to sleep.

The long, low house. He could see it very clearly, and could almost feel the gravel crunching under his feet as he walked out through the gate to the stables; up the ladder to the corner of the loft over the stable where he kept his pigeons. He knew every one of them by name. He could hear the soft sound of their cooing as they puffed out their crops and made little runs, their tails spread and bent downwards, brushing the sand on the floor.

Even as he sat there he heard footsteps coming up the ladder. He called out and received no answer. He tried to look around, but could not. They had reached the top of the ladder and were coming towards him.

Fear held him. He wanted to shout out, but could make no sound. And then that grip on his shoulder!

He woke in a sweat. Thank God he was awake! The jailer came walking quickly down the passage. A key turned in the lock.

The man next door had ceased to snore. He called out, "Shut that flaming row!" and thumped on the wall.

The jailer came up to his bed and touched him on the shoulder. Macrae sat up, rigid and trembling.

"What's the trouble?" The jailer's voice was gruff, but not unkindly.

"Nothing."

"Well, don't yell out like that. You've woken all the rest of them."

Far away a man was swearing obscenely.

"You're not the only one here."

"I'm sorry."

The jailer switched on the light. "First time you've been inside?"

"Yes."

"You'll get used to it."

Macrae felt for a handkerchief and wiped the sweat off his forehead. "What time is it?"

"Quarter-past four."

Macrae watched the door close behind the jailer. Then he kicked off the blankets and swung his feet to the floor. He wasn't going to risk sleep again. The chill of dawn was in the air, filtering in through a square ventilator. He shivered and lay down again, drew up the blanket, but did not sleep.

When Crick had gone, Thompson said to the sergeant: "We'll charge Macrae with the theft of the pearl necklace. What time does the Court sit?"

"Half-past ten, sir."

"Right. I'll come back before that. Don't make the charge until I arrive."

From the police station Thompson went to the Yard with Perry and wrote out a report of the case. It took him an hour to complete it. Then he lay down on a settee and slept till eight o'clock. He was awakened by a messenger who reported that Superintendent Chivers was in his room.

Chivers read through the report and then said: "I'll send this over to the Director of Public Prosecutions. I think myself that we've got a good case against Macrae, but it's not for us to decide. Meanwhile you go ahead with the theft charge."

Thompson returned to Howard Street police station and stood at the desk while the charge was read over to Macrae. When the sergeant had finished, Macrae said: "Is that all?" There was relief and hope in his voice.

"You need not say anything now, and I caution you that anything you may say will be taken down in writing and may be used in evidence."

Macrae moistened his lips with his tongue before he replied: "Yes, I understand. I don't wish to make any statement."

"All right. You will appear in Court in about an hour's time. I'll inform your solicitor."

Thompson went out to a neighbouring café for breakfast, and when he got back he found that Crick had arrived. He asked Thompson what evidence would be given at the hearing.

"Formal evidence of arrest. I shall ask for a remand for eight days."

"I won't make an objection," Crick replied. "But I shall ask for bail."

"I'm afraid I'll have to oppose that."

Crick looked at Thompson for a few seconds without speaking. Then he said, "I understand," and asked to be allowed to see Macrae. He was taken to the cell.

"'Morning, Mr. Crick." Macrae was smiling as he turned from a looking-glass. He had had a shave, his hair was brushed, and he was wearing a clean collar. His tie was neatly knotted. "What's the matter with you?" he said, as he took his coat off the bed and put an arm into the sleeve.

"I've just heard that you've been charged."

"I'll be all right. They can't prove that I had anything to do with the pearls, and besides they've been returned, and Mrs. Keene will never press the charge."

"It's out of her hands," Crick replied. "This is a police prosecution."

"Oh!"

"Yes, and the police are going to oppose my application for bail."

"Well, that can't be helped."

"I don't like it. Even if you get away with this present charge, you may not be out of the wood."

Macrae looked blank and the smile faded.

The jailer opened the door and said: "You're next, Macrae."

Crick took Macrae's hand. "Now, don't forget. Leave the talking to me and keep your chin up." He went back to the charge-room and up a flight of stairs into the Court.

Macrae followed the jailer to the room at the end of the passage. A man was coming down the stairs. He was swearing to himself.

A voice from the open trap-hatch called out, "Eric Macrae."

The jailer said, "Go on up," and Macrae stumbled up the steep steps. At the top a constable took him by the arm, led him to the front of the dock, and stood behind him.

Macrae looked straight ahead of him and saw a tubby little man sitting at a wide table. He was pawing through a litter of papers. He was the Clerk of the Court. Three feet above him sat the magistrate, a man of fifty who might be taken for a Civil Servant, a country solicitor, or a gentleman of independent means whose life-work it was to read The Times and play bridge.

The clerk found the paper he was looking for and jerked to his feet as though some one had pulled a string. He stood on his chair and spoke to the magistrate; then he jumped down and faced Macrae.

"Is your name Eric Macrae?"

"Yes."

"You stand charged on indictment with the theft of a pearl necklace valued at fifteen hundred pounds. Do you plead guilty or not guilty?"

Macrae was about to speak, when Mr. Crick got to his feet. "I represent the accused, your Worship, and on his behalf I plead Not Guilty."

Thompson was called to the witness-box and sworn. He described the circumstances of Macrae's arrest. "I was present when the charge was made. I cautioned the accused, who said: 'Yes, I understand. I do not wish to make any statement.' The police are not ready to proceed with this case, and I ask for a remand."

"Remanded in custody for eight days."

"Your worship, I ask that my client be released on bail. The necklace, I understand, has been recovered."

The magistrate turned to Thompson. "Have you any objection?"

"Yes, your Worship. I oppose the application on the grounds that our inquiries have not yet been completed and there is a possibility that further charges may be made. It is a complicated affair and there are a great number of witnesses."

"I am sorry, Mr. Crick, but I cannot grant bail in this case. You can, of course, renew your application at the next hearing."

When Bert Finch appeared in the dock shortly after one o'clock the police offered no evidence and requested permission to withdraw the charge against him. The magistrate assented, and Bert walked out of the Court a free man, while Macrae made the journey to the remand prison in the tiny cubicle of a police van.

CHAPTER TWENTY-TWO

PEGGY READ the account of the police-court proceedings whilst eating her lunch under the plane tree in Bulmer Court. Suddenly she dropped her sandwich and clutched the paper with both hands. Macrae arrested! Eric Macrae!

Three fat pigeons fought over the sandwich as she ran up the Court. Mrs. Finch was standing outside her door.

"Has Mr. Crick come back?"

"No, deary. I haven't seen him."

Peggy looked up at the open window of Mr. Crick's room and called out. There was no reply.

"He went to the Police Court, didn't he?" said Mrs. Finch.

Peggy stared at her through her tears. "Yes, but he ought to be back by now."

"You're crying. What's the matter?"

"It's Captain Macrae. He's been arrested by the police."

"Arrested!" Mrs. Finch's shrill voice trailed away to a whisper. "Whatever for?"

"Something to do with some pearls. Stealing them. Here, look at this." She thrust the crumpled paper into Mrs. Finch's ready hands.

"Now, show me, deary. Where is it? Oh, dear, I knew there was something wrong. When I went round to Bury Square this morning there was a policeman outside the house and he said I couldn't go in, and I asked him . . . Oh, I see. Yes, here it is." When she had read the quarter-column Mrs. Finch said, "Well, he didn't take it. I'll bet a bob on that."

"Do you really think so?" Peggy almost hugged Mrs. Finch.

"Of course I do. The Captain's a real gentleman. He'd never do a thing like that. Now, Peggy, you come along with me, and I'll make you a nice cup of tea."

"But I must see Mr. Crick as soon as he gets back."

"You can watch out from my window, can't you? Come on, do, there's a sensible girl."

Mrs. Finch drove Peggy in front of her and put a chair by the open window. Then she borrowed sixpence for the meter, put the kettle on to boil, and joined Peggy at the window. "You know, deary, I wish you didn't feel that way about the Captain."

"Why not?" Peggy asked fiercely.

"Well, he's different from you really, and, after all's said and done, you have been carrying on with Bert this five year back, and though I says it myself he's a good boy. Of course he makes me mad at times, not saying what he's doing and all that sort of thing, but he is steady."

"You introduced me to Captain Macrae."

"Yes, I know I did, but I never thought as you'd get to feel this way about him."

"You think I—love him?"

The direct question made Mrs. Finch stumble over her words. "No, I didn't say that, deary, but the way you're carrying on—"

"You do think so, and it's true, and I don't care who knows it."

"After what happened last night?"

"Nothing happened last night—or, at least, nothing much."

"You'd been crying when you came in with the key of his room, and I says to myself at the time there's been trouble, and I was sorry you'd ever met him. Not that I don't like him myself," Mrs. Finch added hurriedly. "And what I always say is—"

"There's Mr. Crick! And Bert!"

Mrs. Finch nearly fell out of the window in her excitement. "He's back! He's back!" She ran out of the room, and to Bert's embarrassment she kissed him in full view of Mr. Crick, Lampy, Peggy, and a man coming out of the saloon bar of the "Goat."

She pawed at his coat and asked questions at the rate of one every three seconds. What had happened? What had he had to eat? Didn't he want a drink? Had he been able to sleep?

Bert, very red in the face, allowed himself to be guided to the "Goat."

Peggy, waiting in Mrs. Finch's doorway, saw him disappear up the alley and then ran towards Mr. Crick. "Have you seen Captain Macrae?" Her eyes were wet and shining, her lips were trembling.

Mr. Crick caught her hands in his. "Yes, I saw hm."

"How is he?"

"Bearing up pretty well."

"Can I go and see him?"

"Yes, I dare say it could be managed, but I'd keep out of it if I were you."

"Oh, you don't understand."

Mr. Crick felt that he understood only too well, but did not say so. "Come up to the office."

Peggy blew her nose and mopped at her eyes.

Mr. Crick opened the door of his room and squeezed round the desk to his chair. He took a cheroot from the box and lit it. "Sit down. There's really no need to be upset."

"I love him."

"I was afraid of that," Mr. Crick said gently.

"And I want to help him. I can."

"He'll need all the help he can get." Mr. Crick's tone was grave. He frightened Peggy.

"What do you mean?"

Mr. Crick was acutely uncomfortable. "I don't know for certain, but from what I heard it may be that Captain Eric Macrae knows more than is good for him about the death of Abie Russ."

Peggy felt very sick. She held tight to the top rail of a chair till her knuckles showed white.

"You had to know sooner or later," Mr. Crick said nervously.

Peggy said, "Yes," faintly. She was looking past Mr. Crick with unfocused eyes; she saw Macrae, smiling at her across a table. He was filling up her glass. She saw him lift his glass, touch hers, and say, "Here's to the next time."

Suddenly she came alive. "It's not true." She fought to keep the picture, to shut the door on reality.

"I think you ought to go home."

"But I must see him."

"There's no hurry. I'll let you know if I hear anything."

"Promise?"

"Yes, of course."

One hundred yards from Mr. Crick's office Mrs. Finch was dipping her sharp little nose into a tankard of bitter. She was beginning to feel comfortable, the stage immediately preceding the desire for half an hour on her back.

Bert, the recipient of sundry liquid gifts, was doing his best to lower them and answer the eager questions of the donors. At no time verbose, he was becoming mellow and almost talkative; almost.

Mrs. Finch regarded him much as a trainer might an animal of uncertain temper.

"Did they knock you about, Bert?" asked a melancholy man with froth on his whiskers.

"No, there wasn't nothing like that."

The melancholy man was disappointed. "My brother what works at Newcombe's wharf was took once, and the way they got on to him was something cruel. He had his arm in a sling for a fortnight and his nose ain't right yet—"

"Aw, can it!"

"Put a sock in it, Cheerful. Now, come on, Bert. Tell us who you think killed Abie Russ."

"I knows who killed Abie Russ," Mrs. Finch said, with alcoholic dignity. "I knows, and if you want to know how I knows I'll tell yer."

The gentleman who had advocated the use of a sock cheered.

Some one else clapped Mrs. Finch on the back, which ill-timed action delayed the recital until she got her breath back and had another drink to settle it.

"You don't think I knows nothing, do yer?" A pause for denial brought forth no dissenting voice. "But I does. Cap'en Macrae and me was very good friends. I did for him. And when I was doing for him I saw it."

The melancholy man asked, "And what *did* you see?" in the voice of an unbeliever.

"I'll tell yer if only you'll keep quiet and let me talk."

Some one gave Mrs. Finch a pint. "I'm sure that's very good of you, Mr. Robbins, and it's me that needs it after all I've been through. I didn't sleep hardly a wink last night, wondering what was a-going to happen to Bert."

"Come on, Ma, tell us all about it. The horrible thing you saw."

"Well, I knows as you won't believe it, but when I was a-turning out of a cupboard in his room—"

"Whose cupboard?"

"Cap'en Macrae's, of course. That's who I'm talking about, isn't it?"

The melancholy man said, "Well, you *ought* to know."

"As I was saying when I was interrupted, I was going through his cupboard, and it wasn't half full of rubbish neither, I can tell yer. I says to him, 'Why, whatever's this?' He gave me a proper nasty look and said for me to leave it alone and—"

"What was it you saw?"

"A revolver."

The effect satisfied Mrs. Finch. Even the melancholy man was impressed. He stood staring at her with his mouth wide open. The barman stopped wiping down the counter.

"Still Life in a Public House" would have been an apt description of the group round Mrs. Finch, and the scene would have provided material for a problem picture entitled "What Had She Said?"

"Coo-er!" was the first noise which broke the silence which followed, and then every one started asking questions. They wanted to know if it was loaded and what it looked like and if it was still in the cupboard.

"It may still be there for all I know, because I never had no occasion to go to that there cupboard again, but if you wants to know what I thinks, it's that there Cap'en Macrae shot Abie Russ."

"You didn't ought to say a thing like that if you haven't got the proof," said the melancholy man.

"What more proof do yer want, you blooming old string of misery? She saw the revolver, didn't she? Now tell us, Ma. Was there any blood on it?"

Mrs. Finch spun a yarn around that revolver that was a masterpiece of fiction. She didn't notice that the barman had ducked out under the curtain, and she was going strong when Leith came in.

"'Afternoon, Mrs. Finch."

Leith's entry had a freezing and then a dissolving effect on the company. They didn't mind listening to stories about a murder, but they had the very strongest objections to being mixed up in one.

"If it isn't my old friend Mr. Leith." Mrs. Finch giggled and said, "Here's how," as she lifted her pint pot.

"I'd like to have a word with you outside."

Mrs. Finch shut one eye and screwed up the other. In her present state she could see better that way.

Bert got her by the arm and said to Leith: "You don't want to bother with her. She's going home."

Leith blocked the doorway. "I'm going to talk to her first. You keep out of this."

Bert said, "Oh, all right, if that's the way you feel about it," and fell back a pace.

"Now, what's all this talk about a revolver?"

"That's right. He had one."

"Who?"

"Why, Cap'en Macrae, of course. I seen it in his room a couple of days ago."

Leith took out his note-book and began to write. "That was in the room at Bury Square?"

"That's right. Number six. First floor front."

"Wait here a minute." Leith rang up Scotland Yard and asked for Thompson, who replied: "Take her to Howard Street. I'll come right along."

Mrs. Finch, who unfortunately lacked complete control over her legs, arrived at the police station only a few minutes before Thompson.

The charge-room had a sobering effect on her, and Thompson had little difficulty in obtaining a coherent statement. Then he produced the revolver which had been found in Abie's left hand. "Is that like the one you saw?"

"Well, I wouldn't like to swear to it, but I can't see no difference."

"All right. Will you sign your name here?"

While Mrs. Finch was doing her best to ruin a pen, Thompson stepped back and said to Leith: "We'll take her along to Bury Square. You'd better come, too."

Macrae's room was hot and smelt of stale air when Thompson unlocked the door and walked in. A beam of sunlight striking through the torn blind was alive with dancing specks of dust.

Thompson walked over to the window and snapped up the blind. Then he opened the cupboard door. He turned to Mrs. Finch and said: "Now I want you to show me exactly what happened when you found the revolver."

Mrs. Finch picked at her skirt with nervous fingers. Leith gave her a push and she took two or three uncertain steps in the direction of the cupboard.

"I'd sooner not, if you don't mind."

"Which was the chair you used?"

"That one."

Thompson picked it up and placed it in front of the open cupboard. "Is that how it was?"

"No, the other way round. I put me right hand on the back of it to steady myself."

Thompson reversed the chair. "Get up."

Mrs. Finch, mumbling a protest, obeyed.

"Now, you had your hand on the revolver when Macrae came into the room? That's right, isn't it?"

"Yes, like this." Mrs. Finch put a hand on the top shelf. "I dropped it on the floor."

"Was he surprised to see the revolver?"

"No, I don't think so. I made the suggestion that the best thing he could do was to let me clear the whole lot out and sell it."

"What did he say to that?"

"I forget exactly what he did say, but he locked the cup-board door after that."

Thompson checked over the contents of the cupboard. It had been searched once and no revolver had been found, but he wanted to be sure in his own mind that there was no gun there.

Peggy didn't go home. She walked half-way along Fenwick Street. If Macrae were accused of the murder of Abie Russ she was the only one who could help him. She could say that she had been with him at the time it happened.

But she must visit him first and tell him of her plan. They must both tell the same story. If he had an alibi already, of course, it wouldn't be necessary for her to do anything, but she must make sure. She must see him.

The lights at the first crossing were red, and as though they were an answer to her question she turned and almost ran back to the office.

Mr. Crick woke from a doze as she burst in without knocking. "What's happened now?"

"Nothing. But I must see Captain Macrae."

Mr. Crick was suspicious. "What's made you decide that all of a sudden?"

"Oh, I can't tell you; but do please take me to him. It's frightfully important."

"All right." Mr. Crick stared at the drift of white ash on his waistcoat and made a feeble effort to brush it off. Then he got up and put on his squashy black hat. "I can't guarantee anything, but I'll do my best."

"We'll take a taxi. I'll pay for it."

"I wish I knew what was in your mind," Mr. Crick said. But Peggy wasn't listening. She ran on ahead down the stairs and waited impatiently in the Court while Mr. Crick made his flat-footed descent.

Fenwick Street was not popular with taxi-drivers, and they had to walk almost as far as London Bridge before they found one.

Peggy sat on the edge of the seat during the long drive. When she saw the prison she caught her breath. She had been thinking of Macrae vaguely as one in trouble; her thoughts, her hopes, and her fears circling in her mind in aimless confusion, but ever returning to the man she loved. The lines of sightless barred windows sunk deep into the stone walls brought home the cold reality of the present. All power of thought was gone.

Mr. Crick pulled himself forward and peered out of the window. "I wish you hadn't come." He looked at Peggy with the faint hope that she would change her mind.

She read his unspoken question. "I'm going through with it."

"Very well. But you'll have to wait here until I make inquiries." Mr. Crick opened the door as the taxi drew up.

Peggy watched him press a bell at the side of a massive double door, and, as a smaller door opened and he disappeared within, she caught a glimpse of a man in uniform with a bunch of keys hanging from his belt.

She sank back on the cushions and tried to imagine what it would be like inside the prison. Would he be wearing his own clothes? Would she have to go to his cell? Her hands pressed hard down on the seat. Would she be allowed to see him alone? To speak to him; to tell him of her plan? If not, then she could do nothing.

It was awful to feel so helpless. The driver was reading a paper, his peaked cap tilted back on his head. He didn't care. The drive was but another fare, and a profitable one at that. The ticking of the meter was, no doubt, music in his ears.

A boy with a basket of bread passed and looked curiously into the cab. Peggy drew back from the window. Why was Mr. Crick so long? She looked at her watch. He had only been gone five minutes. It was stupid to worry; there would be a lot of formalities to go through. She must keep calm. And she wouldn't look at her watch again; not until she had counted up to a hundred.

The hand appeared to have barely moved. Two minutes gone. The driver was on the second page. Peggy could have hit him over the head. He was so supremely oblivious of the trouble which was torturing her. She got out of the cab and walked quickly along the pavement. Before she had gone twenty yards she fought with an absurd desire to look round. She wouldn't! She couldn't! At least, not until she had got to the mail-box at the corner.

And then . . . There was no sign of Mr. Crick. She walked on blindly, and the vigorous movement had the effect of partly stilling the tumult in her brain.

When she turned again and looked back she could not see the cab. Perhaps Mr. Crick had come out and was waiting for her; perhaps *he* was waiting for her. She almost ran back to the cab.

"Has any one been asking for me?"

The taxi-man withdrew his rapt gaze from an advertisement which promised relief to sufferers from half a hundred ills. He looked at her and said, "What?"

"Mr. Crick. Have you seen him?"

"You mean the gent as come here in this here cab?"

"Yes. Yes."

"No, I ain't seen nothing of him."

Peggy got into the cab and sat down. She shut her eyes and began to rehearse what she must say to Macrae. On the night when
Abie Russ was killed they had dined at the—where should she say?
The Savoy? Yes, that would do. They had got there at eight and had
dined and danced and had not left until—

What was that? Footsteps coming towards the cab. She jerked
forward to the edge of the seat. Mr. Crick! She put out a hand to
open the door. And then she heard him say: "Bulmer Court." Her
hand dropped to her side.

Mr. Crick opened the door and she drew aside to let him in.

"I'm sorry, but it's no good. He won't see you."

The world stood still. "He won't see you. He won't see you."

"I did all I could, but it wasn't any use. I'd try and forget, if I
were you."

Peggy laughed suddenly. Mr. Crick gripped her wrist and said
fiercely. "Stop that."

She stared at him for a moment and then burst into a flood of
tears. Mr. Crick had never been in such a ghastly position before.

He thought of several comforting phrases, but they never
reached his lips. He just sat, an elderly man in anguish, and stared
at the meter. The sum it registered, five and nine-pence, made him
feel worse, if that were possible.

And then, when he had begun to fear that the situation was to
continue for ever, the weeping ceased, and Peggy said:

"I'm awfully sorry." Her handkerchief was a sodden rag.

Mr. Crick said, "That's all right," and looked out of the window.
Not far to go now.

"What did he say?" Peggy asked, and there was a sob in her
voice.

"That it would be better if he didn't meet you again."

"Did you tell him that I could help him?"

"Yes." Mr. Crick thought it best not to tell all. How Macrae had
been angrily contemptuous of Peggy's suggestion. That he had said
he wished he had never met her. That she was a silly little fool. That
if you took a girl out once or twice she expected you to marry her.

He was in a hell of a jam and couldn't be bothered with her damn'-fool talk.

Mr. Crick at that moment hated Macrae with an intensity which caused the blood to rise to his head and made his hands tremble. He could hardly trust himself to speak.

"How was he looking?"

"Oh—er—very well."

"Is there anything I can send him?"

"No, I don't think so. He is quite comfortable."

During the last five minutes of the drive Peggy did not speak again. When she got out of the taxi she said, "Thank you, Mr. Crick," and walked quickly away.

CHAPTER TWENTY-THREE

As soon as Macrae's case had been disposed of Thompson left the Police Court and drove to the hospital where Tony Mascati was a patient. Tony was feeling better, and he grinned through a gap in his bandages.

"This is the last time I gives you the office about anything," he said. "The nurse says I damn' near passed out."

"I'll get Tim a stretch. You won't have to worry."

"I hope I'll be in Court when he gets it. I'd like to kiss him good-by. The ruddy swine."

"Tony, you were in the club on Thursday night, weren't you?"

"I was. That night and every night."

"Was Macrae there?"

"No."

"Sure about that?"

"Positive."

"What about Daly and Connor?"

"They were in the place up to the time it shut. That would be about two o'clock."

"Thanks. That's all I want to know."

Thompson went to the office of the Director of Public Prosecutions and saw the man who was working on the case. He gave him the information he had obtained from Tony Mascati, and said: "That seems to tie it up."

"Yes. You can go ahead and charge Macrae with murder."

Thompson arrived at the prison shortly after Mr. Crick and Peggy had left. He took Macrae to Howard Street police station and charged him with the wilful murder of Abraham Russ, aged 28, on July 23rd, at 47 Fenwick Street, by shooting him with a revolver.

Macrae said: "I understand."

"If you wish to make any statement, I must caution you that—"

"I'm not saying anything except that I did not kill Russ."

The sergeant opened a glass-fronted cupboard and took down a pair of hand-cuffs. One link was snapped on Macrae's right wrist and the other on that of a plain-clothes officer. As the cold steel touched his flesh, Macrae said: "Is this necessary?"

"Afraid it is," Thompson replied. "Come along."

They got into the waiting police car. Thompson put a cigarette in Macrae's mouth and lit it for him.

"Thanks. What's the next move?"

"You'll come up before the magistrate to-morrow."

"And then I'll be remanded again, I suppose?"

"Yes. For eight days."

At the doors of the prison the driver sounded his horn. A warder came out, looked at the car, and then swung back the big doors. The car stopped before another door and Thompson got out. Macrae followed him and then came the plain-clothes officer.

Thompson unlocked the hand-cuffs and went into an office with the warder. A few minutes later he returned. The warder said to Macrae, "Come with me," and unlocked the inner gate. "We've moved you to Hall K, near the hospital. You may go there later. It depends on the doctor."

They walked along a concrete path; on one side was a patch of grass and a circular flower-bed. It was planted with pink sweet-williams; a prisoner knelt on the grass weeding the bed; he took a quick glance at Macrae as he passed.

Like spokes of a gigantic wheel, the five halls of the prison radiated from a central tower, grimly forbidding.

The warder unlocked the door of the hall and when they had entered locked it behind them. The warder on duty came up. "All the stuff's been shifted. Number seven-four-two."

It was a bigger cell than the one he had occupied the night before. There was an easy chair and a rug on the floor.

Macrae looked at the narrow window, with its thick glass, almost opaque, and narrow-set bars. If he could forget them he might be quite comfortable. There was a pile of magazines on the table and a short shelf filled with books. His brushes! They had been a twenty-first birthday present. He handled one, a twisted smile on his lips. It was all so damn' funny. So damn' funny. He wanted to cry, to shout, to break his way out of this damn' place.

That smug-faced warder. He would be going home soon, to a smug little home, to tell his wife that he'd got that there Macrae in his Hall. The one who did in Abie Russ. That's what every one would say. "He did it all right. The police never charge a man with murder unless they're sure they've got him cold."

The first warder had gone. The other, a fat squab of a man with a round red face, was standing with a thumb in his belt. "I want your tie, braces, and shoes."

Macrae said: "Why?" And then a second or two later added, "Yes, I understand," and took off his coat. "I suppose I can't have a belt?"

"No. Against the regulations." The warder took the braces and dropped them outside the door.

Macrae sat on the edge of the bed and bent to unlace his shoes. "And the tie."

Bert Finch took his mother home from the police station, and when she got into the house she pulled off her boots and lay down on the bed with an immense sigh of relief. She felt proper done in, what with the excitement of Bert getting out and then her being taken to the station and questioned. As she fell into an alcoholic doze she saw herself in the witness-box at the Old Bailey wearing her best bonnet, the one she had bought for the funeral of her old man, the cape she'd got from her Auntie May. The skirt was the trouble. The hem of her "best" would need turning up. Another sigh, a preparatory whine, and then a snore broke forth to announce to all the world that Mrs. Finch was asleep.

Bert sat for a long time in the front room with his elbows on the table. He was thinking of Peggy. Funny the way she'd run off after Mr. Crick when she must have seen him. And it wasn't as though she'd given him the chuck, because they'd been out together only a couple of days ago and she was all right then, and she'd sent him in a meal when he was at the station.

Twice he got up to leave the room, and twice he changed his mind and sat down and lit a cigarette. Perhaps he had been a bit to blame. He hadn't taken her out much of late. The love he bore for Peggy was awakening now that she appeared not to want him, and the more he thought of her and the more he recalled how she looked, the way she smiled, the way she talked, the more an overpowering desire to see her came over him.

He put on his cap and shut the door gently behind him. He must see her.

At the end of the Court Lampy was droning out a tune which had a family resemblance to "Was It Rain?" Bert felt in his pocket and found a sixpence. He gave it to Lampy, who was so surprised that he didn't say "Thank you" until Bert was five yards past him.

A newsboy was running along the pavement shouting something unintelligible. Bert bought a paper.

CAPTAIN MACRAE CHARGED WITH THE MURDER OF ABRAHAM RUSS

God! That was his mother's doing. Talking about the gun she'd seen in his room. Macrae! Bert tried to remember what he had looked like when he'd identified him at the station. He hadn't looked like a murderer then.

Bert walked back to the mouth of the Court. Lampy saw him and smiled a wide, toothless grin. Maybe there was another sixpence coming his way.

"They've got the bloke that shot Abie," Bert said.

Lampy's mouth hung open. "You mean Tim Daly?"

"No. Captain Macrae."

"I know him. He gave me half a dollar."

"When was that?"

"I forget."

"Well, you won't get another from him."

"Been took for murder!" Lampy muttered to himself. "For murder!" His fingers fell from the keys. Didn't seem right to go on playing, somehow. Gawd! He'd thought he'd had a rough deal, standing all day in the sun playing for coppers, but—took for murder! That did knock a bloke all of a heap. Well, if the rozzers got on to him and asked him what he knew, he wouldn't say nothing. Captain Macrae was a real gentleman. Given him half a dollar he had, and he'd spoken nice, too.

Lampy humped his accordion on his back and shuffled up the Court.

It was a stiff climb up Mr. Crick's stairs, and he had to lean up against the wall and rest when he got to the top. Everything was on the move, turning round and round. He shouldn't have come up so quick.

He beat on his chest. He was feeling better now, but he kept a hand on the wall as he walked, with uncertain steps, along the passage. He knocked on the door at the end and waited. There was no response, and he knocked again, louder.

"What do you want?"

Lampy turned round slowly and faced Mr. Crick. "It's about that Captain Macrae," he said.

"You'd better come in."

Lampy went slowly through the open door.

"Sit down."

Lampy lowered his accordion to the floor and groped for a chair. "I've just heard he's been took."

Mr. Crick fiddled with the pens on his desk. "Yes. What about it?"

"For killing Abie Russ?"

Mr. Crick's hand was still. He looked straight at Lampy. "Who told you that?"

"Bert."

"What do you want?"

Lampy got up and unbuttoned his coat. His hand disappeared into the depths of a pocket and came out with a leather purse. His fingers were trembling as he unfastened the catch. "Six pound ten shillings and ninepence." The notes were much folded and very dirty. He put them on the desk.

"What's this for?"

"For the Captain. Maybe he'll be needing a pound or two, and lawyers cost a lot."

The hint of a smile pulled at the corners of Mr. Crick's mouth. Lawyers cost a lot. He spread out the notes and counted them. Then he pushed them towards Lampy, who drew back.

"No. No. That's for the Captain. You keep it. You'll know what to do with it. He'll want a mouthpiece."

Mr. Crick picked up the money. "Where did this come from?"

"It's mine. All of it. And come by honest."

"All right."

Lampy slung his accordion over his shoulder and went out.

Mr. Crick sat for a time without moving, the money in his hand. Funny old blighter. This was probably his lifetime's savings. Why should he have given it to help Macrae?

Mr. Crick, who knew quite a lot about human nature, was puzzled.

Lampy came out into the sunlight, blinking. He thought he'd never felt quite so happy before. And he had given away every single penny he possessed.

Bert walked the streets for an hour.

When he got back to Bulmer Court he found his mother awake. She was sitting in front of a cracked, misty mirror, combing her hair.

"Well, you've done it this time with your gabbing."

Mrs. Finch was querulous. "Now, for heaven's sake don't start getting on to me the very first minute you come into the house. I've had plenty to worry about, what with you being took by the police and all that. I never slept a wink the whole of last night, and now you start getting on to me about something I knows nothing about."

Bert laughed. "I like that. Yes, that's good. You don't know nothing about it. I don't blooming well think. What did you tell old Thompson this afternoon?"

"Thompson? Who's he?"

"The bloke that's in charge of this murder inquiry, that's all. Don't you remember telling him you'd found a revolver in Captain Macrae's rom?"

"Oh, yes, I remember that all right. I wasn't as bad as all that."

"You've cooked Macrae's goose. He's been charged with killing Abie Russ."

The realization of what she had done broke slowly on Mrs. Finch's understanding. Remorse followed fast. "I wish I hadn't said nothing about it," she whined. Then she turned on Bert. "It was your fault; you shouldn't have let me. You knew I'd had a couple."

"What the hell do you think I care? If Macrae shot Abie he deserves all that's coming to him. He's put me out of a job."

Mrs. Finch became tearful. "Now, Bert, you didn't ought to say things like that." She got up and walked up and down the room; a pathetic figure wearing an old mackintosh, wisps of grey hair straggling down her back.

Bert said he was going to the pictures and strode out into the Court.

When the street door banged, Mrs. Finch went back to the glass and finished doing her hair. Then she took off the mackintosh and put on a blouse and short jacket. Three-and-ninepence. That was all she had in her purse. She wondered vaguely what had happened to the pound Macrae had given her. Three-and-ninepence wasn't no good to nobody.

She went out and walked to the end of the Court, where Lampy was standing. "Lampy, I want you to give me a hand."

He stopped playing and said, "I'd be glad, Mrs. Finch."

"Can you get hold of a barrow somewhere?"

"What d'you want it for?"

"Never mind that. Get me a barrow, that's all, and bring it up to my place."

Lampy shuffled off, saying he'd be back in half a tick.

Mrs. Finch went back to her doorway and waited there impatiently. At last he came in sight, bent over the shafts of a coster's barrow.

"You stop there." Mrs. Finch went into her room and came out a few minutes later with a clock and an armful of clothes. The second journey produced two saucepans, a kettle, and a handful of knives and forks; the third a picture, an eiderdown, a bedspread, and a fender.

"I didn't know you was going to move house," Lampy croaked.

"I'm not. Come on, that's the lot."

It was a long way to the pawnshop in Thistle Street, and Mrs. Finch had to help the old man for the last quarter-mile. He helped to carry the load into the shop.

Mrs. Finch was urgently persuasive, but one pound nine and sixpence was all she could screw out of the pawnbroker. She gave Lampy sixpence.

Mr. Crick was locking his office door when Mrs. Finch arrived, much out of breath, on the landing.

"I'm glad I caught you," she said.

Mr. Crick opened the door. "Come in."

"I won't keep you a minute." Mrs. Finch followed him into the room and put the proceeds of her clothes and furniture on the desk. "I want you to take that," she said. "One pound nine and six. It's for the Captain."

Mr. Crick stared first at the money, then at Mrs. Finch.

"For Captain Macrae?"

"Yes; I've just heard. Bert told me. The Captain's been charged with murder, and this is for his defence. It's not a lot, but it's all I can raise."

Mr. Crick took an envelope from a drawer and dropped the money into it. He wrote on it, "Mrs. Finch. £ 1 9s. 6d.," and put it in the safe.

"He was awful good to me, and I feel real bad about it, seeing it was my fault really that it happened."

"What do you mean?" Mr. Crick asked sharply.

"Well, you see, I knew that he had a revolver in his room; I found it there; and I was talking about it in the 'Goat,' when Leith took me to the station and wrote it all down. After that I was taken to the Captain's rooms and the revolver wasn't in the cupboard where I'd seen it." A tear ran down Mrs. Finch's cheek. Mr. Crick saw it and almost groaned. He'd had his fill of weeping women for one day.

"Well, I'll have to be getting along," he said.

"Then I won't keep you."

Mr. Crick listened to the sound of Mrs. Finch's departing footsteps. Then he got up slowly and went out and down the stairs. He must go and see Macrae and tell him Mrs. Finch's story.

He walked southward half a mile along Fenwick Street and caught a tram which took him to the prison.

CHAPTER TWENTY-FOUR

"I'VE NEVER owned a revolver."

Macrae was sitting on the table in his cell as he spoke the words in answer to a question from Mr. Crick.

"Mrs. Finch has told the police that you did. That she saw one in your room. And it's not there now." Mr. Crick's voice was matter-of-fact and even.

"Mrs. Finch! That old char! She'd say anything. She's always gassing about something. And besides, it's only her word against mine."

Mr. Crick recalled the payment to him of one pound nine and sixpence by the "old char."

"Now, look here, Macrae, you've got to face it. The police have charged you with murder, and you can be quite sure that they've got a case against you; and if I know anything about them, it's a sound *prima facie* case, which is going to take some breaking. You've got to tell me everything."

Macrae stood up and fiddled with the brushes on the chest-of-drawers. Then he picked up a stud-box.

"Funny thing, but I've had this ever since I was a kid. It's not worth more than twopence, but I've kept it all this time. Not that I ever cared a damn for it, but—"

"For heaven's sake take a pull on yourself! Can't you realize that you've got to be ready to meet any attack that they may make? And you've got to tell me everything."

Macrae turned. "Yes, of course; but what is there to say except that I didn't kill Abie Russ?"

"Where were you on that night?"

"At Sammy's Club."

"Who saw you there?"

"I've told you already. Connor and Tim Daly."

"I don't think they'll be much help. They've been arrested."

"Oh!"

"The police'll give me copies of any statements they may have made."

"The club was raided yesterday afternoon. I'd forgotten."

"I don't like it." Mr. Crick put his hands in his trouser pockets and jingled some loose change. "And if your alibi's no good we've got to find something else. It looks to me as though your best line is to say nothing. Leave me to think up a story."

"All right." Macrae picked up the stud-box, looked at it, and then put it down.

"Now I want to get back to the revolver business. Are you sure there never was one in your room?"

Macrae did not speak for nearly a minute, then he said, "Well, as a matter of fact, there was. I'd had it during the war. It was in a cupboard with a lot of junk. I'd forgotten all about it until that interfering old woman found it."

"Do you know what happened to it after that?"

"Yes. I chucked it away. Into the river."

"Why?"

"Well, you know the fuss about licenses. I hadn't any use for it, so I thought that would be the best thing to do. If I'd taken it to a police station I'd have been asked a lot of questions."

"When was this?"

"I forget exactly. About a couple of days ago."

"Did any one see you throw it away?"

"No."

"Have you ever been to Russ's shop?"

"Yes. I went to pop a pair of links. I told the police about it. They produced a man who said he worked in the shop, and he said that Russ had given me a pile of notes. He was lying."

"Did this man say why Russ had given you the money?"

"No."

"Why did you go to this particular pawnshop?"

"It was the nearest one to where I live."

"Now, have you told me everything?"

"Yes."

"All right, I'll have to be going. I'll come and see you again to-morrow."

When Mr. Crick had gone, Macrae stood for several minutes staring at the door. His confidence was ebbing. The story he had told had sounded thin, but it would have been all right—had it been true.

If Mrs. Finch hadn't found the revolver . . . If he hadn't been seen in Abie's shop . . . If he hadn't taken the pearls . . . That was how it had started. If Mrs. Keene had cashed that cheque for him . . . It was her fault. The whole of this business. He cursed her. The tight-fisted . . .

Oh, hell! But what was the good of going over it again? He'd got to make his story water-tight. No one had seen him enter the shop on the night that Abie died. And he'd got away without being seen; he had got rid of the pearls without any one knowing that he'd had them in his possession.

There was really nothing to worry about.

He sat on the edge of a chair and put out his hand to pick up a book, and then changed his mind. He wasn't in the mood for reading. His brain was restless, examining every point in his story. There were no weak links; and then the cold doubts of common sense began to creep in.

The police must know something. As Mr. Crick had said, if they hadn't a case against him they would never have brought a murder charge.

He sat for a long time quite still, while fear took hold of him and sapped at the confidence born of conceit. If only he could find out what they knew he could prepare himself to meet the attack. He felt helpless and frightened.

When the lights were switched off his fears gathered force. He had never been frightened of the dark before, even when he was a kid. But now, with the coming of darkness, he became conscious of something behind him. It was always behind him.

A chink of light from the trap in the door cast a thin line across his bed. It served but to accentuate the darkness.

Last night he had slept—uneasily, but still, he had managed to get an hour or two of peace. But to-night fears were crowding. And he dare not look round.

There was no sound. No warning before he felt that grip on his shoulder. Tighter! Tighter! His legs were as water, but he forced himself to get up off the bed and take a staggering pace to the door. He was sweating and trembling all over. It had gone!

He turned and leaned with his back against the door. He was breathing fast and the palms of his hands were pressed against the cold steel. He could still see the line of light across his bed. It was comforting in an odd sort of way. It was real.

He braced his legs and walked to the bed. Then he took off his coat and trousers. His pyjamas were on the chair. He groped for them and put them on and got under the bed-clothes. The pillow was small and hard; he turned on his back. It wasn't so bad if he lay that way. Chinamen used a wooden block as a pillow. He'd read that somewhere.

He lay wide awake, with the darkness pressing down. It was as though he had gone blind, and at the thought he turned to look at the pencil of light.

Somewhere he could hear footsteps. It was the warder going his rounds in the galleries above.

He looked at his wrist-watch and read the time on the luminous dial. Nine-fifteen. Nine, ten, eleven, twelve. Nine hours to wait. And to-morrow night would be the same. He dare not sleep. Nine-fifteen. In the ordinary way he would have just finished dinner. The night at the San Fresca was as vividly real as though he were there now. If he stretched out a hand he could grasp the glass the waiter had filled. Champagne. And Mrs. Keene was paying. Music drummed in his head. What about a dance? He spoke the words aloud and then laughed.

What the hell was the good of remembering? Of calling up the pictures of a life that was dead? Dead! He knew that he would never dance again, would never sit at a white-clothed table with an attentive waiter hovering in the background.

He knew it, and pitied himself with an all-consuming sorrow. There were tears in his eyes; he felt for a handkerchief.

Then he lay very still for a long time, his thoughts ranging over the years of his life. He'd had a damn' good time, taking it by and large. He forgot the days and weeks when he had gone without a decent meal so that he could pay the rent of his room.

He had always managed to dress decently, and the folding of his trousers had been a rite. To-night he had thrown them on the floor. What did it matter now?

And then the fighting spirit returned. Why should he give in? But he knew as he muttered the words that he was powerless to stop the march of fate.

An hour passed, and then again he heard the footsteps of the warder. Sleep was not far away, but he dared not sleep. He sat up in bed, his hands clawing the thin blanket into folds. God! Would the night never end?

And then, as though some one had spoken aloud, he became conscious of a demand.

"You killed Abie Russ. Tell them. Tell them that you killed Abie Russ."

"I didn't. I didn't mean to."

"Tell them you killed Abie Russ."

"I didn't. . . ." Oh, hell! He raised his two hands to his face and sought to shut out the insistent accusation.

"You killed Abie Russ. . . ."

He kicked back the blankets and put his bare feet on the floor and stood up. He put out a hand to steady himself, felt nothing, and staggered forward. His knee struck against the table. His hands clutched at the cover.

He felt for the wall and edged towards the door. The floor was clear. He could walk up and down. Three short paces each way. Three paces. One, two, three. There was nothing there. He stood still and stretched out an arm. Three paces.

It was more exhausting than a ten-mile walk, and the nervous tension destroyed what benefit the action might have bestowed. He groped for the bed, found it, and threw himself on it face downwards.

He lay there with his face pressed against the hard pillow. God! He felt tired. He turned, crooked an elbow under his head, and dozed.

"You killed Abie Russ. Tell them. . . ."

When the warder came in answer to the ringing of the bell, Macrae was standing with one hand on the table. His shoulders were bowed and he was staring at the floor.

"I killed Abie Russ. I killed him."

The warder grasped him by the shoulders. "What's this?"

"I killed him." Macrae raised his head and stared stupidly at the door. He looked drugged. "I killed Abie Russ. I shot him."

Then peace came to Macrae's brain. It was as though the words he had spoken had exorcised the fear which had held him in its grip.

The warder said, "All right, mate. Sit down and take it easy." He filled a tin mug with water. "Drink this."

Macrae obeyed like a child, and held the mug to his lips with both hands. As he handed it back empty he muttered, "I want to see somebody. I want to make a statement."

The warder backed to the door. "All right. I won't be long."

Macrae got up and stood leaning against the door listening. He could hear the tinkle of a telephone-bell and then the warder speaking.

He could not distinguish the words that were spoken, but he could imagine what they must be. "Macrae has confessed to the murder!" Murder! He hadn't said that. Killing wasn't necessarily murder. Sometimes it was manslaughter. And there had been cases he'd read of where the accused man had put up a plea of provocation and got away with it; sometimes without a sentence, and in other cases with only a year or two.

His brain worked quickly. He pictured the scene he must describe. A sudden quarrel. Abie drawing a revolver. A struggle. His forcing Abie's hand back. The gun going off accidentally.

Macrae nodded approval of this explanation. But he must get the details right or else they'd bowl him out in some silly mistake. He respected Thompson.

He had gone to Abie's house to pay a friendly visit. Abie was sitting at his desk. They had talked for a time and had had a drink or two, and then . . .

What had happened after that? He hadn't much time. The warder would be coming back soon. There'd been a quarrel. Yes, of course. But what about? He couldn't tell the truth, because if he admitted the theft of the pearls from Abie, that would provide a motive. It would have to be something else. About a girl? No. That wouldn't work. He would have to say who it was.

He listened, but could hear nothing. Time was running on. He hadn't got long. Money! That was it. He had lent Abie money and had asked for it back. Abie had refused, and then there had been a quarrel.

Abie, still at his desk, had opened a drawer and had taken out a revolver. He had lost his head and closed with Abie, had tried to get the gun away from him and it had gone off.

When he had realized what had happened he had acted foolishly. He admitted that. He had run away. Later he had meant to tell the police what had happened, but it had been too late then. They would never have believed his story, but it was the truth. As God was his judge, it was the truth!

Macrae felt pleased with himself. It was a simple explanation. They couldn't prove that it was his revolver that had been used, nor that he had taken the pearls from Abie's safe. There was no motive, and without a motive his story of provocation and a quarrel must be accepted. Who could contradict it?

As the minutes passed, Macrae became impatient for the time when he could tell his story. And when at last footsteps approached his cell he got up quickly from his bed.

The Chief Warder was outside, sleepy-eyed and surly. "So you want to make a statement. Is that right?"

Macrae said, "Yes," eagerly.

"You've chosen a lovely time. Why couldn't you wait till the morning?"

"I've got to get it off my mind. I want to tell everything."

The Chief Warder looked sceptical. No one, in his experience, ever told everything.

Macrae buttoned up his coat and felt mechanically for his cigarette-case; he pulled down his coat, then he raised his head as he walked out in obedience to a sign from the hall warder.

Out into the cool night air. The stars were brighter than he'd ever known them to be; there was a faint smell of damp earth and mown grass.

The Chief Warder, a square block of a man, trod the centre of the narrow concrete path. A few yards short of the main gate he turned right-handed into an open space. It wasn't very large, perhaps twenty yards square. Macrae could see the lighter shade of grass and the dark squares of flower-beds. It was the Governor's garden.

There was a jingle and a clinking as the Chief Warder stopped and fumbled with his keys; and as he stood behind him, waiting, Macrae felt that he had gone back twenty years and was standing outside the French windows of the morning-room at Grove Hall. He could see the tall trees which fringed the tennis-lawn and the brick wall of the kitchen garden.

Funny, how one remembered things like that. It was as though time did not exist. He would walk back into the house in a minute, into the lamp-lit hall, say good night to his mother, and—

"Come along. This way." The Chief Warder held the door open and Macrae walked into a carpeted passage. The door was locked behind him. Some one was talking behind a door on the right. The Chief Warder opened it and light streamed out. Macrae went in.

Thompson was sitting in a leather arm-chair, smoking his pipe. He nodded to Macrae. He hadn't been long out of his bed, but showed no signs of that fact.

The Chief Warder saluted the other occupant of the room, who was sitting on a hard chair with his legs crossed. The Deputy Governor half raised his right hand in acknowledgment and said, "He can sit there," and indicated a low chair. When Macrae was seated the Chief Warder took up a stand with his back to the door and looked at the ceiling.

The Deputy Governor said to Thompson, "All right. Go ahead."

Thompson wriggled his shoulders into a more comfortable position. "Well, Macrae. I hear you're ready to talk. Carry on."

It wasn't so easy now to say, "I killed Abie Russ." Even though he had his story clear in his mind, and had rehearsed every word of it, he could not find the words. There was something about the room—he couldn't have defined what it was—which killed the desire to speak.

Thompson worked himself forward in his chair and turned towards Macrae. "You admit you killed Abie Russ?" His tone was almost conversational, and the words were spoken as though the question was the most ordinary one in the world.

Macrae said, "Yes, but I didn't mean to. It was an accident. A pure accident. We had a quarrel."

"Oh, so that's how it was?"

"Yes. I went to see him about some money—"

"Wait a minute." Thompson put his pipe into his mouth and got up. He sat down in a chair at the desk and took a sheet of foolscap from a pile and put it on the blotting-pad. Then he picked up a pen and dipped it in the ink. He wrote three lines and blotted them and read, "'I have been cautioned by Chief Inspector Thompson that I need not say anything, but whatever I do say will be taken down in writing and may be used in evidence.' Do you mind signing this?"

Macrae got up and took the pen which Thompson held out. He signed his name with a firm hand. "Eric Macrae."

"All right. Sit down." Thompson picked out the dead ash from his pipe with a match.

"Now you can go ahead. Start at the beginning. Why did you go to see Russ?"

"I told you. Because he owed me money, and I wanted to get it back. I'd written to him, and—"

"Wait a minute till I get this down. 'I went to see Russ.' Where?"

"At his shop."

"'Because he owed me money.' Go on."

"He let me in and we went up to his room. He sat at his desk. I kept standing. I told him what I wanted and he said he couldn't pay. He asked me if I'd have a drink, poured out drinks. Whisky-and-soda. But I wasn't going to be put off that way, and I said that I must have my money, and I wasn't going till I got it. Then he got nasty. I went over towards the desk and he snatched a revolver out of a drawer and pointed it at me."

"Yes."

"I got hold of his wrist and tried to force his hand back, and then the revolver went off and he fell. It was an accident. All I was trying to do was to protect myself." Macrae leaned forward in his chair as though to give force to his words. His voice had reached a high pitch.

"I've got that. What happened next?"

"Well, I hardly know. I got scared. I realized I was in an awkward position and I cleared out and went home."

"That was a stupid thing to do. If you'd told the police right away there wouldn't have been any of this bother."

"Yes, I know. I was a fool."

"In which drawer was the gun?"

Macrae hesitated for a split second, and then said, "The one nearest me."

"That would be on Russ's right?"

"Yes."

"I suppose he picked it up with his right hand?"

"Yes."

"Do you remember that?"

"Yes. Why?"

"Oh, nothing." Thompson's expression was wooden as he wrote the words.

"Were you wearing gloves?"

Macrae said, "Yes," without thinking, and then stared at Thompson. His hands were trembling. "Why?"

Thompson ignored the question, and asked, "A pair of string gloves?"

"I can't remember that."

"We found a pair of string gloves in your room in Bury Square. I suppose that was the pair you were using?"

"I told you—I can't remember."

"Did you take anything from Abie's flat?"

"No."

"From his shop?"

Macrae stiffened. The palms of his hands were pressed hard down on his knees. "No." His voice was harsh.

"Russ had a string of pearls."

"I don't know anything about them."

"They belonged to Mrs. Keene."

"I told you before. I know nothing about Mrs. Keene's pearls except that they were stolen. I read about the theft in the papers."

"All right." Thompson blotted the words he had written.

Then he read the statement aloud. When he had finished Macrae nodded.

"Do you want to add anything or make any alterations?"

"No. What I've said is the truth."

When he had signed the document, the Head Warder touched Macrae on the shoulder and pointed to the open door.

Macrae slept dreamlessly until the insistent vibrating clanging of a bell awakened him.

Mr. Crick did not arrive at his office in Bulmer Court until eleven o'clock on Saturday morning.

Five women, chatting at the street door, awaited him. He drove a way through the group, and he did not smile as he returned their greetings.

Peggy came out of her room as he reached the landing. She said, "There's five of them to see you." There was a tremor in her voice.

Mr. Crick made a dive for the door of his office. "All right, send up the first."

Usually attentive to the stories of his clients, this morning Mr. Crick found that he had to force himself to take in the meaning of the stream of words. Impatiently he asked questions, and hardly listened to the answers.

It was a quarter-past twelve when the last one had gone. Peggy came into the room.

"Mr. Crick, I must see Captain Macrae—I must!" When she stopped talking she pressed her lips together and grasped at the back of a chair. Mr. Crick said, "Why?"

"I told you I could help about the murder. It was done on Thursday night, wasn't it?"

Mr. Crick nodded.

"About eleven o'clock?"

"I don't know the exact time, but it was probably about then."

"Well, then, Captain Macrae couldn't have done it. I was with him. He took me to a—a—dance. I didn't get home till after one. He was with me all the time."

"It's no use, Peggy."

"What do you mean?"

"You're too late. Macrae confessed last night."

"Confessed!"

"Yes. He has admitted that he killed Abie Russ."

"Oh!" Peggy turned and took a staggering step to the door.

Mr. Crick heard her enter the office, heard a chair scrape across the floor, and then the sound of crying came to him.

He got up and walked to the door, stood listening for a minute, and then went back to his room. Outside Lampy was playing his accordion. Mrs. Finch was leaning out of her window gossiping. A man with a basket of milk-bottles on his arm came whistling up the Court.

Mr. Crick looked at the marble clock which said twenty minutes to seven and bit a cheroot. It was going to be a difficult case to prepare. He sighed as he dipped his pen in the ink and began the draft of his instructions to Counsel.

Macrae sat on a chair in his cell. He was going through his story for the hundredth time. "I went to ask Russ for the money he owed me.... I went to his room.... We had a drink.... He got nasty...."

The lock snapped back and the door swung open. "Come along."

Macrae braced himself. There was a smile on his lips as he followed the broad blue back of the police constable. Another fell into step behind him. Along a short passage, through a doorway, and up a short flight of wooden steps.

The whispering in the public gallery died away as his head appeared above the floor level of the dock.

As he walked to the rail it broke out again. "That's him. Looks quite a decent sort of chap, too. You'd never think he'd kill any one, would you, now?"

"Silence in Court." An usher intoned the words and held back a curtain.

Mr. Justice Hascomb came in—a womanish, dumpy figure in a gown which fell to his ankles, tied with a broad sash.

Counsel bowed. The judge bowed. There was a rustling and a scraping of feet as every one sat down.

Then the Clerk of the Court rose.

"Eric Macrae, you stand charged upon indictment that on the 21st July, 193—, you murdered Abraham Russ. Are you guilty or not guilty?"

"Not guilty."

The jury was sworn and filed into their seats.

The Clerk of the Court turned to them. "Members of the Jury. The prisoner, Eric Macrae, stands charged on this indictment for that he on the 21st July, in this present year, murdered Abraham

Russ. To this indictment he has pleaded not guilty, and it is in your charge to say, having heard the evidence, whether he be guilty or not."

Counsel for the prosecution was a tall, thin man with the face of a horse crossed in love. His chin and jaws were blue-black. He spoke with an incisive harshness which commanded attention. Sometimes he repeated a sentence, for he was well-aware of the capacity of a jury to miss points.

As he listened Macrae thought: "Hell! He's making a water-tight case." He sagged in his chair. It was like watching a man working at a jig-saw, the completion of which was inevitable.

"There can be no doubt, members of the jury, that the prisoner desired the death of Abraham Russ. He had in his possession a revolver. . . . Mrs. Finch will tell you that she saw it in the room in Bury Square. Ammunition was found identical in make to the bullet taken from the head of the murdered man. . . . There is a motive which will be made clear to you when you hear the evidence of Mrs. Keene and. . ."

Macrae roused himself and scribbled two lines on a scrap of paper, folded it and signed to the usher. "Give this to Mr. Wearing." He watched eagerly as his Counsel read the words he had written, saw him purse his lips and then crush the note into a ball and toss it aside. He began to sweat and his hands clutched on the skirts of his coat.

Forty minutes later the first witness for the prosecution was ushered into the witness-box and sworn. It was Mrs. Finch, acutely nervous and barely audible in her replies. Yes, she recognized the revolver she had been shown by the police as the one she had seen in the cupboard in Macrae's room. She also said that prior to the murder Macrae had been hard up and failed to pay her wages.

Then Macrae's Counsel rose to cross-examine. To him she admitted that she was not familiar with revolvers, that she didn't think she had ever had one in her hands before the time she found the one in the cupboard, and that she only saw it for a very short time.

Macrae began to feel better.

Mrs. Keene kept her eyes carefully from the dock as she gave her evidence. Cross-examined, she said that she had no reason to believe that the prisoner had stolen her necklace. She had not missed anything from her flat since she had known the prisoner.

Macrae began to breathe more easily. He sat erect in his chair listening to every word that was spoken.

Bert Finch admitted that he had not seen Abie Russ give the prisoner any money but he had been under the impression that a payment had been made by the pawnbroker. He had not seen a pearl necklace in the shop nor had he seen any entry relating to one in the pledge-book.

Macrae cursed himself for ever having made the statement in prison. If he hadn't admitted having been present when Abie had died they couldn't have got him even for manslaughter. He paid little attention to the evidence of Mr. Broderick who told the Court that the necklace had been found in Mrs. Keene's flat shortly after the prisoner had been there, nor to Danny Levine's account of his betting transactions.

He was confident that he would be acquitted and eagerly awaited the moment of his call to the witness-box when he would be able to explain everything. He had his story clear in his mind. Impatiently he listened to the conclusion of Danny's evidence. He heard his Counsel announce: "I will now call the prisoner to give evidence, my lord."

A warder put a hand on Macrae's arm and led him down the steps of the dock and across the well of the Court.

"I swear that the evidence that I shall give shall be the truth, the whole truth and nothing but the truth." His voice sounded strange and very far away. It was as though some one else was speaking, but as he answered the questions put to him by Counsel his nervousness receded.

He admitted that he had kept a revolver in his room, but insisted that he had got rid of it long before the date of the murder. He knew nothing whatsoever about the loss of the pearl necklace. As for the tag which had been at one time attached to the necklace, he had picked it up from the floor of Abie's room and had put it in his pocket without realizing what he was doing. He denied that at the time he visited Abie he was wearing the pair of string gloves which had been found in his room.

The next question was: "What took place in the room over Russ's shop on the Thursday night?"

Macrae took a long breath and gripped the sides of the witness-box. "Well, it was just as I said in my statement. I went to Russ to ask him to pay me the money he owed me. He said he hadn't got it. We had a drink and he tried to get me to wait a month. I said I couldn't."

Macrae paused. His brain suddenly refused to work.

"Yes, and then?" prompted his Counsel.

Macrae forced himself to think. Where was he? What was he saying? He saw faces, faces, faces, staring at him. Some one was talking very far away.

The judge moved in his chair. "You have told us that you asked Russ for money he owed you, and he said he couldn't pay you. Now, what happened after that?"

"Oh, yes." Macrae mumbled. It was coming back to him, the story which had seemed so convincing when he had rehearsed it to himself, but now . . . "He asked me if I would have a drink and walked over to the cocktail cabinet and poured out drinks. I told him again that I must have the money; he turned nasty. He pulled open a drawer in the desk and took out a revolver. I was frightened. He pointed it straight at me. I caught his wrist. I don't know what happened after that. We must have struggled. The revolver went off and Russ fell. I lost my head and ran from the room. I went straight home."

Counsel for the prosecution rose to cross-examine. He began quietly with questions about Macrae's relations with Mrs. Keene, then he said: "Now I want to come to the Thursday night when you visited Russ at his flat. You have told us that you asked him to pay you a sum of money and that he refused. What you said was: 'We had a drink, and he tried to get me to wait a month. I said I couldn't.' If you had won money betting, why couldn't you have waited a month for the repayment of the loan?"

A. "I only said that to make him pay."

Q. "The desk in Russ's room was of the roll-top kind, was it not?"

A. "Yes, it was."

Q. "Was the top down or up?"

A. "It was down."

Q. "Right down?"

A. "Yes. Just before he went to the cocktail cabinet Russ pulled it down and I heard the lock catch."

Q. "Are you quite sure about that?"

A. "Yes. Positive."

Q. "Russ then poured out drinks and came back to the desk?"

A. "Yes."

Q. "What happened then?"

A. "He got very angry and told me to clear out. I said I wouldn't."

Q. "And then?"

A. "He sort of stooped down and pulled out the drawer and took out a revolver."

Q. "Which hand did he use?"

A. "His right, I suppose. I didn't notice particularly."

Q. "Which drawer was it he opened? Was it on the right or left-hand side?"

A. "The side nearest me."

Q. "That would be on the right-hand side?"

A. "Yes."

Q. "Before he did that, did he touch the roll top?"

A. "No."

Q. "He didn't unlock it?"

A. "No."

Q. "Then how could he have opened the drawer?"

A. Macrae wet his lips with his tongue and mumbled, "I don't know what you mean."

Q. "Don't you know that in this type of desk, if the top is down, all the drawers are automatically locked?"

Macrae's grasp on the edge of the witness-box tightened and beads of sweat broke out on his forehead. He tried to think, but could not. From that moment his fate was sealed. The story which he had built up had crumbled and fallen in ruins.

In the public gallery a woman whispered hoarsely, "He done it all right. You've only got to look at his face."

Mr. Crick exchanged a glance with Wearing and shook his head. What he had feared had happened. He got up and walked to Counsel's seat. "What can we do now?"

Wearing said:

"He's sunk. Do you see the jury?"

Mr. Crick nodded and went back to his seat. A profound depression seized him. He thought of Peggy Nichol.

Counsel waited while sixty seconds ticked away, then he said, "All right, we'll leave that. I have only one more question. Why did you tell Mrs. Finch that Russ had committed suicide?"

There was no answer.

The jury retired to consider their verdict at half-past four in the afternoon and returned fifty-five minutes later.

As they filed into their places Macrae eagerly searched their faces for some sign of what his fate was to be. He drew no comfort from his scrutiny. Ice-cold fear seized him, and crowding in his brain were all the arguments that he wanted to shout aloud; to shout so that they must listen. They must. He had had no reason to desire the death of Abie Russ. He had never had the necklace. No one had seen it in his possession. No one—

The Clerk of the Court rose to his feet. "Members of the Jury, do you find the prisoner, Eric Macrae, guilty or not guilty of the charge of murder?"

"Guilty."

"Eric Macrae, the jury have found you guilty of the crime of murder. Have you anything to say or know you of anything why the Court should not give you judgment of death according to the law?"

Macrae tried to speak, but his throat was dry and the words would not come.

The Judge: "Eric Macrae, the jury, after a most careful and patient hearing, have found you guilty of the crime of murder . . ."

Piccadilly was more than ten thousand miles away. Never in his life before had he longed with all his heart to be walking along the crowded pavement as he did at this very moment.

". . . the sentence of the Court is that you be taken to a lawful prison and thence to a place of execution. . . ."

It couldn't be. It wasn't true. In a minute he would wake up and . . .

". . . within the precincts of the prison in which you shall have been last confined before your execution, and may the Lord have mercy upon your soul."

The Chaplain: "Amen."

Peggy was sitting in Bulmer Court with her back against the plane tree. A pigeon eyed her with his head cocked on one side, and seeing no signs of food withdrew with short, jerky steps.

A newsboy came up the Court. He was shouting: "Verdict in the Southwark Murder. Verdict—"

Peggy snatched a paper from his hands.

Her eyes were blurred with tears as she ruffled through the pages.

"Guilty!" The finality of the word stunned her. The pages fluttered to the pavement and tears rained fast as she said over and over again: "If only he had let me help him! If only—"

Bert Finch followed Mr. Crick out of the Old Bailey, down the steps to the street. He caught him by the sleeve. "I say, Mr. Crick, do you know where I can find Peggy?"

"Yes," Mr. Crick replied. "But I think if I were you I'd leave her alone for a bit." He gave a little smile. "Later—I'm sure everything will be all right."

THE END

Lightning Source UK Ltd.
Milton Keynes UK
UKOW05f2357010517
300289UK00015B/570/P